# RISKY MATCH

## ROYAL SPIES
### BOOK ONE

## J. D. CAROTHERS

DREAMLIFIC PUBLISHING

ISBN: 978-1-957997-55-1 (eBook)

ISBN: 978-1-957997-57-5 (Paperback—model cover)

ISBN: 978-1-957997-58-2 (Paperback—discreet cover)

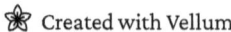 Created with Vellum

*To my amazing husband and incredible readers*
*for encouraging me to continue writing*

# 1

## BLAKE
### TWO YEARS AGO

Standing in line to enter the gala, I'm still bloody mad at my manager, Noah. I can't believe he forced me into attending tonight.

This is the Champions Dinner at Wimbledon. Yes, I scored a ticket, which makes me the envy of the tennis world. But it's for the winners. I'm not one. I bloody lost. I have no right to be here.

Would he listen to reason? Absolutely not! He practically shouted that I had no choice because I'm the top-rated British player. Otherwise, he claimed the press would have a field day with me, insinuating that I'm a sore loser with no manners and probably worse.

Finally, I relented and agreed to attend under protest.

After a shower and a double whiskey, I put on my custom tux and got into the car Noah sent for me. On the ride to the venue, I plotted a survival plan for the evening, which primarily consists of smiling at everyone, avoiding conversations about losing, and escaping as early as possible.

As I stand in line, the only thing left to do is wait my turn to enter and hope this awful evening ends early.

Ten minutes later, I finally reach the entry and display the ticket on my phone. The attendant scans it and grants me admission.

It's showtime, so I throw my shoulders back, straighten my cuffs, and walk into the crowded, dimly lit grand ballroom.

Unfortunately, the first thing I hear is the lyrics to *We Are the Champions*. My stomach clenches. That's the last thing I needed, but I tune it out and press on.

My eyes take a moment to adjust to the light from purple and green towers surrounding the perimeter of the room. The stage at the front displays a giant neon Wimbledon logo between two equally large tennis racquets. Below the stage, a dance floor is nestled amongst a sea of tables. Each table is set for ten with white linens, white flowers, and glowing white candles. The white, purple, and green décor is the epitome of Wimbledon tradition.

The evening will feature extravagant food, fine wine, dancing, and tales of the spectacular shots that led to victory. It's a befitting celebration for the winners and dignitaries at the conclusion of the summer Grand Slam tennis tournament at Wimbledon.

Galas like this are a rare chance to mingle with VIPs, players, and guests. I usually enjoy them while dressed in a tux, and smelling of my favorite woody cologne. It's a welcome change from taking selfies and signing autographs when I'm covered in sweat and worried whether my deodorant is working.

But tonight is different. I don't deserve to be here, so I'd rather be anywhere else. Unfortunately, tradition and respect require my presence and the pretense of enthusiasm for the evening. Fulfilling my duty, I'll oblige one more time. Next year, I'll earn my invitation.

As I make my way through the crowd, I'm repeatedly stopped by well-meaning individuals who want to commiserate with me about my Wimbledon loss. Others stop me for selfies and tell me to keep my chin up. My jaw tightens more with each conversation, but my brittle smile stays in place as I promise to do better next year.

When I thought it couldn't get worse, an elderly lady steps in front of me and pats me on the shoulder, saying, "Laddy, winning isn't everything. We know you tried. Don't worry, we still like you."

My fists clench at my sides as I try to hide my disappointment and dejection. Not knowing how to respond, I simply say, "Thank you," and walk toward my table.

Comments like that fuel the self-doubt that's creeping into my head. I know everyone means well, but each of these encounters is a sad reminder that I not only let myself down, but I also let them down.

I should fire my manager. Why I gave him a second chance after the business fiascos escapes me. I'd have thought he would be more accommodating to my preferences after that. But no. Noah still insisted I suffer through tonight. He worried it would look bad if I didn't show up. I hate to tell him, but it will look even worse when everyone realizes how irritable and depressed I am.

This was an enormous mistake, but I'm stuck now.

Reaching my table, I push down my annoyance and exchange pleasantries with those around me.

At this point, the festivities proceed according to a pre-prescribed agenda. The photographers arrange traditional combinations of people for photos. Speeches are made. Congratulations are offered. Then the dancing begins.

If I didn't know better, I'd think it was a wedding reception. But here it's the winners and runners-up who pose for photos, raising trophies instead of flowers. The speeches are to congratulate the winners and present them with coveted honorary memberships to the All England Club, which is the venue for the Wimbledon Championships. And instead of a bride and groom sharing a first dance, the men's champion joins the women's champion for a twirl around the dance floor.

The evening proceeds in a slow-motion blur as I count down the minutes until I can sneak away. I check my watch and the corners of my mouth upturn slightly. It's almost time. Once a few more people leave the tables for dancing and mingling, no one will notice if I disappear.

Ten minutes later, I take a last sip of my wine, say goodnight to the only remaining couple at my table, and stand to leave.

As I turn around, I'm stopped by Chris Chadsworth, the CEO of my shoe sponsor, WheelCovers. Once he spots you, there's no escaping his bigger-than-life persona.

Chris isn't the typical, clean-cut American CEO. He doesn't wear dark suits, nor does he sport a serious demeanor. Instead, he demands attention with his forceful, booming voice and unique style. Tonight is no exception. His shoulder-length wavy blond hair hangs against his purple satin tuxedo jacket. And no one will miss his black, sequined sneakers with the company logo on top. Saying he has a presence is an understatement.

"Blake, I was looking for you. There's someone you need to meet. Come this way."

Before I can answer, Chris is walking away, expecting me to follow. If it were anyone else, I might let the crowd separate us and beg forgiveness on another day. But he's my sponsor, and Noah already warned me that Chris would be looking for me, so I follow.

Chris pauses at a table filled with dignitaries. I stop beside him and begin scanning the table, nodding at two people I recognize.

My eyes stop when they encounter one of the most beautiful women I've ever seen. Her long hair shimmers in the candlelight. It's a deep brown with red tones, reminding me of fine mahogany. Her lips are plump and cherry red. Her skin is smooth as velvet.

My desire stirs as my eyes follow the plunge of the V-neck of her dress, offering a hint of what hidden treasures lie underneath the satiny material.

As Chris begins to speak, my gaze locks with the sparkling, emerald eyes of this enchantress. That's when it hits me. I know who she is, and she won't be going home with me tonight no matter how much I wish otherwise.

Tuning into Chris's words, I hear him say, "I'm not sure if you two have met before, but I wanted to formally introduce you. Blake, this is Her Royal Highness, Princess Brianna of Catalinius. Your Royal Highness, this is Blake Knight. He's Britain's highest ranked tennis player."

Having tamped the desirous feelings that were entirely inappropriate for off-limits royalty, I bow to the princess. While we've never officially met, our paths have crossed at tournaments because she's also a part-time pro tennis player. She's quite attractive in her tennis attire, ponytail, and baseball cap, but I've never seen her dressed up for a gala. That's why I didn't initially recognize her.

"It's a pleasure to meet you. I'm a huge fan," she says in a silky, warm voice.

Chris nudges my arm, asking, "Blake, don't you want to ask Princess Brianna to dance?"

"Of course. Your Highness, would you like to dance?"

"I'd love to."

As she stands, someone jostles me from behind, unexpectedly pushing me even closer to her. It should be awkward, but for some unexplainable reason neither of us immediately pulls away. Maybe it's her intoxicating scent that holds me close while her eyes study my lips.

Realizing that decorum calls for a little distance, I take a step back, extending my upturned hand to her. We don't exchange any words as she rests her hand in my palm. Her touch sends a warmth up my arm that reaches my shoulder and then cascades into a wave of heat traveling down my body.

What was that? I've never felt that before. It wasn't like a quick zap of electricity, but instead it was slow and powerful. My first reaction is to pull my hand away, but I stop myself, instead staring at her with narrowed eyes, trying to solve the mystery.

She looks at me questioningly as though she sensed something unexpected as well.

I just smile and pretend everything is normal. After all, that's part of my plan for the evening. I hadn't expected the night to include dancing with a princess though.

Her table is next to the dance floor, so a heartbeat later, we step onto the wooden surface as the music slows from a pop hit to a love song.

I'm not sure if that's good timing or bad timing given the thoughts I had when I first saw her tonight. Somehow, I'm going to have to control my body's involuntary attraction to her. Otherwise, this dance could be embarrassing.

I shake my head at myself. What's wrong with me? I'm a grown man, not some teenager.

"What's wrong? Don't you want to dance?"

She's definitely perceptive.

Smiling, I face her, placing my right hand on her back well above her waist while maintaining a proper distance.

"I do. That's not it. I just never expected to be dancing with a princess tonight."

"Can we agree that tonight I'm just another tennis player?"

"Okay. You are a particularly lovely tennis player though," I say as I guide her around the floor.

She squeezes my shoulder slightly and smiles with what seems to be genuine happiness.

She fits nicely in my arms, and I notice she inches a little closer to me, forcing my arm farther around her back and an inch or two lower.

"You look great in that tux too. This is quite a change from our usual tennis clothes, isn't it?"

"It is. Everyone looks so different tonight. It's almost hard to recognize people. But you're lovely on and off the court."

"I'm sure you say that to all the princesses."

She tilts her head, giving me a view of the mischievous glint in her eyes as she pats me on the chest, again sending a wave of warmth through me. How does she do that?

Feeling her eyes still on mine, I answer, "No. You're the only one.

And even if I meet another one someday, I promise not to say the same thing." I chuckle.

She throws her head back and laughs softly.

"I'll hold you to that. By the way, I really am a huge fan of yours. I love watching you play. I particularly admire your serve. That's something I'm always working to improve in my game."

"Thanks. I was fortunate to have a great coach when I was younger. You are an excellent tennis player yourself. You don't compete year-round though, do you?"

"No. I play in as many tournaments as possible, but my royal duties preclude participating in a full schedule. It's frustrating."

It never occurred to me that she wanted to play more. It seems we all have others dictating how we conduct our lives.

Without thinking, I share, "Believe it or not, I understand that meeting expectations and following traditions can be difficult. But we persevere to keep up appearances, don't we?"

I'm normally not that open with a stranger, but she's so real and easy to talk to. It came out before I could censor myself.

She looks at me as if searching my eyes for the story behind my statement.

As she's about to speak, the music stops. I'm not ready to let her go, so I whisper into her ear, "Would you like to continue dancing?"

I'm relieved when she nods.

The dance floor is crowded now, so I have an excuse to pull her closer. Before long, there's no room to move. She rests her arms around my neck, and I wrap mine around her waist, as we stand in place, swaying to the music. We chat, laugh, and tease as song after song plays. Eventually, we fall into an enjoyable silence with her head resting on my shoulder and my arms wrapping her in a gentle hug.

When the music stops for more announcements, I'm forced to take a step or two back from her. I immediately miss her warmth, and my arms feel uncomfortably empty as I offer, "Would you like me to show you back to your table now or would you like to join me on the patio? It may be cooler out there.

"I'd love to join you. I could use a breath of fresh air."

I'm surprised, but happy, that this beautiful princess wants to spend more time with me. "I'd love your company. Do you need to let anyone know where we'll be?"

"My bodyguards will figure it out. They don't let me out of their sight."

"Okay. We'll need to weave our way through the crowd. There's a patio through the side doors."

She was right about her bodyguards. We've barely started across the room, when one of them steps in front of us and parts the crowd while another one shields us from the phones attempting to snap photos.

It's a relief to step through the door and feel the light breeze on my face and smell the fresh scent of recent rain that permeates the night.

"Let's step near the glass wall. We'll have a better view," I suggest.

From the wall, we have a clear view of the night sky with its twinkling stars and the softly lit flower garden below.

Without realizing it, my hand has been on the small of Princess Brianna's back since we left the dance floor. She hasn't complained but it's probably not proper protocol. It just seemed natural.

As I'm pondering whether to remove my hand, she firmly, but politely, tells her guards, "Please give us some privacy. We'll be fine here."

One of the guards stares at me with piercing, dark eyes and clenched teeth silently conveying his threat of what will happen to me if I harm Brianna in any way.

The other guard nods, saying, "We'll be nearby if you need anything."

"Thank you."

Turning to face me, she shrugs her shoulders. "I'm sorry about the need for security, but my parents insist."

I wave off her apology. "It's not a problem. They saved us from being stopped twenty times on our way here, so that's a definite positive. It's a relief to have a break from shaking hands and more small talk."

Her shoulders relax.

"Thank you for understanding. And I completely agree about needing a break. You're the only person tonight who has had a normal conversation with me." She sighs, sadness passing over her face.

My eyes narrow. "What do you mean?"

"I must have had a dozen people ask me why I'm not wearing a tiara tonight. Others curtsied to me so many times it was making me dizzy. Then some wouldn't talk to me at all because they were under the impression that they were only allowed to answer questions I asked. And there's a limit as to how many times I can ask someone if they are enjoying the food, the wine, the evening, etc."

I want to hug her and erase the frustration she's feeling. Instead, I gently push an errant strand of her hair behind her ear and stare at her intently, saying, "That sounds exhausting."

She shrugs. "I don't mean to sound ungrateful. I was born into a wonderful life. But, sometimes, I just wish I could have normal inter-actions with people. Tonight, you were a shining light. You were respectful but treated me like a real person. I'll be forever grateful for you saving me at this event."

I can't imagine what it's like to be treated the way she describes. No wonder she was desperate for normal conversation. Is she hungry for intimacy too, I wonder? That's none of my business though. I remind myself that princesses don't date tennis players, even wealthy ones.

"I'm happy to have been of service. Let me know if I can do anything else to make tonight better." I wink, unable to resist flirting a little.

She blushes, saying, "I'll have to give that some thought."

I wonder if she likes the idea of something more. With that thought, my mind quickly conjures the most inappropriate options.

"You do that," I suggest.

"It's getting cool." She shivers.

I remove my tux jacket and wrap it around her shoulders, pulling her closer as I say, "The rain cooled the air down more than I expected."

Enjoying the moment, my hands linger on her upper arms, holding the jacket in place.

She stares into my eyes as if judging my intentions and finally says, "Thank you. I should have brought my wrap with me, but I assumed it would still be warm. You never know what to expect this time of year though. It can go from warm to cool and rainy in an instant."

"This works. I don't mind keeping you warm." I smile.

"You are quite the charmer, aren't you?"

"Not always. Most people think I'm too serious. I'm just enjoying your company. This has been an exceedingly difficult two weeks for me. I must say I was dreading tonight. You've made it worth it for me," I admit, looking away in an attempt to hide just how hard it's been.

"I can only imagine what it's been like for you. I was sorry to see you lose your semifinal match here. It was a nailbiter. You played well. I thought you were going to win, but your opponent had a couple of lucky bounces in the last game."

"He did, but I had other opportunities to win that I let slip away."

If she only knew how much that loss sucked the energy from me. I've always been a fighter, but I'm starting to wonder if I have what it takes to conquer this battle on grass courts.

She reaches up and tenderly rubs her palm against my cheek, saying, "There's always next time. At least that's what I tell myself. Each year, I keep hoping for a wild card invitation to Wimbledon, but it hasn't happened yet."

There's a longing in her voice that tugs at my heart.

But she's a princess. Her parents should be able to fix this. I ask, "Can't you or your family pull some royal strings?"

A fierce, hardness forms on her face as she practically growls, "I'd never do that, and I gave my parents strict instructions not to even think about using their influence to get me an invitation. I only want to play at Wimbledon if I earn the opportunity. I take my tennis very seriously. I don't cut corners. The problem is that I'm not able to play enough tournaments during the year to raise my ranking enough to automatically qualify. Therefore, I'm left hoping that one day I'll receive a wild card invitation."

Talk about integrity. I'm overwhelmed with admiration. But I'm confused. "I don't mean to be insensitive, but how did you end up at the Champions Dinner tonight?"

I can only describe her expression as resigned.

After a pause, she answers, "I've been watching Wimbledon as a guest in the Royal Box this week. As a visiting royal, I'm sure they felt obligated to invite me tonight. It would have been impolite not to attend. What about you?"

"Technically, invitations are only given to the winners and runners up in singles, doubles, and mixed doubles. But as the highest-ranking British player, I'm also given an invitation each year regardless of how I do in the tournament."

Realization dawns on her face. "I see. And like me, it wouldn't be acceptable to skip the dinner even if it's hard to watch the winners celebrate."

"Exactly. We have more in common and understand each other better than I would've ever imagined."

"We do. This dinner is bittersweet for both of us."

It's so rare for me to be able to have such a candid conversation with anyone. Brianna and I have so many parallel, yet different experiences.

"Brianna, I can't think of a better word than bittersweet. To be honest, If I hadn't met you, I would have already left to mourn my loss."

"I'm sorry if I've made it harder for you."

Squeezing her shoulder and pulling her closer, I say, "You've done the exact opposite. You're the best part of tonight."

"I could say the same thing about you. Can I share a secret?" she asks as she rests her head against my chest.

"Absolutely."

"I was looking for an excuse to leave too. My plan was to go back to my hotel suite and drown my regrets in a gigantic bowl of bacio gelato with a flute of champagne."

"Great minds think alike. Escape was my answer. But what flavor is bacio?"

She pulls back, looking at me like I'm from outer space. "I can't believe you've never had bacio gelato. You have to try it."

"If I can find some, I will. The smile it puts on your face tells me I wouldn't want to go through life without tasting it."

She pushes back from me, exuding elation and excitement, saying, "I have the perfect idea. Come to my hotel suite. I could use the company. We'll drown our sorrows in gelato and champagne and watch old movies."

Is she really inviting me back to her hotel for ice cream? Her security detail will never let that happen.

"Are you serious?" I ask.

"Absolutely."

She looks at me with such determination that I can't question her motives or her intent.

Without hesitation, I say, "I can't turn down an offer like that."

"Excellent. We must be careful though. The last thing I need is the tabloids writing more stories about me. That means we can't leave this dinner together. I'll go with one of my guards. The other one will stay behind and arrange for you to meet me."

A hint of jealousy burns through me, causing me to ask, "Do you arrange such clandestine meetings often?"

She looks at me in shock. "Never. But I'm tired of living by the rules all the time. I'd like to be naughty for just one night.

"You're amazing. Let's do this."

"Okay. I'll tell Oliver to find you in the ballroom."

---

FORTY-FIVE MINUTES LATER, I STAND OUTSIDE BRIANNA'S HOTEL SUITE IN somewhat of a daze. I'm not sure what I'm doing here. Was her invitation for gelato nothing more than that or was it an unspoken request for more? I'm assuming the former given that she was so direct in our interactions at the gala. Part of me hopes I'm wrong.

There's something special about her. She's like a siren beckoning me. There was no way I would have turned down her request, so I'm here.

I knock on the door. I wait.

As I raise my fist to knock again, Brianna opens the door, looking at me with what I sense is a combination of questioning and longing. Does she regret extending the invitation? Or is she also confused about the chemistry between us?

My thoughts are interrupted as she says, "Come in. I'm so glad you're here."

"Thanks."

I walk into her spacious hotel suite. Taking in the expanse, most would consider this a luxury apartment with its marble floors, plush furnishings, and glass wall of windows overlooking the Thames.

My gaze quickly returns to Brianna though. I thought she was hot in her fancy clothes at the gala, but she's even more inviting in her casual purple top and white cotton trousers.

"Let me have your jacket. I'll hang it up, so you'll be more comfortable for our movie night.

"Okay."

She doesn't take her eyes off me as I slip out of my tux coat and hand it to her. It's as if she's trying to figure out our connections as much as I am.

Taking my coat, she hangs it in the entry closet and says, "Take a seat on the sofa. I'll get the gelato and champagne."

I follow her instructions, sensing a tension in the air. The last thing I want to do is make her uncomfortable after we've shared such a bond over our similar situations tonight. But it's as if we're both nervous not knowing what to expect from each other. Does she want more as much as I do?

A couple of minutes later, she hands me an overflowing bowl of a luscious, frozen chocolate treat topped with fresh strawberries. She also sets a flute of champagne on the coffee table, saying, "Get ready to be blown away. The strawberries are the key to taking it over the top."

I take a bite, and the flavors explode in my mouth.

"You weren't kidding, the fresh strawberries with the chocolate are a definite winner. And I should have figured out that bacio means chocolate with hazelnuts. It's like candy. Forgive me, but I was thrown off because I thought bacio meant *kiss* in Italian."

"It does mean *kiss*. Don't you think that this flavor combo is just like a wonderful kiss?"

I stare at her plump red lips trying to decide how to answer. I finally say, teasing, "The gelato is delicious, but certain kisses might be even better."

"I guess they might, but for now, focus on the food. Take a bite of the gelato with a little bit of strawberry, and before you swallow, add a sip of champagne. It will definitely make you smile."

"I'm already smiling," I say, not sharing that one reason is the thought of actually kissing her gorgeous lips.

"See, I told you this was the perfect way to turn a sad evening into smiles. There's a well-known chef in the U.S., who said no one can be miserable while eating a chocolate chip cookie. I don't think that's an exact quote, but it's something like that. For me, I can't be too sad when eating bacio gelato with fresh strawberries while sipping champagne." She laughs.

"Thanks for sharing your secret. It's definitely turning this evening around for me."

I lean toward her to give her a peck on the cheek as a thank you. But just as my lips are about to connect, she turns her head and our mouths collide. Neither of us pulls away. Instead, we both lean into the kiss.

Her lips are warm and sweet. I can't resist a taste, letting my tongue gently slide across the seam of her mouth.

"Mmm. The chocolate and strawberries taste even better on you," I whisper.

She wraps her arms around my neck, pulling us together again. This time I don't hesitate to deepen the kiss. My breathing quickens as our tongues tangle and explore.

Wrapping my arms around her, I slide her across my lap so she's straddling me. She snuggles into place as if we were made for each other.

"I can't get close enough," I moan while nibbling her earlobe.

"More. Please," she begs.

"You're killing me." Taking a deep breath, I manage to ask, "Are you sure you want this? We can stop now."

"I'm sure. Don't. You. Dare. Stop."

I let out the breath I was holding in anticipation of her answer.

"Can we get rid of this?" I ask, pulling on the hem of her T-shirt.

"Only if yours comes off too."

She leans back and undoes my bow tie, slipping it from my neck and tossing it on the floor. Her fingers move down to the studs on my shirt, removing each one. A moment later, she frees my cufflinks and slips the shirt off my shoulders.

"Next time you change shirts during a match, I'll remember this." She glides her hands across my pecs and abs. "You're pure perfection."

"My turn," I grin, lifting her shirt over her head. I can't help staring reverently at her chest as I cup my hands over her amazing, perky breasts.

"You look pleased."

I squeeze her breasts. "That's an understatement. Who knew these were hiding under those tight sports bras you wear for tennis? I wish you were the one changing on the court. I'd be watching every single match you play."

Leaning forward, I take one of her already hard nipples into my mouth. She's rocking against my hardening cock and running her hands through my hair as I move my mouth to her other breast.

Rolling her to my right, I lay her back against the sofa, peeling off her trousers.

"You're beautiful."

"There's a problem . . . I don't have any condoms. Do you?"

"Shit. Hold on."

I grab my wallet from my back pocket, hoping like hell that there's one hiding in it.

I pull out two foil wrappers, holding them up and grinning like they're winning lottery tickets.

"Get over here," she says. Taking the condom from my hand, she reaches for my shorts.

"Now, let's see what you've been hiding," she says seductively, reaching for my zipper.

I can't stop gazing at this perfect woman as I help her strip off my shorts and boxer briefs in record time.

"Oh my god!" she exclaims.

"What?" I ask in confusion

"Umm. It's . . . It's so . . . big. It's been a long time for me. And even then . . . "

Feeling confident, I say, "Ohhh. Don't worry. I'll take it slow."

She smiles and nods as I lean over her, parting her legs with my knee. She's glistening and ready for me.

"Love, are you this wet for me?"

I barely insert my finger when she pumps her hips, needing

more. I hold her still, then add a second one, and then a third, making sure she'll be able to accommodate my size.

"Yes. It's all for you. Quit teasing me. Please," she moans.

"Princess, I just want this to last," I say, pressing my mouth against hers as I remove my fingers and tease her entrance with my cock.

As our tongues tangle, I do my best to ease into her tight wetness as slowly as possible. It takes every trick in the book to keep me from losing it quickly. I've never felt this level of need and desire for any woman before.

Watching her face closely for any sign of discomfort, I slowly push deeper into her.

"Mmm, that's soooo good," she whispers between panting breaths.

That's my signal to press fully in. I hold still, giving her time to adjust, but she begins moving her hips begging for more. I'm happy to give her everything she wants.

Slipping my hands under her, I lift her slightly as we move together.

"Yes, yes, that's the spot. Don't stop!" she screams.

Keeping our rhythm, I pump in and out of her tightness. She feels so good, it's taking every last bit of my restraint to hold off my own pleasure. Needing her to let go first, I move my lips to her breast, letting my teeth graze her nipple as my hand reaches between us.

Circling her clit, I command, "Come for me, now."

"Ohhh! Yesss!" She arches, letting go, pulsing hard against my cock.

With that, I'm no longer able to hold on as my orgasm releases with an intensity that's beyond anything I've experienced before.

Collapsing on top of her, I quickly roll us onto our sides and hold her tight as we each recover.

Once our breathing evens out, I ask, "Where's your bathroom?"

"In the bedroom. It's on the left."

After quickly disposing of the condom, I return with a warm wet cloth for Brianna.

I gaze at her, knowing that I'll always remember the connection we had tonight.

"Are you okay? I hope that wasn't too much for you," I say.

"It was wonderful."

I search her face, making sure she's being honest with me. The look on her face is mystifying. It's one of contentment but confusion. It's as if neither of us knows what just happened. It's as if we've shared something more than sex. We've shared an understanding of what it's like to be different and have a need for something as simple as pleasure and compassion outside the public eye.

"Listen, this has been great, but I should go. You know this can't be more, right?" I say with a hint of apology.

She squints her eyes in confusion. "Did I ask for more? My life doesn't have room for a relationship any more than yours does."

I'm stunned. That's not the reaction I expected. Before I can respond, she shocks me again. "It's good we're in agreement. This was a one-time thing. Although I'm sure you're eager to get going, it's late, and we could both use some sleep. Would you like to stay until morning?"

I wasn't expecting that invitation. With any other woman, I'd headed out the door, but more time with her is something I won't turn down. She provides me with a sense of calm and comfort that I've rarely felt. If I could bottle this feeling, I would.

Those thoughts are too personal to share. Instead, I say, "If you want me here, I'm not going to leave."

The words are barely out of my mouth when she says, "Stay then." Her face relaxes, and her lips turn up in a soft smile. It's funny how happy she looks at the mere idea that I'll be keeping her company tonight when she's a princess that supposedly has everything she could ever want at her fingertips.

Her smile brings me satisfaction too and is all the encouragement I need. I stand, slipping my arms underneath Brianna, and carry her to the bedroom. Gently placing her on top of the silky sheets, I crawl into bed beside her and cradle her back against my front, relishing that we have a few more hours together.

Before closing my eyes, I whisper, "Rest, Love. It's been a long day."

"It has, but I'm not ready for it to be over yet. Did you happen to bring that other condom with you?"

I laugh. "I did. Should we save it for morning?"

"No. We'll figure something else out then."

"You really are perfect, aren't you?"

"Quit talking and show me more of your masterful moves."

"Your wish is my command."

For the rest of the night, our limbs entangle as we explore each other. Fireworks explode like never before.

I can't get enough of her.

Waking the next morning, there are only two problems. First, I lost Wimbledon. As wonderful as last night was, I still must come to terms with the loss. Second, we both know this will never happen again. For some reason, that bothers me more than it should.

# 2

## BLAKE
### TODAY

My heart rate soars. Sweat coats my palms. My chest tightens.

No! Please, not now. Not again.

I take a deep breath, exhaling slowly.

It doesn't help. My heart continues to pound. I can't catch my breath.

Think. What did they tell me to do?

Repeat calming thoughts. That's it.

*I'm going to be okay.* Breathe in.

*Winning is not everything.* Slowly exhale.

*I'm not in real danger.* Breathe in again.

*This is temporary.* Slowly exhale.

Unfortunately, repeating my mantras only helps a little. My brain is on autopilot, inserting unsettling thoughts between the positive ones.

*"This time has to be different."*

*"I can't fail again."*

*"Everyone is counting on me. I can't let them down."*

The overwhelming sense of anxiety is more than I can handle. I need out of this bloody car, so I can sprint down the road until I'm too tired to think. Unfortunately, there's nowhere my driver can pull over, and I don't want him to know what's happening to me.

Trapped in the backseat, I keep taking slow, deep breaths and hope the calming thoughts will eventually prevail, allowing my heart rate to slow to a reasonable level.

This predicament is all my fault.

I shouldn't have let my business manager talk me into hiring a driver today. But I didn't want to explain why I preferred to drive myself to the rental house near Wimbledon. It's none of Noah's business, but the last thing I needed was all this quiet time to think.

If I hadn't been hellbent on protecting my secret, I wouldn't be stranded in this freaking car where I can't escape.

So far, I've hidden my recent panic attacks from everyone except my coach and my new sports psychologist. I can't let the press or my opponents know. If my anxiety makes headlines during the upcoming tennis tournament, my opponents will have an advantage, and that will make my anxiety even worse.

Unfortunately, I'm sitting alone in the back seat for the hour-long drive from the center of London. It's only about ten miles, but heavy traffic allows time for my mind to repeatedly play worst-case scenarios, letting self-doubt creep in yet again. Until recently, I've never experienced these frightening physical manifestations of stress. I've always been the strong, determined winner that everyone feared on the court. How could this have happened to me?

I grab my mobile phone and start the app that's supposed to calm my thoughts. I should have remembered it sooner. As the app plays sounds of nature and guides me through a counting sequence, my heart rate slows.

Finally, the rental house comes into view. Thank fuck.

The luxury, three-story-plus-basement home built with tan brick, accents of yellowish stones, and white-rimmed windows matches the photos Noah emailed. The best part is the parking for six or seven cars inside the wrought-iron gated entrance that will provide privacy.

As the car passes through the gate, relief floods over me with my escape in sight. I practically jump out of the backseat when the vehicle comes to a halt. The fresh air hits my face, and my breathing eases further.

The driver emerges from the front of the car, and I ask over my shoulder, "Can you bring my bags in? If you don't mind, they go in the primary bedroom at the top of the first flight of stairs." At least that's what Noah's email said.

"Of course, sir."

Fortunately, I don't think the driver noticed my situation. That gives me some solace. I can't afford him gossiping to the press.

Hustling to the door, I pull out my phone to search for the keypad code. At first my sweaty fingers slip on the buttons, so I dry my hand on my shirt and try again.

As I successfully punch the numbers in, my pulse and breathing are finally back to normal. It's amazing that the change of focus helps. I'm still struggling to understand what is going on with me, but I'm grateful that the current attack is fading.

Walking inside, I call out, "Anyone home?"

Silence.

Where's my team? They arrived last night, so someone should be here. My frustration grows as I wander around the ground floor in search of them with no luck. I was counting on a chance to talk with my sports psychologist followed by a hard workout to reset myself.

Until recently, I was a laid-back guy off the court because I work hard and expect the results to follow. My nerves before and during tournaments have always been just enough to keep my energy level high so that I play well. Players have even called me the Ice King because I don't get frustrated during tennis matches even when I'm behind. That is, except at Wimbledon.

In the past, I've shaken off the Wimbledon losses as mere flukes.

There was always a viable explanation as to why it wasn't my year to win. Each time I've assumed that I'll win the next year.

That changed about eight months ago with the arrival of the first of several mysterious emails. Ultimately, they led to me parting ways with my old coach and hiring a new one. Beginning this year with a new coach meant he wanted to change things about my game. Changes often mean I play worse before improving. That sucked and added to my stress.

Then things went further downhill two or three months ago when I started having nightmares where I was a gray old man who still hadn't won Wimbledon. The crowds boo me, the press harangues me, and little kids point and laugh at the old man still trying to win the one Grand Slam tournament that has eluded him his whole life.

Soon after the nightmares began, I had my first panic attack. I didn't know what was happening. I'd never experienced anything like it before.

I thought it was a heart attack, so I went to the nearest Urgent Treatment Centre in London. While my symptoms could have signaled a heart attack, I learned that in my case, the heart palpitations, sweating, churning stomach, and overwhelming sense of dread were the result of a panic attack.

Relieved, I assumed this was a one-time thing and went back to my normal life. Then it happened again when I was practicing with my coach. A young boy pointed to me and loudly asked his dad, "Isn't that the guy who's never won Wimbledon?" Suddenly, my nightmare was a reality.

I rushed off the court. For 30 minutes, I stood in the shower, letting hot water rain over me as I tried to calm myself.

Now I'm struggling with my fear of playing in front of strangers. It's complicated. Not only are the panic attacks debilitating and draining, so is the fear of having one in front of fans. Josh, who has been my coach for a few months now, and Doc, who joined my team recently, are helping me through this, but it's difficult.

Noticing a fruit basket on the kitchen counter, I grab an apple and head upstairs, climbing the steps two at a time. My legs are tight from the leftover tension radiating through my muscles.

This must stop. Wimbledon begins in a week. I can't let the opportunity to finally lift the trophy slip through my fingers yet again. It's time to focus on the most important tournament in my career, which starts with a strategy session with Josh and a talk with Doc.

Reaching the top of the stairs, I text my coach.

> Me: Can we go over strategy this afternoon?

> Josh: Absolutely. When do you want to meet?

> Me: I just arrived at the house. Where are you?

> Josh: Running an errand. Will be back at the house soon.

> Me: I'll unpack and meet you in the study in an hour. Can you also let Doc know that I need to talk?

> Josh: I'll message Doc. See you in an hour.

I set an alarm on my phone and walk into the bedroom that Noah assigned to me. My bags are waiting, thanks to the helpful driver. Surveying the area, there's a king-size bed, a desk with a chair, and a door leading to a private bath. It's yet another perfectly nice place. I'll spend two or three weeks here and then promptly auto-erase it from my memory as I move on to the next tournament in a couple of weeks.

Part of me longs for more time at my permanent home in London surrounded by my own things. To have that would mean my tennis career is over. The end is coming soon enough, but I'm not ready to call it quits yet.

Banishing the desires for another life, I start unpacking. I hope it was the right decision to arrive at Wimbledon this early. My team thought it was too soon, but I wanted sufficient time to settle into a routine. In the past, I've always felt rushed here, and the results weren't good.

By changing things up, nothing will get in the way of my success this year. It's worth every pound I'm paying to rent this enormous house for three weeks because it has a gym, hot tub, study, enormous kitchen, and enough bedrooms for my entire team.

My coach and Doc are critical to my training, strategy, and mental health. But ultimately, they aren't the ones who have to win on the tennis court. That's the beauty of playing singles instead of doubles. I'm in complete control of the outcome of my matches. If I play my best, I win. If I don't, then I lose and only have myself to blame. I like it that way.

Unfortunately, my current obstacle is me, but Doc is helping.

As I put away the last of my toiletries, the alarm sounds, so I go downstairs to the study, which is near the front door.

Josh has his back to me, concentrating on his tablet. I know he's in a serious mode when his white baseball cap is on backwards containing all the long ends of his wavy, dark brown hair. He may be a retired-player-turned-coach, but based on his level of fitness, most would think he's still playing. He can still give me a run for my money in the gym. That's one reason we've been a good team so far.

"Coach, you're early."

He turns quickly, saying, "I knew you would be anxious to begin. How was the trip from London?" Josh asks.

Not wanting to reveal I had another panic attack, I say, "Fine. Let's get started. I need a win here. Let's not waste any time."

"Have you forgotten that you won the Wimbledon Junior's title at seventeen."

"That's not the same thing."

"It's still impressive. More importantly, you've won each of the other three Grand Slams multiple times in the last fifteen years. Very few players can say that."

"That may be true, but winning the men's singles title at Wimbledon would mean everything to me. For some reason, since my junior's win, grass court tennis has been my nemesis. That's changing now. We need to solidify a bulletproof plan and implement it. I'm not going to let the press or my past losses distract me this time."

"Your game is perfectly suited to grass, but you don't have much time to transition from clay at the French Open to grass here. Hell, you only play on grass about five weeks a year, and two of those are at Wimbledon. It's a tough adjustment for everyone."

"I know. There's not enough time to get comfortable on this surface. But someone wins each year. This time it will be me."

"The transition is as much mental as physical. You know what to do. You psych yourself out. That's one reason I recommended the sports psychologist. She's helping you mentally prepare, which I believe will make the difference."

"And it's why I insisted we arrive here much earlier than usual. I'm not taking anything for granted, particularly given my recent panic attacks. When the matches start, I'll play every point as well as I can. In the end, I plan to hold up the trophy," I say, slamming my fist on the desk.

"I know. Calm down. We've got this."

Clenching my fists, it takes everything in me not to scream. Calm down, my arse. I'm not having a panic attack now. I'm merely focused on winning. Even if I were having an attack, doesn't he know I wouldn't be able to control it by merely *calming down*?

I know he wants to help, but he's never experienced what I'm dealing with. It's futile to try to explain. Instead, I simply say, "Good. What's on the agenda for today?"

"I've mapped out a strategy for your workouts and court time that should have you peak at the right moment. Give me a second to pull up the spreadsheet."

While I wait for his computer to boot, I try to push away my negative thoughts. The problem is that I almost dread this tournament each year for fear that I'll fail again. I'm sick of answering the same questions year after year and seeing the headlines that suggest I'm not as good as the players who have won all four Grand Slams. Or even worse, they imply that I always choke at this tournament.

This year I'm determined to overcome the obstacles one way or another.

Pointing to the screen, Josh says, "Here we go. Look at this. I've divided each day into four parts."

As I'm about to ask a question, Josh's mobile phone rings.

"Hello. It's Josh."

He listens and then responds, "I'm not going to tell him. That's your job. I'm putting you on speakerphone."

"Who is it?" I ask, frustrated by the interruption.

"It's Noah. He has an update for you."

I can't imagine what my manager wants that can't wait.

"Hey, Noah. We're in a meeting. Let's talk when you arrive for the tournament."

"No, this can't wait. It'll impact your schedule."

Scheduling hassles are the last thing I need now. Rubbing my neck to relieve the building tightness, I ask, "What do you mean?" I ask.

"Your clothing sponsor insists that you play mixed doubles as well as singles this year."

"No!" I bark.

"No isn't an option. You *will* play mixed doubles," Noah commands.

Who the hell does he think he is? He works for me.

At this point, I'm pacing the room, attempting to control my response. Josh doesn't need to hear what I really want to say to Noah. That will happen after Wimbledon and in private.

For now, I count to ten—twice, and finally bite out, "They can't make me do that."

"Unfortunately, they can. There's a clause in your contract that says they can make this request at one Grand Slam event per year. If you don't comply, you'll be in breach of contract, and they will sue you. They will also terminate their sponsorship deal with you."

What is Noah good for if he can't properly manage my schedule and contracts? He's supposed to protect me from these distractions.

"Noah, I'm not playing doubles at Wimbledon, period. They can pick another tournament—just not this one. Tell them."

"I already tried. That's when they pointed to the contract and mentioned calling their lawyers. You don't want the bad publicity, and you don't want to lose a sponsor that pays you millions per year. Your contract is up for renewal. They've made it clear that the renewal depends on you playing doubles at Wimbledon."

What a cocked-up mess. I continue pacing, weighing my options. Then a solution pops into my head.

"Fine. I'll play in the first round."

Noah is grating on my nerves. We've been going through this song and dance for years. I'm tired of it. Soon I will take the plunge and hire a new manager who negotiates tighter contracts for me. That can wait until after Wimbledon though.

Noah adds, "And you'll play to *win*. There are sizable monetary incentives the further you make it in the doubles bracket. They also have a penalty if you lose in the first round. In other words, you must play your best."

"Shite. I don't need this hassle. I was willing to play one round, but no more. I'm going for a run. When I get back, I expect to hear how you found a way out of this mess. Fix it!"

"Don't you want to know who your partner will be?" Noah asks.

"NOOOO!!!! I don't give a flying flip who the sponsor wants me to partner with. It's not happening."

I storm out, slamming the door with a loud bang.

Is the universe against me? Why am I always screwed at Wimbledon? I've been plagued with ridiculously tough draws, innumerable rain delays, twisted ankles, back spasms, and even the stomach flu once. Why do these things always happen here? Not that I want them to happen at the other tournaments, but it's uncanny how many things go wrong here.

Now it's an unreasonable sponsor insisting I play doubles. I don't have time for relationships, not even a working relationship with a doubles tennis partner.

*It's not going to happen. I can't let it.*

# 3

## BRIANNA

Chills run down my arms as I stare at my parents with wide eyes. Could it finally be true?

"I'm one of the wild cards? Are you serious?"

They nod in unison.

My heart's beating out of my chest, and my body's shaking with excitement. It's really happening. My lifelong dream is coming true.

*I'm going to play at Wimbledon.*

It takes all my restraint not to jump up and down. But proper protocol for a twenty-eight-year-old princess prohibits such displays, particularly when standing in my dad's—or more accurately, the former king's—palace office.

But damn, I'm human, and this is the best thing that's ever happened to me during my tennis career. With my royal duties, it's impossible to play in enough tournaments to rank in the top 100 and automatically qualify for this prestigious Grand Slam event. For a long time, I've known my only chance was to be granted one of the handful of coveted wild card slots that are given to players the tournament deems deserving.

As I'm riding on a cloud, I notice my parents look worried rather than pleased at the news. What's up with them?

Reeling in my emotions, I ask, "Aren't you happy for me? It was a long shot, but you knew I was hoping for this."

"Of course we're happy for you, dear," Mum says.

She's still frowning though. Then it hits me.

"Ohhh! I know what's wrong. You're concerned about my safety. Don't be. The royal box on Centre Court is always packed with British royals and celebrities. Not only would they be the first targets for any threat, but security will also be first rate. I'll be fine."

The problem is that Mum and Dad have fewer royal duties since they stepped down as the rulers of Catalinius, letting my oldest brother, Xander, become king. They soon learned there weren't enough events to keep them occupied in our small island nation during their retirement. Once they tired of vacations to nearby Italy and France, they jetted around the world but soon became weary of constant travel. And when charity work wasn't enough to fill their downtime, they decided to take more of an active interest in my tennis.

Their first suggestion was for me to employ the extra staff they no longer needed. My parents explained that these people could manage my tennis engagements and travel while my current assistant could manage my royal duties.

I didn't want those people to lose their jobs, so I agreed. The side effect of this arrangement is that my parents now hear about my schedule from their loyal staff and worry every time I'm off to a crowded event.

Mum shakes her head, saying, "That's not it. There are a couple of conditions on the invitation."

"What do you mean? Wild cards don't come with conditions."

"Your mother is referring to the fact that you'll be playing mixed doubles, not singles."

My eyes narrow and I twirl my ring, considering what my dad just said. It's disappointing, but it also doesn't make any sense. Sure,

I've played doubles quite a bit over the years, but this year my focus was on singles.

And even if they invited me to play doubles, why mixed doubles? I've usually played doubles with Sara as my partner. I can't remember the last time I played doubles with a guy. So, why in the world would Wimbledon give me a wild card in mixed doubles? Something doesn't ring true, but it's not like I can challenge their decision. They might realize their mistake and withdraw the invitation entirely.

That thought sends a chill through me, so I resolve to accept the situation, saying, "That's unexpected and disappointing, but if that's my only option, it'll be okay. It's still Wimbledon, and I'm a strong doubles player. Wait—something doesn't add up. I don't have a regular, mixed-doubles partner. It doesn't make sense."

"That's not a problem. You're partnering with Blake Knight. It's all set," Dad says.

I shake my head. I can't have heard him right.

"Did you say Blake Knight?"

"Yes. You know him, don't you?" Dad asks.

That's one way to put it—we spent a steamy night together two years ago, but Dad wouldn't know about that—at least, I don't think he would. We were very discreet.

Hopefully, I'm not blushing at the sudden memory of Blake's warm, athletic body wrapped around mine.

I carefully answer, "Yes. We've crossed paths and interacted at various tournaments over the years. Enough for me to know he hates playing doubles. He's not going to agree to this."

"He will. One of his sponsors wants him to play with you. They've made it a condition of continued support. He'll come around to the idea."

"Why on earth would his sponsor do that?"

"The sponsor wants the royal connection on the court. They like the idea of a top male player and a princess both wearing their clothes at Wimbledon," Dad says.

"Are you allowing me to wear their clothes? As a royal, you've never permitted me to have a sponsor."

"That relates to the other condition," Mum says.

"I'm afraid to ask but tell me."

"You'll be on a CRM," Dad says.

My mind is racing. "Are you joking? A Covert Royal Mission? Does that mean the wild card invitation isn't real? I'm not actually going to be playing, am I?"

"Slow down. We'll explain. The wild card is real, and you *will* be playing. At the same time, you'll be spying on your tennis partner," Dad says with a straight face.

*What the actual fuck?*

My eyes widen, and my jaw drops. I'm utterly speechless, which is rare for me.

That means I slept with the guy I'll now be spying on.

"May I sit?" I ask, but I move toward a chair before my parents have a chance to answer.

"We know this isn't exactly what you had hoped for," Mum says.

It's hard to fathom that Blake is a suspected criminal, or worse, a terrorist. That would be the only reason for the Covert Royals to be involved. But it can't be too serious. They would never send me into danger despite my repeated requests for more meaningful missions. My parents wouldn't allow it. That must mean that Blake's involvement is rather benign.

Even if that's the case, there's still something suspicious about this wild card invite.

My name wasn't on the list when Wimbledon announced the majority of the wild card recipients a couple of days ago. Saying I was crushed would be an understatement. I'd thought my dedication and success in tournaments over the past year would've been enough to garner a merit-based invite. But the last thing I wanted was for people to think the privileged princess was pouting, so I plastered a smile on my face, pretending not to be bothered.

There's a limit to my ability to fake it though, so I'd decided not to attend Wimbledon this year. It would be too painful to watch, knowing that at my age the chances of ever playing in my dream tournament are quickly fading.

Regaining my voice, I say, "As you know, I've always wanted to receive an invitation based on my tennis success, not because I'm part of a royal family. I also never envisioned being invited to play as part of a covert mission. Please be honest with me. I need to know. British intelligence orchestrated my invite, didn't they? I didn't earn the spot."

"Dear, we need to tell her even though she'll be upset," Mum says to Dad.

He nods. "Bri, please understand that this mission is very important not only to our country but also to several of our allies, including the UK."

"So, you and British Intelligence *did* arrange for my wild card slot."

"Not exactly. You see, you were originally on the list to receive a wild card to play singles at Wimbledon this year. But we needed you close to Mr. Knight. That required changing your invitation," Dad says.

"How do you know I was on the list of wild cards for singles?"

"If the tournament hadn't already chosen you, British Intelligence wouldn't have been able to get you in. You earned your spot."

Thank god.

"That's a relief, but you know how hard I've worked to earn a spot for singles. I've had my best year of tennis ever. This was probably my only chance. Now, it's gone because someone wants me to collect information and pass it along. It's like someone punched me in the stomach," I say, hugging myself. I'm feeling sick.

"We know it's not fair, but this isn't one of *your* typical missions. We were against your involvement in the beginning. Ultimately, we agreed you're the best person for the mission. In fact, you're probably the only one who can do it."

"You've clearly known about this for a while. Why wasn't I told sooner?"

"Your father and I have spent hours trying to find a way to keep you out of this mission. We wanted to protect you from danger and let you experience your well-earned honor," Mum says.

"And we weren't sure they would find a way to force Blake to play doubles. If he refused, we wanted you to receive your original invitation for singles. But he'll play, so duty calls. You've trained for years with the Covert Royals. You're ready," Dad says.

He's right. I've been trained in the use of electronics for surveillance, martial arts, survival skills, weapons handling, and covert communication. We update our training in the classroom and with field exercises every year, so I am ready.

Mum nods solemnly.

"I've been ready for a long time, but no one would assign me to real missions. Are you saying this one involves more than just passing information?"

"It does. When you return to your apartment, log in to your secure laptop. Your contact is waiting to give you a video briefing. You'll receive further instructions when you reach the UK. You also need to talk with your coach and team about the invitation. Be ready to leave at the end of the week. Mr. Knight is already at the home he's rented in Wimbledon."

"Okay. I have a lot to prepare. I'll sign in for my briefing, if there's nothing else you need to tell me."

"That's all. We'll talk again before you leave," Dad says.

After quick goodbyes, I start the long walk from my parent's palace apartment back to mine, which is in another wing. Along the way, I console myself with the knowledge that I earned a singles invitation even if I can't tell anyone. At least I'll finally set foot on the sacred grass courts even if it's not for the reasons I'd hoped.

This whole situation is ironic. For the last decade, my occasional covert assignments have been mundane. Now, I finally get my opportunity to play singles at Wimbledon, but it's spoiled by the fulfillment of my desire for a more important mission. I should've been more careful about what I asked for, I guess.

I've put in the work at the annual covert training. I'm ready for whatever threats cross my path—at least as ready as training can make someone. It's doubtful, though, that this mission will involve real threats. My parents think eating at a restaurant is a significant security risk, so it's hard to believe this mission will be particularly exciting despite their reassurances that this is more than an info exchange.

There is one threat, or more accurately, a complication that my parents don't know about. I have a history with Blake. That means I have mixed feelings about seeing him again. No one has ever made my pulse race like he did that night. We shared personal feelings and stories and connected over our shared struggles.

It's too bad we didn't stay in touch. If we had, I'd know more about his current situation. But at the time, we parted amicably with no plans to contact each other. It worked out well because neither of us was looking for a relationship. We were both concentrating on our tennis.

A warmth passes through me as I remember how special he made me feel that night. But for all I know, he would have done whatever it took to be able to say he slept with a princess. Not that there have been any rumors that he's said anything to that effect, but I've learned that's a thing for some guys. My title and money make me a target. Unfortunately, I can never be certain who cares about me for me rather than for what I represent.

I can't help but wonder whether Blake will be glad to see me or if he'll be annoyed that I'm showing up to play doubles with him. Knowing how much he hates doubles, he'll probably tank the first match to avoid the need to play again.

If so, my time competing at Wimbledon will be short and won't earn me respect from my tennis peers. More importantly, losing early would make it hard to spy on him.

But those aren't my only concerns. What will I do if he wants to pick things up where we left off? I can't sleep with a criminal suspect I'm surveilling.

What a mess!

My mind is jumping from topic to topic. This is not like me. I'm usually organized, methodical, and rational. It's time to snap into mission mode.

---

ARRIVING BACK AT MY PALACE APARTMENT, I LOCK THE DOOR AND RETRIEVE my encrypted laptop from its secure hiding place. I log in using three-factor authentication and click the link for my briefing.

An avatar fills the screen, obscuring the identity of the real person on this video chat.

Following the next step in the verification protocol, I say, "The sky is gray, but the sun may shine soon."

"Unless the stars appear first."

"That will never happen."

As I wait for the authentication process to complete, I think back to when I first became part of the Covert Royals. We're a unique group of highly trained members of European royalty who act as intelligence agents for our home countries and our allies. Our royal parents formed the group over a decade ago to provide an option for their children who would not be ascending to the throne. They wanted us spares to have the opportunity to play a significant role in assisting our countries rather than feel left out as some have in the past.

We were all given the choice to opt-out, but most of us were pleased to have a path of service that involves more than ribbon cuttings, building dedications, and charity events. Until now, my roles for the Covert Royals have been rather tame, but I've made it known that I'd like to do more. This may be my chance.

Finally, a series of beeps sound, confirming my identity, and the avatar fades to an image of Walter with his familiar bald head and gray mustache. Walter has been my primary contact with the Covert Royals since I finished my initial training.

He says, "Agent Brianna, welcome to Operation Denarius. You have been selected to play a key role in tracking down smugglers of ancient antiquities. Specifically, rare gold and silver coins have been disappearing from European museums and private collections. Some have reappeared months later in museums around the world. We suspect others have been acquired by private collectors who do not wish to risk detection."

"When you find the coins, are they returned to their rightful owners?" I ask.

"Not necessarily. That process can take years and return of the coins is not always possible due to differences in international laws."

"I see."

"Most recently, a superb collection of ancient Roman gold coins was stolen. They're known as the 12 Caesars. Each coin features the portrait of one of the Roman rulers on one side. The opposite side depicts a symbol, mythological character, or person relevant to the time period."

"I gather the coins are extremely valuable."

"They are. These coins are small. Each one has a diameter of about 20 mm and weighs about 8 grams. But they are each worth hundreds of thousands of British pounds."

"Wow. These crimes sound like common art thefts. Why are the Covert Royals involved?"

"Yes, theft of ancient coins is a form of art theft. There are also laws prohibiting the export of ancient coins and antiquities from certain European countries without permission. These crimes alone would not necessarily call for the involvement of intelligence agencies. These incidents rose to our level when we learned that the stolen coins are being used to purchase weapons for certain terrorist organizations."

"That definitely elevates the crime. How is Wimbledon and tennis involved?"

"We have reason to believe that certain pro tennis players or members of their teams receive the coins at tournaments in the countries where the coins are stolen. Those people then pass the coins on to couriers at the next tennis tournament in another country. Using this procedure, the players are smuggling the coins from one country to another."

"I see. Do you suspect any particular players or team members?"

"Yes. Based on our investigation so far, we suspect two teams are orchestrating the movement of the ancient coins across the borders as they move from one tournament to the next. At this point, we're not sure if it's the players or people on their team who are handling the coins."

"Am I to understand that Blake Knight's team is under suspicion?"

"To be clear, Blake and his team are suspects. That's why we've arranged for you to play as Blake's tennis partner. That will give you the opportunity to plant surveillance devices, question Blake, and hopefully, retrieve the coins that recently disappeared."

"How do I obtain the electronic surveillance devices?"

"Upon arrival in the UK for Wimbledon, you'll be contacted. At that point you'll be provided another briefing along with the devices for the mission. We have also sent encrypted images of the missing coins to your phone. Please review them, commit them to memory, and then permanently delete the images."

"I will. That's standard protocol. Is there anything else I should know."

"One more thing. We've lost two agents assigned to expose the people involved in the arms purchases. Our current intel suggests their deaths were unrelated to the theft of the coins. However, we cannot be certain at this time."

"Have you lost anyone investigating the coin thefts?"

"No, but please proceed with caution throughout this mission. We don't want you to be the first. Your bodyguard will be your backup if necessary."

"Does that mean Erin can be given the details of the mission?"

"No. As always, she will know you're on a mission and will be on heightened alert. That's all."

"I understand."

"Good. May you succeed in secret. Good luck."

After reciting this Cover Royals motto, the screen goes blank before I can respond.

Before viewing the images of the coins, I take a moment to process the contents of the briefing.

After mentally reviewing the call and committing the details to memory, my mind settles on the fact that two agents have been lost. It's possible they were killed in unrelated accidents, but that sounds unlikely to me. I can only hope that Walter is correct that the coin smuggling part of this conspiracy is less deadly. That thought sends an ominous chill through me.

No wonder my parents weren't keen on my involvement in this CRM.

My training may be more important than I'd thought.

# 4

## BRIANNA

*our days later.*

Standing outside my parents' palace apartment, I wait for their butler to let me in. The delay gives me time to mentally run through my list of remaining questions about the mission. Hopefully, my parents will answer them during breakfast this morning.

With a click, the door swings open, and the familiar, silver-haired gentleman ushers me inside.

"Good morning, Grayson. Are my parents in the dining room?"

"They are, Your Royal Highness" he says, bowing his head to me. He's old school like my parents and believes in maintaining tradition, but his formality feels awkward given our history. I've known my parents' butler since I was a small child. He used to slip me pieces of chocolate in exchange for promises to behave. As I grew older, it became a game. I'd threaten to do something egregious to extract chocolate from him. His wink told me he knew I was kidding, but it was our secret.

The memory makes me smile. Holding my hand out, I say, "Perhaps I should knock over the pitcher of orange juice this morning for old times' sake."

He wags his finger. "Tsk, tsk. There will be none of that today."

A foil-wrapped square drops gently into my palm. It's better than a hug from a favorite uncle.

"I guess I'll have to be good today," I tease.

It sounds childish, but this exchange is our way of showing affection.

"Enjoy your breakfast and good luck at Wimbledon. I'll be watching," he calls after me.

"Thanks. I'll do my best," I say over my shoulder, hurrying to the dining room. I'm anxious for answers. It's my last chance to learn more details before my team's flight leaves for London later today.

Entering my parent's private dining room, my plan instantly goes up in smoke. In addition to my parents, my older brothers, Xander and Evan, are waiting for me.

"Surprise!" Xander says as he gives me a hug.

"I thought you two were both traveling."

"We were, but we had to congratulate you in person and give you a proper send off," Evan says.

We've always been close, but it's touching that my brothers flew back just for breakfast. I appreciate their support even if I'd hoped to corner my parents alone this morning.

"Exactly. We're so proud of you. You deserve this," Xander adds.

Technically, I deserve a chance to play singles, but they can't know that. My brothers have no idea that I've spent six to eight weeks each summer for the last eleven years, training as a Covert Royal. They thought I was at an intensive tennis camp between tournaments each summer. I was, but it was much more than just tennis.

My brothers never knew about the program because they weren't eligible for it. Evan was already in graduate school and on a different path when it started. Xander was the Crown Prince, destined to be king. It wouldn't have been an option for him because the program was designed for the *spares*—not for royals who would ascend to their respective thrones.

Our parents wanted the spares to have a unique opportunity to serve our countries that consisted of more than cutting ribbons, dedicating hospital wings, and raising money for charities. They recognized that prior royal children in our situations had had a difficult time finding their place and value in life. They wanted to fix that dilemma.

But very few people in the world know about the highly secret program. And I don't want my brothers to learn about it yet. I feel guilty hiding it from them, but they are too overprotective and would try to keep me from doing anything useful. As king, Xander now has the power to prohibit my involvement, which makes it even more important to keep my role secret.

My parents are bad enough, but they've had years to get used to the idea that I'm trained to spy. Besides, they agreed to my participation in the first place. They can't complain too much now.

After I've proven my worth on more substantial covert royal missions, I'll share my role with my brothers. By then, it will be too late for them to stop me. At least, that's what I hope.

---

A FEW HOURS LATER, I BOARD ONE OF THE ROYAL JETS WITH MY COACH, MY physio, my regular bodyguard Erin, and Fausto, who is a new addition to the team.

My parents insisted on a second bodyguard. He's disguised as my personal chef. Clearly, they're worried about the danger of my mission.

It's amusing that my parents are sending bodyguards to keep me safe when I'm the spy with as much or more special training than my guards. Normally, I'd object, but given the loss of two agents on a related mission, I'll accept the extra backup protection this time.

There's another upside too. If *Chef* Fausto's cooking is as outstanding as they promised, then we'll eat extremely well.

This may be one of the smaller jets my family owns, but it's still luxurious with polished burled wood that shines like a mirror, along with plush, cream-colored leather chairs and a sofa.

Erin and I like to chat during flights, so we take our preferred seats facing each other. We could almost pass for sisters if not for her light brown hair and brown eyes compared to my mahogany hair and green eyes.

The others are on the sofa near the back, already watching a football match on the TV.

As we sink into our seats, the flight attendant appears with our customary drinks. She hands me my favorite mocktail: sparkling water with a splash of pomegranate juice and an orange slice. I'd rather be sipping a martini, but I'm limiting alcohol for Wimbledon.

Since learning about Wimbledon and my mission, my mood swings are epic. One minute I'm fuming mad. The next I'm consumed with disappointment. Then I'm excited about having a real mission and playing at Wimbledon, even if it's doubles.

Unfortunately, the darker thoughts dominate.

But at the end of our two-and-a-half-hour flight from Catalinius to London, I'll need to bury any trace of negative thoughts. As far as the world will see, I'm thrilled to be playing doubles at Wimbledon.

After all, who wouldn't want to play with Blake? He's not just one of the best players in the world, he's also drop-dead gorgeous.

"What's up with the lopsided frown?" Erin asks. "I thought you'd be ecstatic about the invite to Wimbledon."

"I am."

"You could have fooled me. We've known each other since we were six. That frown means you're frustrated. Is it the mission?"

Erin would see through any lie, so I admit, "It's more than the mission."

She'll assume it's another low-risk CRM, involving a basic info exchange. Due to the confidentiality of the mission, she doesn't know the details. She only knows to be on higher alert.

"Do you want to talk about what's bothering you?"

"I'd hoped for an invitation to play singles, so it's a letdown."

I can't tell her the mission is why I didn't get the singles invite.

"I suspected as much. At least you weren't left out entirely."

"True. But it's more complicated than that. I'll be playing with Blake Knight."

"Is he a jerk?"

"No. We got to know each other *extremely* well a couple of years ago."

"Do you mean what I think you mean? Are you saying you two did the twisted-sheet tango?"

I laugh. "That's a new one, but yes, we spent a long, incredibly enjoyable night together."

"How did I not know? With you that's frontpage news."

"God, I hope not. That's one reason I've been selective. But I know what you mean. You were on vacation at the time, so my parents sent two other guards. I gave them strict instructions not to mention my guest."

"Are you hoping to rekindle the relationship?"

"It wasn't a relationship. Neither of us wanted that. And even if I did want to hook up again, I can't. He may be involved in my mission. I'll know more when I'm fully briefed. Regardless, I can't let emotions distract me."

"Let's hope he's on the periphery of your mission. If that's the case, there's no reason not to have a little fun." She waggles her eyebrows.

"Not this time. I'm worried it's going to be awkward though."

"Keep an open mind. If the chemistry is still there, who knows what will happen."

"We'll see." I sigh.

# 5

## BLAKE

Josh is doing double duty on the practice court today. He's nagging me about minor flaws in my game while also serving as my practice partner. The drills he's taking me through are particularly brutal—my punishment for insisting we play during the warmest hours of the afternoon. But that's part of my new plan. If I practice in the harshest conditions, any other time of day will seem easy.

During a quick break, I grab a towel to mop off the copious sweat running down my face and neck. Pulling the cloth away from my eyes, I notice two women walking toward us from the far end of our court. The glare from the sun makes it hard to recognize them, so I don't pay much attention. There must be a mistake, though, because we reserved this court for another hour.

I'm relieved when Josh jogs toward them. He'll take care of the scheduling mix up before they reach me.

While he deals with the women, I hustle back onto the court to practice my serve.

I've only served half a dozen balls when Josh shouts, "Blake, come over here for a minute."

"Can't you handle the scheduling problem? I need to keep practicing."

"It's not about court reservations. We need to talk."

"Give me a minute."

I toss a ball into the air and swing with my full strength, lunging into the court. At impact I let out a loud "Grrr," releasing my annoyance at the unwelcome interruption. My perfect serve skims across the net at over 135 mph, landing exactly where I aimed.

With that satisfying result, I take my time walking to the side of the court where Josh is.

"What's the problem?" I ask Josh, ignoring the uninvited guests.

"There's no problem. I want to introduce you to Her Royal Highness, the Princess of Catalinius."

My jaw drops as I finally take a closer look at the women standing next to Josh, my focus landing on the one with the silky, mahogany hair tied back in a bouncy ponytail. Involuntarily, my scowl turns into a smile.

"Bri. What a surprise," I say, ignoring all proper formalities.

I haven't seen her up close for two years. I'd forgotten the mischievous light in her stunning emerald eyes and the way her smile exudes energy and a love for life.

It looks like she just finished a practice session, but she's gorgeous even with a sweaty sheen coating her lightly tanned skin.

I can't help noticing that her arm and leg muscles are more defined than they were the last time I saw her. That would have required a significant amount of time in the gym. She may be a princess, but her work ethic must be stellar, which is a hot surprise. I'd love a chance to have those long legs wrap around me again while I pull her tempting ponytail.

Bri interrupts my fantasy, saying, "It's good to see you, Blake."

"It's been too long. Were you looking for *me*?"

"I was hoping we could set up our practice schedule. We need time playing together before our first match."

"What are you talking about?"

"I know you're ranked in the top five for singles, but as you know, doubles tennis is different. And we've never played as partners before. We need to get comfortable with each other and coordinate our signals before our first-round match."

I point at her and then back at myself. "Are you supposed to be my doubles partner?"

That can't be possible. Partnering with Brianna would be too strange after our one-time encounter two years ago. It would be awkward at best and more likely extremely frustrating, at least to my cock. I don't have time for distractions like this.

I look at her, almost pleading for her to tell me I'm wrong.

Instead, she looks hurt yet defiant, as she responds, "I'm a solid doubles player. I promise that I won't embarrass you."

Shite. I've just insulted her. That wasn't my intention.

"That's not what I meant. I didn't realize you were supposed to be my partner. Of course, I'd be honored to play with you. But the problem is that I need to focus on winning singles this year. And you need to focus on your own singles matches. Shouldn't we skip the mixed doubles?"

A look of horror crosses her face but is quickly replaced with a neutral expression.

Looking upward, she bites her upper lip, clearly deciding what to say next. After an awkward silence, she lowers her eyes to mine, saying, "I'm not playing singles. My wild card is only for mixed doubles."

Did I hear her correctly?

"Are you saying you can only play at Wimbledon if we play together?"

"Exactly."

"Fuck."

"Don't you dare speak to Her Royal Highness in that manner," says the other woman, whom I now recognize as Martina, Bri's coach.

"Martina, it's fine. Blake and I are friends. Give us some space to discuss this."

"As you wish, but I'll be nearby as will your guard."

"Thank you. Blake, let's walk to the back of the court so we can talk privately."

"Of course."

I walk by her side, taking in her intoxicating scent. It's a mystery how she smells so sweet after a workout. I accidentally drift closer, and our arms almost brush, but I catch myself just in time. Reaching the back of the court, we stop. We're far enough away from the others to talk privately.

Brianna turns to face me.

Before she says anything, I need to clear the air.

"I'm sorry, Bri. I wasn't intending to be disrespectful to you. It's the situation. This is the only major I've never won. I need to focus. But if I do that, I'll let you down."

"We can make this work. We only need a little practice time. You'll still have plenty of time to prep for your singles matches. I'd love to see you win this year."

"I don't see how this could work."

"I've wanted my chance to play at Wimbledon my entire career. This may be my only opportunity. And it would be a disaster for me, and my family, if the press reports that you don't think I'm an acceptable playing partner. My career would be over. No one would ever invite me to any future tournaments. Please don't do that to me."

Her eyes well with unshed tears as her head falls in defeat.

A tear rolls down her cheek. I step closer, gently lifting her chin with my index finger so our eyes meet.

The genuine hurt on her face rips at my heart. If someone told me I couldn't play after years of waiting for an invitation, I'd be crushed.

I pull her into a hug, which is probably not allowed—but hell, what's a bloke to do?

"I could never deprive you of your opportunity here. Of course, I'll do it."

Heaven knows my ache to win here is crushing me. I can't be responsible for inflicting that level of pain upon her.

"Thank you."

As we pull apart, our coaches approach.

Josh asks, "Have you two worked things out?"

"We have. Can you and Martina set up a couple of practice sessions this week?" I ask.

"Will do," Josh says.

"Mr. Knight, you've cursed, made the princess cry, and engaged in inappropriate PDA with her. If this partnership is going to work, it will take more than a couple of practice sessions," Martina chides.

"Don't worry. We'll figure it out. We've meshed well together before," I say, winking at Bri.

She blushes, which ignites a different type of fire in me.

Detailed memories of our prior night together resurface. There's no doubt she's a distraction I don't need right now. I'd love to spend more time with her, though. The timing is just off.

"Where are you and your team staying?" I ask.

"Martina and my physio have a small place nearby. Tonight, I'll be at the castle with Stephen and Adrian. I'm not sure where I'm staying after that. I've been told not to worry about it."

"We have an enormous house with plenty of extra space. We're only using 4 of the 7 bedrooms. You can stay with us if you would like."

Why did I blurt that out? Us staying in the same house would be a disaster.

"The palace is insisting that I stay somewhere that can accommodate me, my bodyguard, and my chef, but thanks for the invitation."

"Let me know if you change your mind."

"I'll let them know that it's an option, but I'm sure that they've made arrangements by now."

I barely keep myself from saying I hope not. I'm definitely warming to the idea of having Bri around for the next two and a half weeks. I wouldn't mind a repeat of two years ago.

Wait a minute. Have I lost my mind?

Playing doubles is enough of a distraction without having Bri living under the same roof. I have to find a way to remain focused on singles while allowing Bri to fulfill her dream of competing at Wimbledon.

Bloody hell! How will I do that?

This whole situation has thrown me off-kilter. My mind is racing through options.

"Did you want to practice a little now?" I ask, hoping to get it over with, so I can get back on schedule and execute my plan.

What am I saying? I'm not through with my singles practice. She needs to go—even if a certain part of my body disagrees.

"I can't today. I have an hour drive to dinner tonight."

"Are you meeting friends?"

"Yes. I'm catching up with Adrian and Stephen."

"Prince Adrian and Prince Stephen?"

"That's right. We've known each other since we were teenagers, but we don't see each other very often. They live in a castle not too far from here part of the time, so this is the perfect opportunity. I'll be too busy after the tournament starts, so they invited me to dinner and to stay at the castle tonight."

I'm not sure what to say when someone nonchalantly mentions having dinner at a castle to chat with a couple of princes. I go with, "That's nice."

"It will be. Oh, and before we go, let me give you the contact information for me, Erin, and Martina.

She hands me a card with their information and says, "See you soon."

Smiling and waving, she turns and leaves the court.

My eyes follow her perfect, swaying bum. It's a visible reminder that I need to stay away from her except for tennis. She's trouble.

Hell, her friends are British princes, and her temporary hotel is a castle. I can't offer her that level of luxury. What was I thinking, inviting her to stay at my house? She wouldn't want to have dinner with me, much less spend another night in my bed. Our prior night was meant to be a one-off.

I wonder if she regrets it. Why do I even care?

Shaking my head, I realize it's for the best that I'm reminded of our differences. We'll keep our tennis partnership purely platonic and limit our time together.

"Josh, let's get back to work. We've wasted enough time on that foolishness."

# 6

## BRIANNA

I let out a long sigh as Martina, Erin, and I leave the court.

"Are you okay?" Martina asks.

"That was tough. I knew Blake wouldn't be excited about playing doubles, but I thought he had agreed to it. I felt like an idiot when he said he didn't even know I was his partner. Then he tried to talk me out of playing."

"I didn't know. If I had, I wouldn't have let you walk into that situation."

"I know. Blake and I worked it out though. It's fine."

"Fine isn't enough. I'll talk with Josh. He will get Blake in line."

"No. Don't. I have this under control."

"Are you sure?"

"I am. I need to hurry now, or I'll be late for dinner."

"This way. Your car is waiting," Erin says.

As we walk in silence, I process how small I felt having to talk Blake into playing doubles with me. Tears threatened to fall, but I managed to hold them back. The thought of not playing at Wimbledon was overwhelming. Even worse, I couldn't fathom blowing my CRM before it even started. I had to convince him to play, even if it meant swallowing my pride and begging, which was rare for me. Usually, people beg me to do something for them.

Then he comforted me with a hug, engulfing me in his lean six-foot-three frame and holding me tight with his bulging biceps and muscular forearms. Damn, he felt good. I swear I could feel his eight pack through our tennis shirts, and I'm fairly certain that wasn't the only part of his body that was hard. His warm body against mine sent shivers from my head to my toes, conjuring memories of our hot night together.

Why does he have to be so damn attractive? I'd love to run my fingers through his thick, dark hair, lose myself in his deep blue eyes, and let his faint five o'clock shadow tickle me as we kiss. It's going to take all my fortitude not to give in to those desires. And based on our hug, I suspect it's not going to be easy for him either.

I'll have to repeatedly remind myself that I'm spying on him because he may be a criminal. No way can anything happen between us. I can't sleep with someone who may be part of something illegal.

"What time do we have a practice court tomorrow?" I ask.

"Josh is double-checking their schedule. I'll text you when they confirm," Martini answers.

"Make sure I have enough time to drive here from the castle. I'll do my gym workout there if we're practicing in the afternoon."

"I'll let you know."

My coach and I part ways as Erin and I slip into the black Range Rover. Recalling the look on Blake's face when I mentioned dinner with Adrian and Stephen, I smile. Blake is such a celebrity that I think of him as tennis royalty. But his reaction was a reminder that he's not accustomed to dining with titled royals and staying at castles.

My life isn't normal even for a tennis star like him. Hell, my life isn't normal for most royals. Only a handful of us are part of the Covert Royals program, and I'm the only one trying to have a tennis career while keeping up my royal duties. That's why Adrian, Stephen, and I are such good friends. The three of us were the sole members of the first Covert Royals class, and we still train together in April and May each year, along with those who joined after us.

While I told Blake that dinner tonight is for catching up with the princes, it's only been a couple of weeks since Adrian, Stephen, and I were sweating our way through martial arts drills, practicing our sharpshooting, running an obstacle course, and learning about the latest listening devices.

Somehow, I managed to meet Martina at the adjoining tennis facility for two hours each day as well. I couldn't afford to skip that training in case the Wimbledon invite came through. Looking back on those weeks, Covert Royals camp makes my regular tennis training seem like a breeze.

That's why Blake's life, with only tennis to think about, seems like a dream to me. I owe my parents so much for allowing me to pursue tennis along with fulfilling the duties of my birthright. Most royal parents would have quashed my pro tennis career before it began. Fortunately, mine were more open-minded.

***

AFTER A QUICK SHOWER, I SLIP INTO A LITTLE BLACK DRESS AND APPLY SOME makeup. Transformation complete, I go in search of the dining room. It's a bit of a memory test because I haven't been here for a while. But I don't mind. It's a rare pleasure to wander around somewhere on my own. That's the luxury of staying at the castle. I'm perfectly safe and don't need Erin shadowing me tonight. It's almost like being at home in the Catalinius palace.

Hearing familiar voices, I walk through the double doors at the end of a long hallway and am instantly enveloped in the arms of my good friends.

Prince Stephen is two years older and an inch shorter than his younger brother Adrian. They both have golden hair with brown streaks, but Stephen wears his slightly shorter. That's where the similarities end, though. Stephen is serious but empathetic, like his father. Adrian, on the other hand, finds interesting ways to have fun while still achieving his goals. They're both wonderful guys I'm lucky to have as friends.

"We're so excited you're at Wimbledon this year," Adrian says.

"Thanks. It's been a long time coming."

"We know. And that's why we're horrified that you were denied the invitation to play singles. You clearly earned it," Stephen says.

"You know about that?"

"Of course, and we're upset for you. I can't imagine how disappointed you must be," Adrian says.

"Extremely. Thanks for understanding. Tennis is important to me, but I love my family and country more. That's why I eagerly embraced the opportunity to prepare for covert missions with the two of you when I turned seventeen. It made me feel special that I could do something for my country and our allies. I also knew there would be personal sacrifices, but this one hit particularly hard. How did you find out?"

"We're your contacts for the mission. Tonight's your follow-up briefing," Adrian says.

"I should have known. Hopefully, the briefing includes dinner though. I'm starving."

Stephen laughs. "We promise to feed you. We can't have the next mixed-doubles champion collapsing from lack of food."

"Definitely not. Can you imagine the tabloid headlines? *Princess Collapses on Tennis Court Due to Food Deprivation!*" Adrian teases.

"You two are such jokesters. It's like being around my brothers, except they would never approve of the covert part of our lives."

"I'm surprised you've kept that from them. I was sure they would find out when Xander became king," Stephen says.

"I made a deal with my parents that we wouldn't tell him unless it became a matter of national security. It took a bit of persuasion, but they eventually agreed."

"You always have been persuasive," Stephen says with a wink.

"I'll take that as a compliment. Now, I'm ready for dinner and the briefing. The video briefing only gave me the basic outline of the mission. I'm still in shock that I'll be spying on my tennis partner."

"I'm sure you weren't expecting that part," Adrian says.

"Not in my wildest dreams. By the way, who's here from British Intelligence?"

"Matt is on his way. He should be here any minute," Adrian says.

"Matthew Harrington? The Deputy Director?"

They nod.

That's a new development. This mission must be more serious than I thought if someone in his high position is handling the briefing tonight.

"My prior missions have never involved anyone at his level. I should have guessed though. The briefing suggested that this mission isn't like any of my prior ones where I was a glorified messenger."

"Your Royal Highness will be much more than a messenger this time," Deputy Director Harrington says as his shoes click across the polished hardwood floor.

We turn and watch as the middle-aged gentleman in his finely tailored suit and tie approaches. He's noticeably aged since I last saw him. I wonder if it's stress that added the wrinkles to his face and the extra gray to his salt-and-pepper hair and mustache.

Reaching us, he stops and bows his head to each of us in turn, showing his respect for our titles.

Extending my hand, I say, "Deputy Director Harrington, please call me Bri."

When we arrived for our first training, we were disappointed to learn that British Intelligence doesn't use Double-O designations for its agents. Apparently, those designations only exist in movies. Instead, we go by our first names unless a mission requires aliases, which are usually common names that no one we encounter is likely to remember.

It's not that we wanted a license to kill, but we liked the idea of being special agents with secret identities.

"Thank you, Bri. And please call me Matt tonight."

"I'm anxious to hear about the mission. I gather it's serious and potentially dangerous."

"Before we discuss the details, let's have dinner," Matt says.

Adrian leads us to the table for four, and servers magically appear with heritage tomato and burrata salads accompanied by glasses of sauvignon blanc.

When the staff leaves, Adrian says, "Bri, I know you're probably avoiding alcohol during the tournament, but it's customary to toast the beginning of each mission for good luck. Will you join us?"

"Of course. One sip won't hurt."

"Then raise your glasses to completing this mission safely and, in doing so, protecting the history and integrity of our countries. Cheers."

We each take a sip. My nerves are on edge with his mention of safety and protecting our countries. Just how much danger will there be? This is what I've wanted, but I thought the missions would ramp up slowly with each mission slightly more serious than the prior one. It sounds like I'm being thrown into the Arctic Ocean when I've only stepped into a shallow hot tub before.

"I'm ready to hear the details. I'm the one surveilling the suspect but seem to know less about the mission than everyone else here," I say.

While I wait for Matt to begin, I take a bite of my salad. Yum. Without thinking, I reach for the wine and take a sip, letting its acidity cut through the creaminess of the cheese. Then I remember that I'd only planned to have a sip for the toast, so I set the glass back on the table. I need to stay sharp.

Matt says, "Many European countries prohibit the export of certain ancient coins even if privately owned. They are considered national treasures and must remain in their homelands."

"Catalinius has such a law. Too many of our coins were lost before we enacted laws to protect them. In some instances, our national museum doesn't even have an example to exhibit, or if they do, it's an inferior one," I say.

"A number of ancient coins started appearing for sale at various auctions around the world without proof of a legal origin. In other words, the sellers cannot show that the coins were legally exported from their home countries. In some instances, we're certain the exportation was illegal because of the timing. We know they left their home countries within the last year." Matt says.

"How did that happen?" I ask.

"Smugglers," he replies flatly.

"What does that have to do with Blake?" I ask, wanting to hear Matt's version of the story Walter told me in my video briefing.

"We have evidence that the coins are leaving the affected countries at the end of tennis tournaments and being passed to intermediaries for the buyers at other tennis tournaments. We don't know how they're hiding the coins to smuggle them between countries."

"That's terrible, but again, why am I watching Blake. What does he have to do with it?"

"There were only two pro players who were at all the tournaments. Blake was one of them."

"It can't be Blake. He doesn't need the money. He's one of the top players. It must be the other player or someone who travels with one of them. It would more likely be one of them, wouldn't it?"

"We have someone watching the other player and his team. As for Blake, we believe he lost a significant amount of money in a bad investment. He may be in need of money, so we're taking a deeper look into his finances now."

"I've spent time with Blake in the past. It's hard to believe he might be a criminal. Do you have any other evidence that points to his involvement?"

"He's been seen having dinner and meeting with people we suspect are receiving the coins."

How can my judgment have been so bad? He comes across as a dedicated tennis player and good guy. Sure, he can be somewhat of an arsehole if you interrupt his concentration, like we did today. But I'd never suspect he'd be involved in illegal smuggling. Wouldn't that be the ultimate distraction if he were always worried about being caught?

There must be another explanation, and I'll be in the perfect position to find it.

Rather than share those thoughts, I say, "I'm shocked, but that explains why Blake is a suspect. What do I need to do?"

"I assume you know the top players on tour, but how well do you and Blake know each other?" Adrian asks.

I cough, almost choking on a bite of tomato. That's a loaded question. He doesn't need to know that Blake has an adorable birthmark on his left butt cheek or that he has "Love means nothing" tattooed across his lower abdomen in reference to "love" being a score of zero in tennis.

Clearing my throat, I simply say, "I've always been one of his fans. We met at Wimbledon a couple of years ago and danced at the gala. He was smart and enjoyable to be around but extremely focused on tennis."

"It's good that you're not strangers. As his tennis partner, you need to gain his trust and convince him to talk to you. Find out if he's stressed about money. Figure out if he's hiding something. See what he knows about coin collecting. Any information you can gather will be helpful," Matt says.

"Blake and I met briefly this afternoon. It was difficult to convince him to practice with me. It will be even harder to find opportunities to talk. He keeps a strict schedule from what I can tell. Will I be staying anywhere close to the house he rented?"

"We haven't found anything as close as we would like yet."

"I should have taken him up on his offer for me and my bodyguards to stay at his house." I laugh.

"Did he actually invite you to stay at his place?" Matt asks.

"He asked where we were staying. When I told him the details weren't confirmed yet, he said he had three extra bedrooms we could use. I'm not sure if the invitation was real, but I knew no one would want me to be that close to a suspect. I was joking about taking him up on the offer."

"Staying with him would be perfect," Stephen says.

"It would. Call him and accept the offer. You can move in tomorrow afternoon," Matt orders.

"Should I be staying with someone who may be involved in criminal activities?"

"He's not suspected of any violent crime. Don't tell me you have cold feet. You've been begging for a more substantial assignment. Have you changed your mind?" Matt asks.

"That's not it. I was concerned about what people would think. Blake and I aren't a couple, but you know the tabloids love to crucify me when they suspect I'm spending nights with someone. It will be even worse if he turns out to be involved in smuggling."

I leave out the fact that I don't trust myself living in the same house as Blake. The fiery desire he ignites in me is off the charts. My body doesn't seem to care that he may be a criminal.

"Don't worry about the tabloids. We'll take care of them. It's more important for you to be close to him. We also want you to plant surveillance devices. This will give you the best opportunity. It's a brilliant solution!" Matt smiles.

"I told him other arrangements were being made. Won't he be suspicious if I change my mind now?"

"Tell him that those arrangements fell through and now you're desperate for a place to stay closer to the venue. Remind him that you can't commute from the castle. It would take too long," Adrian says.

Out of excuses, I say, "I'll take care of it."

We may have to share a house, but that's all we'll share. I can't let my walls down.

"Excellent," Matt says.

"How do I report what I learn?" I ask.

"You'll use the encrypted app on your phone. We've also devised a backup plan in case that doesn't work. That way you'll still be able to exchange messages with these two even if you can't text," he says, pointing to Adrian and Stephen.

Adrian says, "That's right. We've arranged for all your doubles matches to be on Centre Court as part of the backup plan."

"How did you manage that?" I ask.

Stephen says, "It was simple. We reminded the organizers that people love seeing a princess on the court, and Blake is a top seed. You two will be a popular draw."

When I'm focused on tennis, I forget that royal watchers don't care that I'm not a high-ranking player. Sometimes it's like I'm a sightseeing attraction rather than a competitor in their eyes, which is discouraging. I want people to respect my hard work and my tennis wins.

Shaking it off, I ask, "I assume you've worked out a signaling mechanism for when we can't use the app. Is that right?"

Adrian says, "We have. Either Stephen or I will be in the Royal Box on Centre Court each day. If one of us is wearing a purple tie, then we need to talk to you. You'll be invited to a private room after the match."

"That works. No one will be surprised that royals are greeting each other away from the cameras. How do I signal you when I need to pass information to you?"

Stephen says, "During the first set of the match, lay two tennis racquets on the ground in front of your bench before you serve the first time. We'll then arrange an invitation to meet at the end of the match."

"Okay. What if the app fails and we need to reach each other on days Blake and I aren't playing?"

Matt says, "We have a plan for that as well. Attend an afternoon match on Centre Court if you need to talk. We've reserved a seat for you at all the matches. Adrian or Stephen will notice and invite you to meet. If we need to reach you, then we'll have purple roses delivered to your house that morning. You'll show up at the afternoon match on Centre Court, and at the appropriate time, you'll be taken to meet one of the princes."

"You've thought of everything."

"We hope so. And you know the drill. Don't remove your tracker for any reason," Stephen says.

"I won't."

"Which tracker are you wearing," Adrian asks.

"It's the newest model. While we were at training camp a few weeks ago, the techs inserted the tracker into the pendant I'm wearing. I'll keep it around my neck throughout the mission. You can follow me on your smartphone."

"We'll sync our apps to your tracker tonight."

"Sounds good. Who is the other player you suspect?"

"For now, we think it's safer if you don't know. If it becomes important, we'll tell you," Matt says.

"Understood. What else should I know?"

"We need to go over the devices you'll be installing and make sure you remember how to clone a phone," Matt says.

"We went over it in training earlier this summer."

"You did. But we'll be going over it again tonight. There's no room for error."

Adrian says, "Bri won't make any mistakes. Now, let's head to the study. The devices are set up there."

His confidence in me as a Covert Royal is reassuring.

Adrian and Stephen are like brothers to me after the tough training we've endured together. We've had each other's backs at the camp for years. Now, we'll take care of each other in the real world. I won't let them or our countries down.

# 7
## BLAKE

My phone buzzes as I'm heading out the front door of my rental home.

I ignore it.

It rings again.

No one is going to interfere with my morning run. I pull my mobile from my pocket, ready to send the call to voicemail—until I do a double take.

Bri is calling.

Without thinking, I answer, "What's up, Tennis Princess?"

She laughs. "Hello, Blake."

"I couldn't resist. Hope you don't mind?"

"Not the way you say it. Umm . . . never mind, that came out wrong. I'm calling to ask a favor. I need to take you up on the invitation to stay at your house. It turned out to be impossible to find a place that can accommodate me, my bodyguard, and my chef at the last minute. Can we move in later today?"

I swallow hard.

What the hell was I thinking? The last thing I need is the perfectly toned goddess living under my roof while I try to break my losing streak at Wimbledon. She is distraction personified. I never should have invited her to stay here.

Who would have thought she would accept my offer? Sure, my cock was hoping, but she's a real-life princess. She doesn't stay in the house of a mere tennis player—not even a rather wealthy one.

Shite. I'm screwed. I can't exactly uninvite royalty.

I could get rid of her if I refuse to play mixed doubles. That won't work though. Noah says my clothing sponsor insists that I play. They'll cancel my multi-million-pound contract if I back out. I'd also be extinguishing Bri's first, and maybe only, chance to compete here. I can't do it.

This situation will require me to rein in my emotions. I can do that, but I'm worried that her mere presence in my home will impact my focus. Will I have the same effect on her?

Given my body's reaction to her when we met on the court, the close proximity definitely will be a challenge. Not only is she beautiful, but she's also intelligent, witty, talented, and kind. She makes me want to break my self-imposed ban on long-distance relationships. But I can't—not for anyone.

What am I thinking? She's not going to want me anyway—she's a damn princess.

Whew. I'm safe—for now. But I can't let her keep sending my thoughts into a spin like this.

Letting out a deep breath, I finally answer, "Sure. Glad to help out. I'll let my team know you'll be arriving."

"Brilliant. Thanks so much. I'll owe you for this."

I don't say it, but I wouldn't mind collecting that debt with another weekend like two years ago if it were after the tournament. The problem is our chemistry. The electricity between us is palpable even over the phone. It's going to be difficult to stay away from her.

But I'm in my gentleman mode, so I say, "No worries. We'll enjoy your company. I'm hoping your chef can cook for all of us. Our catering service cancelled at the last minute."

"Of course. I'll let Chef Fausto know that he'll need to stock the kitchen and prepare meals for your team too."

"Perfect. See you soon."

At least I'll eat well.

*Then again, there are other things I'd like to savor besides the chef's cooking.*

*I'm in so much trouble.*

# 8

## BRIANNA

Deep breath. I've got this. I have to, or they'll never trust me with another mission.

I just wish Operation Denarius didn't involve spying on the guy I've spent far too many nights thinking about.

Truth is, no one since Blake has stirred passion in me the way he did. Thankfully, he'll never know how many times he's starred in my fantasies on lonely nights.

He may be a criminal though. I don't know how to process that information. It doesn't sync with anything I know, or have heard, about him. I'm probably relying too heavily on my brief encounter with him.

Of course, it's also possible that something happened after our night together. Maybe he needed money. Maybe he was forced into the smuggling business. Matt mentioned a bad investment. I suppose that could explain it.

But why does it matter? I can't let myself get emotionally involved. I don't need a broken heart, and he could rip mine to shreds in a fast second.

The problem is that everything about him excites me—from his laser focus to his hard, cut body and his sexual prowess. I have no idea when he had time to hone those skills, but boy did he learn them to perfection. I guess that's his thing. He strives to be the best at everything he does. I chuckle to myself at that thought.

There won't be a repeat.

There can't be.

With a sigh, I attempt to banish any desires for Blake from my consciousness. Ready for the next phase of Operation Denarius, I ring the doorbell accompanied by Erin and Fausto.

Oops—mental note: stop thinking of Fausto as my protector. He's playing the role of chef to hide that I'm traveling with extra security. We don't want anyone to ask questions.

The front door swings open, and I'm face to face with a six-foot-tall, rail-thin blonde who looks like a model.

"Hello. Who are you?" she asks.

Jealousy flickers. Just a twinge—but it's there. It hadn't occurred to me that Blake would have a live-in girlfriend, much less one who would be here. So much for worrying about how I'll handle amorous advances from Blake. There won't be any with this beauty in the house.

I push the disappointment aside. Personal feelings don't belong on a mission. She poses an unexpected challenge. As his girlfriend, she'll keep him busy during downtime. How will I find excuses to spend time with Blake other than on the practice court?

Before the silence stretches too long, Erin steps in. "This is Her Royal Highness, Princess Brianna of Catalinius. I'm her bodyguard Erin, and this is Chef Fausto. Mr. Knight should have told you to expect us."

"Of course, I should have recognized you. Your Royal Highness, welcome. I'm Dr. Anastasia, but please call me Natalie. Your rooms are at the top of the stairs on the left. We've taken the rooms to the right. Blake is up there now if you need to speak with him."

I reach out my hand. "Natalie, it's nice to meet you. In private, just call me Brianna. Titles are too awkward when we're sharing a house."

"Perfect. How long have you known Blake? He never mentioned he's friends with royalty," she says.

Erin interrupts, "While you two chat, I'll check out the bedrooms upstairs. Chef, you should inspect the kitchen."

He nods, and they walk away. That's their excuse for doing a discreet security sweep before they let me venture farther into the home.

For now, I'll wait with Natalie in the large modern foyer. From here I can see into open spaces ahead as well as a study through the double doors on my left and a sitting area through an archway on my right. The interior of this large home has been completely renovated from what I can tell. It's bright and modern with light-colored floors, sleek décor, and clean lines. The fresh feel and inviting vibes are welcoming.

"Great. I'll be up in a minute," I say before turning back to answer Natalie. "Blake and I met a couple of years ago here at Wimbledon. This will be our first time as doubles partners though. How about you? When did you two meet?"

"About three months ago. His coach introduced us to each other. Hopefully, my presence will be calming for Blake. Winning this tournament means the world to him."

"It sounds like you two have a strong relationship."

"It's built on trust. That and good communication."

"True. Please excuse me though. I need to unpack and get ready for practice."

"Forgive me for monopolizing your time. It's wonderful to have two more women in the house with all these men."

I wave and walk up the staircase, pondering the sincerity of her comment. With looks like hers, I guess she doesn't worry much about competition. Personally, I've never been that sure of myself when it comes to men.

It's not that I can't attract men, I just never know if they're worth it. Men usually want me for my title, money, or the publicity that comes with dating royalty. That's one reason I've sworn off relationships for now.

At least with Natalie here, I won't be tempted to fall for Blake because I honor girl code. I'd never steal someone else's boyfriend. I also don't like showing up on the front page of tabloids as the butt of a joke about a relationship gone wrong. Been there. Done that. Never again.

Erin is waiting for me at the top of the stairs.

"Which room is mine?" I ask.

"This one," she says, pointing to the first room on my left.

"Great. Please tell me it has a tub."

Before Erin can answer, Blake joins us on the landing. "Sorry— just a walk-in shower. Unfortunately, my bath is the only one with a soaking tub. But you're welcome to use it any time you like," he says.

Hmm. That might come in handy.

"Thanks. I wouldn't mind a hot bath while you're out practicing."

"You don't have to wait for me to leave." He winks.

"I'm sure Dr. Anastasia would object to that."

He frowns. "Why would Natalie care?"

"Most women wouldn't appreciate another woman taking a bath in their boyfriend's room."

Blake laughs, "Natalie is my sports psychologist. She's helping me stay in the right mindset and avoid another failure at Wimbledon."

"Isn't it unusual for doctors to date their patients?" I ask.

"What gave you the idea we're dating? Don't tell me you're jealous." He smirks.

"Of course, not. Something she said made me think you two were together."

"Natalie's wife, Cecilia, would strongly object, so that's not happening."

Oops. I completely misread the situation, and I just made it worse. Now, Blake has a mischievous sparkle in his eye as if he likes the idea that I'm jealous.

I pivot. "Thanks again for letting us stay. I need to check on Chef Fausto."

"Why not let Erin handle that?"

"Fausto speaks Italian, and I'm the only one on our team who can translate. Do you or anyone on your team speak Italian?"

"No."

I smile inwardly. Perfect. People rarely pay attention to servers or kitchen staff and talk freely in their presence. Conversations will flow even more freely given that Fausto is Italian. While his English is perfect, he won't be sharing that fact with anyone in the house. That means he can eavesdrop without anyone knowing he understands every word.

"That's too bad," I say.

"Did you grow up speaking Italian?"

"English is the primary language in Catalinius, but we're near the coast of France and Italy. My parents insisted my nanny teach me both languages when I was very young. I went to uni in Paris, so my French ended up stronger, but I'm fluent in both."

"I wish I'd learned more than Italian growing up. It would come in handy at times like these. How will we tell Fausto what we need to eat?"

"I'd be happy to help with that. What would you like him to prepare for you?"

"I'm sure my diet is much like yours—whole grains, lean proteins, fresh fruits and vegetables, and healthy fats. I avoid processed foods as much as possible."

"That makes sense. Are you allergic to any foods?"

"No. But please tell him I don't eat raw fish or raw meat. I'm not willing to risk food poisoning during a tournament."

"A lot of tennis players love sushi as part of their match-day routine, but I agree with you. I'll let him know."

I walk down the stairs wondering what types of food Fausto

knows how to cook. He's a big, burly man who looks like he lives on fish and chips, pizza, and burgers. Hopefully, healthy meals are in his repertoire. If not, his career as a chef will be short-lived, and his cover will be blown.

# 9
## BLAKE

Josh and I warm up on the practice court while we wait for Bri. I'm not thrilled about spending time on doubles practice, but I don't really have a choice. If we're not in sync, we'll fail miserably and embarrass ourselves.

The joint session is cutting into my regular workout time. I want to keep it short, then work on my singles strategy.

I'm just starting to sweat when Bri appears, making me miss what should have been a perfectly placed drop shot. Instead of falling just over the net, it clips the top and drops back onto my side.

Bloody hell. She's a distraction I don't need.

I can't stop staring at her. Her short white tennis skirt and sleeveless, body-hugging top hug every delicious curve.

"Good morning. It looks like we won't have rain today," she says, stretching her arms above her head. Her shirt lifts enough to flash a strip of smooth skin.

I nod, avoiding eye contact. No need to give away what's in my head.

Fortunately, Josh jumps in. "We can be thankful for the nice weather. Martina and I have a practice plan for today, but take a few minutes to warm up with Blake first."

That's when I notice Bri's coach, Martina, standing courtside.

"Perfect," Bri says with a grin, jogging to take Josh's place across the net.

I'm tempted to slam the ball across the net to release tension, but Bri shouldn't be the target of my frustration. This isn't her fault. The blame falls on my sponsor—and the Wimbledon committee that denied her the singles wild card she deserved.

We work through a standard warm-up: baseline shots, volleys, overheads, and serves. Her serve is powerful. Two years ago, she said that she was focusing on it. Clearly, it paid off.

We'll see if the rest of her game holds up. I've heard she's become more competitive, but I haven't seen her play lately.

Ten minutes in, Josh stops us. "That's good. Let's play a couple of doubles games. Martina and I will be your opponents."

"Fine. I'll serve first," I say.

Bri asks, "Shouldn't we coordinate hand signals? Or do you prefer to talk between points, so I'll know where you're placing your serve?"

"For now, let's just play and see what happens."

She shrugs but her narrowed eyes reveal her frustration. Serious doubles teams always coordinate on every point. But right now? I can't be bothered.

Especially with her bent over in front of me, ready at the net, her tight bum directly in my line of sight. Whispering strategies would push me over the edge. I'll be needing a cold shower after this.

My plan: serve aces and avoid the need for strategy.

It doesn't work. Our first two games are a disaster. Martina and Josh return most of my serves. Bri and I have run into each other, left parts of the court wide open, and let balls pass us assuming the other would hit them.

After the second game, Martina and Josh motion for us to meet them at the net.

Shaking her head, Martina says, "I doubt it was your intention, but you two are putting on a hilarious comedy skit. You're more likely to hit each other than the ball. Unless you get your heads in the right place and start working together, you'll have everyone laughing at you. Start talking between points. Share strategy. Act like you're partners with a common goal. Otherwise, it'll be a disaster."

Josh adds, "She's right. Blake, you can't play like you're the only one out there. Move together. Sync up. Let's try this again."

Walking away from the net, I lean toward Bri. "We were in sync a couple of years ago. Timing was perfect, if I remember right." I grin and raise my eyebrows.

Her cheeks flush, and she swats my arse as I pass.

I do like her spunk.

At the back of the court, I realize she followed.

She says, "Let's keep our focus on the game. Our coaches are right. We have to talk between points."

"Fine. I rarely play doubles, so I'm rusty. I can't believe I'm saying this, but I need your help with doubles strategy."

"I understand. Doubles is different. It's all about constant communication and teamwork. I need to know where you're serving, and you need to know where I'm moving. Chemistry's key."

"We've got chemistry. We just need to apply it to tennis," I say with a smirk.

She playfully punches my shoulder. "That was a one-time thing. But we can use our history to work together better. We aren't strangers, so that's a benefit."

"This will take work, and time is tight. Do you have ideas for a plan?"

"Today, let's focus on the basics. First, if I move toward the sideline during a return, you shift toward center. Second, most doubles players stand farther from the centerline to serve. That's your decision though. And finally—"

I interrupt. "I know the last part. Don't play hero. We're a team."

"You got it. Let's make this work."

"Aye, aye, captain," I say, saluting. I can't resist swatting her cute bum with my racquet as she jogs past me on her way to the net. Turnabout is fair play. I smile.

Erin storms toward us, eyes flashing, but Bri waves her off.

Apparently, my racquet on Bri's arse summoned her bodyguard. I shake my head, amused that no one flinched when Bri did it to me.

We start talking more, before and during points. The awkwardness slowly fades. We're still not perfect, but there's progress. We're starting to gel, so there's hope. We'll work together even better when I get over my infatuation with watching her move around the court.

By the end of practice, we're teasing, bumping shoulders, and fist pumping when we win a point.

Finally finished, we plop down on the benches at the side of the court.

I grab a towel, wipe my face, and down a bottle of water while chatting with my coach.

A couple of minutes later, I turn to Bri. "Are you ready to go?"

"Almost. First, I have a question about your racquets," she says, grabbing one from my open bag.

"How do you like this one? It's a new brand for you, isn't it?" she asks, spinning the racquet in her hand, testing the weight and feel.

I reach across to take it back. "Hey, put that down." Annoyance sharpens my tone.

She switches the racquet to her other hand, holding it farther away, flashing one of her wide, infectious smiles.

"What's wrong with you? I'm not going to steal your precious racquet. I'm just looking at it," she teases.

I shrug, chuckling at myself as I run my fingers through my hair to hide the heat rising in my cheeks.

"I don't like people touching them," I mumble.

"That's weird. You do know how many people handle your racquets when you send them for restringing, right?"

"That's a brand new one. I haven't even tried it yet. Never mind. Forget it. It was an involuntary reaction. I usually don't let other players handle my racquets."

"I promise not to steal any secrets." She winks.

"I doubt those racquets will be winners anyway, so I'm not worried about anyone copying them."

"What do you mean? Why use them if you don't like them?"

"That's not what I meant. I'm happy with the power and control overall. But that specific one just won't work for me."

"Huh. That's strange. It's heavier than I expected. Let me hold the one you played with today."

"Here." I hand it to her.

"Wow. There's a huge difference."

"My coach wants me to experiment with different weight distributions. He adds tape on the head and grip. Your coach must do the same, right?"

"She does, but your coach is making larger weight changes in your racquets."

"I still haven't tried the heaviest one. I already know I won't like it, but Josh wants me to test it anyway."

"A couple of these don't have dampeners to minimize vibration. Would you like some of mine? My parents ordered a whole case with our royal seal. I'll never use them all."

"Sure. Why not? Put them on the two heaviest racquets. Then I won't grab them by mistake."

Marco walks up, calling out, "Good to see you, Blake. Why are you complaining? I love my heavy racquets, especially at tournaments like this. Wouldn't want to lose those!"

"If you say so." I wince as he slaps me on the back.

His grin reminds me of a clown's—too big, too fake. That's why we'll never be friends. I'd bet anything he's only buddying up to me to get close to Bri.

Not a heartbeat later, he proves me right.

"Your Highness, I don't think we've officially met. I'm Marco. Welcome to Wimbledon. It's your first time playing here, right?"

Bri's eyes dim as she bites her lip, visibly keeping her emotions in check. My chest tightens at the flicker of pain in her expression. It hurts her to be reminded how long she's waited for this invitation—and it's not even in singles. His insensitive comment mirrors the ones reporters throw at me about never winning Wimbledon. What an arse.

After a brief pause, she says, "I'm happy to be here. It's also a pleasure to meet you. I had the opportunity to watch you play in Paris."

He coughs, caught off guard.

I suppress the laugh that's threatening to escape. He tanked in Paris and lost in the first round. And somehow, she poked him while making it sound like a compliment. *Touché.*

She's no pushover. Her calm poise is a major turn-on.

Eventually, he says, "Unfortunately, I was dealing with a painful hamstring injury. But my sponsors insisted I play. You know how that is."

"You hid it well. You must have a high tolerance for pain. I would have never guessed. Please excuse me, though. I have to go. Good luck with the tournament." She grabs her bag and walks off with a quick wave.

I grin appreciatively. We all know Marco pulls the injury card whenever he plays poorly. It's his go-to excuse.

Only a princess could humble him and leave unscathed. Watching her take Marco's ego down a few notches makes her even more attractive.

It's too bad I can't waste time on doubles. Bri and I would make a dynamite team.

# 10

## BRIANNA

While Blake talks with his coach, I quickly lay a towel over my lap and grab his phone, hiding it under my leg next to mine. With our phones close, a special app on mine starts downloading spy software onto his phone.

The app hasn't finished installing and configuring the software, so I reach for one of his racquets and start asking him questions to delay him.

Fortunately, he doesn't suspect what I'm really doing, and I successfully install the software. Now we can track where he is, capture his text messages and his emails, and so much more.

I betrayed him by invading his privacy. My guilt is offset by the possibility he's involved in criminal activities. But if he's innocent and finds out, he'll never speak to me again.

The vibration pattern on my leg signals the upload is complete. I need to leave before Blake becomes suspicious but use all my restraint not to bolt from the court. Instead, I carefully slip his phone back into his bag before he notices it's missing.

Fortunately, Marco provides an added distraction, but my nerves are starting to fray as I make a hasty departure.

Erin rushes to keep up with me.

Once we slip into the waiting SUV, I let out the breath I'd been holding.

Erin waits until the driver pulls onto the road before asking, "What's up with the hurry?"

"I'd had enough of Marco. He's a bit of a jerk."

That's true even if it's not the whole truth. It's so hard keeping Erin in the dark when we've been friends since childhood and now she also keeps me safe. It's unsettling to think I'm betraying her too, just in a different way.

Erin nods. "I see your point. Your schedule looks fairly open this afternoon. Is there anything you need my help with?"

"No. I'll be staying at the house for the rest of the day. You should take some time for yourself. I plan to work out in the home gym, rest, and then meet with Blake and our coaches for a strategy session later tonight."

"Excellent. I'll see if Fausto needs anything."

Once we reach the house, I hustle up the stairs.

Fortunately, Blake stayed behind for singles practice with his coach. That gives me a chance to search his room.

I grab my cosmetics bag that's loaded with miniature electronics and slip into Blake's room. Soon we'll be monitoring more than just his phone.

In his bathroom, I pull on a pair of latex gloves and start setting up my cover story in case someone walks in. Blake gave me the perfect excuse when he offered me the use of his bathtub. I turn the faucets on full blast and pour in enough bath gel to build mountains of bubbles. While the tub fills, I carefully lay out the surveillance devices on a towel on the bathroom counter.

A quick glance confirms I have a USB drive device to download information from Blake's laptop, plus two listening devices, three cameras, and five trackers. I double-check that my phone app connects to the devices. Fortunately, it works perfectly.

With that done, I turn to see the tub is nearly full. Perfect. I shut off the water and get to work.

Moving quickly, I attach a listening device behind the toilet. A camera in here will be even more invasive, so I search for a spot that will still afford him a little privacy. Noticing some decorative items on top of the cabinet, I hide the camera there and aim it at the sink. That should cover the bathroom.

Back in the bedroom, I tuck the second listening device into a crevice behind the bedside lamp.

I look around the room for the best spots to hide the two remaining cameras. One needs to face the door, the other the bed. Yes, the bed. So much for protecting that part of his privacy.

My heart races, remembering that Blake didn't bother with clothes when we were together. I wonder if he wears anything when he sleeps alone. That thought sends a wave of warmth between my legs.

There's no time for that. I have a mission to complete.

I place a camera in the artwork hanging over the bed. It's the perfect angle to capture the rest of the room, including the door. The other camera fits snugly in a visible black bracket holding the TV that faces the bed. He'll never notice the tiny device.

I'm glad someone else will be monitoring the video feeds. Watching Blake in bed—especially if he brings someone back—would be way too awkward.

Now for the search. I start with the antique two-drawer desk. It doesn't match the rest of the modern furniture. I'd guess it belonged to the homeowner's grandmother, and they can't bear to part with it. Every nick and scratch probably holds a memory.

I rifle through the short stack of papers on top. It's a jumble of receipts, schedules, and a few random notes with dates and times. I snap photos just in case they turn out to be useful. I'll take a closer look at them later. The drawers hold blank notepads, crossword puzzle books, and old greeting cards. It looks like Blake hasn't touched them.

Dropping to the floor, my gaze catches an envelope taped to the underside of the desk. A muffled gasp escapes me. In training, they always told us to check under desks and drawers, inside refrigerators, and under mattresses. But I never expected to actually find something in such a cliché hiding place.

Running my gloved hand over the envelope, I feel the outline of a key. Why would Blake hide a key?

Luckily, the flap is loose. I slide the key out, snap a photo, and grab paper from the desktop to trace its shape. That should be enough information for our team to figure out what type of lock it fits.

Crawling back under the desk, I tuck the key back into the envelope. As I push the flap inside, heavy footsteps pound up the stairs. My body freezes as adrenaline courses through my veins. I listen intently while holding my breath, not daring to make a sound.

It can't be Blake. He's still practicing.

A deep, slightly muffled voice says, "I need to answer some emails. It'll be easier on my laptop than my mobile. When I'm finished, I'll meet you in the study."

It's Blake. What's he doing back so soon?

As silently as possible, I roll out from under the desk, narrowly avoiding bumping my head. I dash into the Blake's bathroom, push the door nearly closed, and drop the key tracing and remaining devices into the wastebasket to retrieve later. I slip into the tub fully clothed just as Blake's bedroom door clicks open.

Unfortunately, the tub isn't deep enough. My wet shirt shows above the bubbles. Ripping it off along with my bra, I tuck them into my tennis skirt and close my eyes, pretending to be relaxed. Let's hope I'm a good actor because my pulse threatens to set a record.

The adrenaline rush is both exciting and overwhelming. This mission is finally putting my training to the test—but nothing could have prepared me for the reality. It's intense. It's exhilarating. And it's terrifying because if Blake figures out why I'm really here . . . well, I'll be totally screwed.

He's just checking his email, I remind myself. That should be quick. I'll sneak out as soon as he leaves.

Through the cracked door, I hear rustling papers and the click of laptop keys.

I lay perfectly still with only my head above the bubbles. Thank goodness I had the bath ready. Worst case, he finds me soaking in his tub. That's totally normal, right?

His footsteps echo across the hardwood floor. They stop. But I don't hear the door close.

Suddenly, the hinges squeak on the bathroom door, and Blake shouts, "Wow!"

I lurch forward, instinctively covering my bare chest. Blake stands in the doorway, wearing nothing but tight black boxer briefs that leave little to the imagination—and are quickly revealing even more.

"What are you doing here?" I screech.

He smirks, eyeing me with a familiar, but unexpected, hunger. A shiver runs down my spine. It's killing me that we can't have another night together. If he's innocent, I'm going to regret this missed opportunity. He knew exactly how to make my body hum.

I blink. He's saying something. "What did you say?"

"Umm. If I remember correctly, this is my room."

"Yes, but you were practicing. You said I could use the bathtub. I thought I'd be finished before you returned."

"I can help you *finish* if you're having trouble," he says, eyebrows dancing.

"Very funny. You know what I mean. Don't be an arse. Why aren't you on the court?"

"Rain cut my practice short. A warm bath sounds amazing. Would you like company?"

"Not this time. Besides, I've been in here too long. The water's already cool. Please give me a little privacy so I can dry off. And no, you're not helping with that either." I smirk.

"That's too bad. But I have one question before I go."

"What's that?"

"Why are you wearing gloves?"

I stare at my hands, stunned. How did I forget to ditch the gloves?

"It's to protect my hands from chapping," I say, not missing a beat. "I love soaking, but I can't mess up my tennis grip."

"Interesting. I've never heard of that being a problem before."

"Trust me. It is. Now, a little privacy."

"Okay. Okay," he says, backing out.

Once alone, I bury my face in my still-gloved hands, letting my heartbeat settle.

My excuse about the gloves was lame, but every tennis player has at least one eccentric habit. Hopefully, he bought it.

Now the bigger problem—wet clothes and no robe.

Climbing out of the tub, I peel off my soaked clothes and hide them in a towel. I wrap another towel around me, retrieve the hidden items from the trash, and pack everything into my cosmetics bag.

Clutching my belongings and channeling confidence, I stroll out of the bathroom. With a tone of cheery nonchalance, I say, "Thanks for letting me borrow your tub. It's all yours now."

I freeze. Oh no!

Blake is standing between me and his bedroom door, eyes blazing with fire and mischief

Gripping my towel a little tighter, I smile and step forward, expecting him to step aside.

*He doesn't. What the hell!*

We're standing mere inches apart. His dark gaze hovers on the gap at the bottom of my towel. Slowly, his eyes follow the seam upward, stopping on my upper chest. His eyes seem to follow the water droplets falling from the ends of my hair, running over my exposed skin, and disappearing into the top of the towel.

My eyes track his, hypnotized by his heated stare. My cheeks flush. My breath catches. I don't move.

Blake reaches out and drags his index finger down my arm, leaving goose bumps in its wake. His voice is low and gravelly. "You can use it anytime, Princess."

I bite my lip and lunge for the door, fleeing before I do something I'll regret.

———

THE TENSION FINALLY BEGINS TO EASE ONCE I'M SAFELY BACK IN MY ROOM. I dry off, dress, and turn to the evidence I gathered.

I start with the photos of the notes. The notes are cryptic but seem harmless. One mentions a play in London. I doubt that note is his. Another refers to someone wanting tickets—maybe for Wimbledon or the play. There's a reminder to have Josh regrip all his racquets. That note is clearly Blake's. The rest are similar. None seems helpful.

Still, I send encrypted messages to the princes with the photos, the key info, and a summary of where I planted the devices. I'll have to copy the data from Blake's laptop and place the trackers later.

I check the time. It's an hour until dinner, so I lie on the bed to relax and plan my next move.

But my mind drifts back to our time on the practice court. I smile at the way he made me laugh. His casual touch sent chills down my spine. And after the first two disastrous games, he suppressed his annoyance about playing doubles and even showed respect for my game.

*If only he weren't a suspected criminal.*

# 11

## BRIANNA

W aking up, I double-check my phone to make sure I'm not dreaming. It really *is* Monday—the official start of Wimbledon. For the first time, I'm here as a player, not merely a royal spectator.

While not every player competes today, the energy and anticipation of opening day are unmistakable.

I sigh and smile, stretching beneath the plush comforter, savoring the last peaceful minutes before the chaos begins.

There's still a pang of regret that the mission derailed my singles invitation. But even so, playing here in any capacity is a dream come true. I'll cherish every moment—even while carrying out my mission.

Our first mixed doubles match isn't until Friday, but Blake's opening singles match is tomorrow. With that on his mind, there's no chance he'll practice with me today.

Hopefully, Martina found someone else for me to hit with. I'd better check in with her.

Me: What time do we have a practice court?

Martina: 11 a.m. Meet you there.

Me: You know Blake won't be there, right?

Martina: Yes. Josh and I are coordinating practices. I've made other arrangements. Don't worry.

Me: This isn't ideal.

Martina: No, but you're both excellent players. We'll make it work. We can talk during practice.

Me: Thanks.

I'm trying not to stress over our lack of doubles practice, but it's hard. I'm competitive by nature. Even if the mission is my top priority, I'm still playing to win—and that's tough when my partner doesn't seem to care.

But Martina is right. I need to stay positive and work on a strategy to maximize our chances. Doubles isn't usually the main focus at Grand Slams, and players often split attention with singles. My not playing singles gives us an advantage. I can concentrate on our doubles game and study opponents' matches to spot weaknesses we can exploit.

---

LATER THAT MORNING, ERIN AND I APPROACH THE PRACTICE COURT. SHE grins. "It looks like Martina found you two handsome hitting partners."

I follow her gaze and can't help but agree. "They are rather handsome. I gather you wouldn't mind an introduction."

I'd rather have eyes on Blake though. They aren't as fit as he is and don't have his perfect facial features.

"As much as I'd love that, it wouldn't be appropriate while I'm working. They are easy on the eyes though. Did you see the thigh muscles on the taller one? You know what that means."

I laugh. "Do I want to know?"

"Probably. I'll tell you later."

"Sounds good. Time to focus on practice."

Erin steps aside as I greet Martina with a nod.

"Perfect timing," Martina says. "Paulo and Rafael just arrived. They're from Brazil, supporting a few of their country's players. They had free time today and agreed to hit with us."

"That's fantastic, guys. Thanks for helping me. My partner is prepping for his singles match. Now, please help me with your names. Which of you is Paulo and which is Rafael?"

The taller, leaner one steps up. "I'm Paulo. It's an honor to meet you."

I nod and smile. Turning to the more muscular one, I say, "So you must be Rafael."

"Correct. Thank you for the invitation, Your Highness."

"There's no need for titles on the court. I'm Brianna here. Let's get started."

Martina steps in. "Rafael is going to partner with you, Bri. He'll mimic Blake's style as closely as possible. He's also been briefed on the hand signals."

"Excellent. That will help me adjust to his playing style."

"Trust me, Josh and I have a plan to get you both ready—even with limited practice time."

"Okay. I'm ready."

Rafael turns out to be an excellent player and remarkably familiar with Blake's game. The practice is far more productive than I expected. I'll have to ask Martina how they plan to help Blake adjust to mine.

Time flies. As another player and his team arrive for the next slot on our court, I pack up my gear and turn to Paulo and Rafael. "It was a pleasure to work with you both. Thanks again for your help."

"You're welcome. I'll be around if you want to practice again," Rafael says.

"Me too," Paulo adds.

Martina thanks them, and I wave goodbye as they leave.

I say goodbye to Martina and turn to Erin, saying, "I'm heading to the locker room for a shower. Then I'll watch the match on Centre Court."

"Understood. The press is asking for you. What should I tell them?"

"Can you delay? I don't have anything to say yet, and I don't want to miss the match."

"I'll text the coordinator to let them know you'll be available later this week. We'll take the tunnel to the locker room to avoid them."

"Thanks, Erin. You're a gem. Lead the way."

"The tunnel entrance is at Aorangi just north of No. 1 Court. Follow me."

Fans line the entrance, eagerly hoping for autographs. It warms my heart to know they're excited to meet me because I play tennis— not just because I'm royal.

I stop to sign a few giant tennis balls and pose for selfies. As I turn to go, a girl with long braids steps in front of me, holding out a ball.

I can't refuse her pleading eyes. "What's your name?" I ask, taking the ball.

"I'm Samantha. You're my hero."

What a sweetheart. She must be eight to ten years old.

"Do you play tennis?"

"Yes. I practice almost every day. I want to be just like you and play here when I grow up."

Her words hit me hard. I remember being her age—dreaming of meeting the players I idolized. Most were kind. One brushed me off . . . until she learned I was a princess. I swore I'd never be that kind of person. Every child matters.

I hand back the ball with a smile. "I'm so proud of you for working so hard. Keep it up. You're going to do great."

Samantha's smile grows wider as Erin gently nudges me down the stairs.

I'm blanketed by the warm and fuzzy feeling from my interactions with the fans as we swiftly jog down the stairs into the underground maze of tunnels. They allow the players and staff to move quickly between the various buildings and tennis courts without being stopped by well-wishers and autograph seekers.

Thanks, Erin. If you hadn't pulled me away, I'd still be out there. I just love seeing the young fans, especially the girls."

"That's what I'm here for."

As we walk, I say, "I still can't believe they upgraded me to the Women's Members' Area instead of the dungeon with the majority of the players."

"You deserve it. And with fewer people, it makes my job much easier."

"I didn't earn it. It's for the top sixteen players and prior winners. That's not me."

"If you played more tournaments, you'd be one of the top players. It's not your fault you're a princess with other responsibilities."

"I just hope no one resents me receiving special treatment. Otherwise, it will be awkward."

"Ignore the rude ones. Some people will always resent you—royal or not. You're a good person and an outstanding player. Let your actions speak for you."

"That's not always easy, but it's my mantra. Thanks for the pep talk."

"What are best friends for? We're here." She opens the door leading from the tunnel to the locker room.

We climb the stairs. At the top, she motions toward the double doors to the Women's Members' Area. "I'll wait outside."

I nod, pausing to commit this moment to memory. I've dreamed of playing at Wimbledon but never expected this additional honor—an invitation to the legendary sanctuary for the Wimbledon elite.

I'm almost expecting angelic music to play. This is every female player's dream. It's the ultimate sign of having *made it*.

It's palatial with perfectly polished, parquet floors, dark wood trim, plush sofas, elegant chairs, and fine rugs. It's not a locker room —it's a spa.

I recognize two players who are lounging with their eyes closed and headphones covering their ears. Others are watching matches and chatting. They don't pay much attention to me, but their surprised looks and whispers don't escape my notice. I nod and smile as if it's nothing unusual for me to be here.

My princess training is useful in situations like this. I've been taught to have confidence, put others at ease, and ignore awkwardness. Only Erin would sense that I'm pretending to be comfortable here.

A table with silver trays holding exquisite biscuits and pastries draws my attention. Nearby, attendants busily arrange fine china for what looks like a formal tea rather than a tennis tournament.

I pass on the tea but can't resist selecting a biscuit on my way toward the individual bathrooms.

As I'm finishing the slightly sweet, crisp treat, an attendant asks, "Welcome, Your Highness. Would you like me to draw you a bath?"

"No, thank you. I'd like to take a shower, though."

"Of course. This way please. We have warm towels and other amenities for you. Do you prefer a specific scent of soap?"

I blink. "I'm not sure I've ever been asked that question before. Do you have anything citrusy?"

"We do. I'll get that for you, along with the matching shampoo and conditioner. Do you need anything else?"

"That's all. Thank you."

After a quick shower, I change and sit at a dressing table to dry my hair and apply a touch of makeup. This space is luxurious—

nothing like the typical gym-style locker rooms I'm used to at tournaments. No wonder everyone covets a spot here.

Once I'm ready, I thank the staff and head out to find Erin. She's talking with Prince Adrian.

"Adrian, what a surprise," I say.

"I heard you arrived and wanted to welcome you to Wimbledon."

"Thank you. That's very thoughtful."

"I understand your partner plays on Centre Court tomorrow. Will you be watching?"

I catch his almost imperceptible nod. Message received. I'm expected to be there, which isn't a problem. I already planned to go —it's a chance to study Blake's game more closely.

"I will. I'm looking forward to it."

"Excellent. Prince Stephen will attend as well. He hopes to speak with you."

"It would be a pleasure to see him. I'm sure we'll have much to chat about."

"What are your plans this afternoon?"

"I'm headed to Centre Court to watch the next match—and calm my nerves before it's my turn to play there on Friday."

"You'll do well. We're all cheering for you."

"Thank you. I appreciate the support."

"You're welcome. I hope you'll excuse me now. I have another appointment."

"Of course. Please tell Stephen that I'll see him tomorrow."

"I will."

As he leaves, I turn to Erin. "Can we walk outside for a minute? The flowers are always beautiful here. This may be my only chance to enjoy them."

"You love worrying me, don't you?"

"You know how much I love flowers."

"No worries. I've been expecting this request. There are two great viewing spots nearby. Follow me."

"You know me so well," I smile broadly.

A few minutes later, we're standing on a second-floor balcony overlooking the walkway between Centre Court and No. 1 Court.

The famous hill is such a vibrant green that it looks artificial. To my right, pergolas draped in hanging baskets of purple, yellow, and white petunias line the walk. Guests are resting on wooden benches tucked underneath them. Dense vines of ivy blanket the walls of nearby buildings. It's stunning.

"I never tire of the flowers and greenery here," I say.

"It's breathtaking. When you have another break, we can walk to the area above Court 18. I'm told the gigantic hot-pink and purple hydrangeas are gorgeous this year."

"We definitely have to see those while we're here."

I soak in the vibrant scene. Families picnic on the hill. Cheers ripple across the grounds. Positive energy fills the air.

It's a shame something darker is brewing beneath all this tradition.

That thought breaks the moment. I turn to Erin. "Let's go. I don't want to miss the next match."

# 12

## BRIANNA

For dinner, my housemates and I meet at the dining table adjacent to the kitchen. The table technically seats six, but it's a tight squeeze because Blake's manager, Noah, joins us. He just arrived and was eager to sample our Italian chef's cooking.

Blake slides into the seat beside me. When he inches his chair closer, our thighs brush and a spark shoots up my spine. He leans closer, his arm brushing mine. "How was your day?"

Now, my arm is tingling too. I'll never survive dinner this close to him. My knickers are already wet, and we just sat down. Why does he do this to me?

Rubbing my forearm where we touched, I meet his eyes. Our faces are closer than proper, but I don't have any desire to move away.

"Today was good," I manage, heat rushing to my cheeks.

He nods and falls silent. As we wait for food, Blake is twisting his cloth napkin and biting his lip. The tension rolling off him is virtually impossible to miss. How can no one else see it, not even Natalie?

My own tension rises with my worry for Blake. I'm about to reach under the table and place my hand on his in the hope of calming him when Fausto arrives. He approaches the table with two platters: one has melon wrapped in prosciutto and drizzled with balsamic vinegar while the other holds a glistening caprese salad.

I'm relieved to see that Fausto understood Blake's request for a healthier menu, and fortunately, Blake relaxes enough to compliment the tomatoes. I "translate" for show, and the chef rewards us with a grin and a theatrical chef's kiss.

Then Fausto announces that we have a choice of lasagna or eggplant parmigiano for our main course.

I grimace. It looks like only the appetizer was on the healthy side.

Blake bristles. "Fuck that. What's wrong with him? Is he out of his mind? I can't eat those fatty carbs the night before a match. I need complex carbs and lean protein. Tell him to make something else for me."

Although Fausto's English is perfect, I keep up the ruse. We're still hopeful Fausto will overhear something useful if they continue to think he doesn't understand. *"Blake ha bisogno di mangiare pasta con un sugo leggero e proteine magre la sera prima di una partita di tennis. Puoi cucinargliela?"*

"È ridicolo. È un buffone . . ." He rants and gestures wildly with his hands as he continues to explain that he used lean meat in the lasagna and that any child knows aubergine is a vegetable.

I'm not sure if Fausto is actually angry or if he's merely playing his role to perfection. I assume it's the latter and play along. Eventually, he mutters something about ungrateful athletes but agrees to prepare the requested meal.

"Blake, he's going to prepare grilled fish, a vegetable, and a side of pasta for you. The rest of us can enjoy the other food he cooked."

"Fine," Blake huffs under his breath.

Blake's clearly tense about his match tomorrow. He probably has certain superstitions as well. Many players think they have to eat the same meal, wear the same clothes, or fall asleep at exactly the same time the night before critical matches. That's probably part of his problem tonight, but it doesn't excuse his rudeness.

I wonder if something else is going on too, but that's for another day. I hope to lift the mood with a change of subject. "I watched a match on Centre Court this afternoon. Did you see anyone play today?" I ask.

"No," Blake says.

I stare at him hoping he'll expand on his answer, but I'm met with silence.

Josh fills the void. "We had a great practice on court and then did weights. Blake's ready to kick ass tomorrow."

"Of course, he's ready. Blake's the best player here. Hell, he could probably win his doubles matches single-handedly," Noah adds, pounding his client on the back.

Water spews from Blake's mouth. I may not be one of the top five players in the world, but Blake won't need to carry me in our doubles matches. I have far more experience than he does in doubles. Unfortunately, decorum requires me to swallow the zinger on the tip of my tongue rather than send it straight through Noah.

"Hey, don't damage the talent," Josh half jokes.

The overly gregarious manager waves off the admonishment. "Blake's tough as nails. The opponent tomorrow doesn't know what's coming."

"Don't jinx me. And no, I couldn't win doubles alone. Let's talk about something else," Blake huffs.

I smile at the subtle support from Blake.

Fausto serves our main course as Noah says, "Sure thing. Do you have the gifts for Chris and David? You're scheduled to present them at the sponsor event in a few days."

Blake ignores him.

While I consider how to change the tone of the conversation, I take a bite of the aubergine. The flavors explode in my mouth as the spicy marinara sauce hits my taste buds. The light crunch of the breading quickly gives way to the unctuous smoothness of the vegetable. "Mmm."

Blake turns to me. "Did you say something?"

"Just enjoying the food. It's not on my typical diet during a tournament, but you should at least taste it," I say, offering him a forkful.

"No, thanks."

"Okay. What's the sauce on your salmon?"

"Lemon and probably white wine. It's good."

"Hopefully, Fausto will make it for all of us one evening. And don't worry, I'll have another conversation with him about the type of food we need. He's new to my staff. My parents hired him. Whoever briefed him must have conveyed the wrong instructions."

Noah grimaces, clearly annoyed that Blake ignored him to talk with me. "Can we skip the food talk and let Blake answer my questions? Do you have the gifts for Chris and David?"

"Remind me which stuff he wants? Was it shoes or racquets?" Blake asks.

Josh asks, "Wasn't it both?"

"This is important. You should have two pairs of shoes and two racquets for him. He also wants to take photos with you and the trophy from your latest win. You can't just ignore the business side of tennis. Your sponsors pay the bills," Noah growls.

Blake clenches his jaw, and the air crackles with tension.

"Back off. I have the crap they want, and I'll pose for the photos. Now, drop it."

"Who's the sponsor?" I ask Noah, hoping to take the focus off Blake. He needs a minute to cool off.

"It's really two sponsors. David is CEO of ProLuxe, and Chris is CEO of WheelCovers" Noah says.

"WheelCovers makes high-end tennis shoes, but I don't think I've heard of ProLuxe. What do they do?" I ask.

"It's a travel company that books luxury excursions to the top athletic events around the world. They have a high-end clientele," Noah says.

"That's interesting. Do the owners of the companies collect tennis memorabilia?"

"Not really. They'll use the photos with Blake, along with the shoes and racquets, as gifts for their best clients."

Trying to draw Blake back into the conversation, I ask, "Blake, have you, Josh, Noah, and Natalie worked together for long?"

Before he can answer, Natalie says, "Oh no. I'm new to the team. I knew Josh before, but Noah and I just met tonight."

"Well, I'm sure we'll all be good friends before the next two weeks are over," I say.

"Absolutely," Noah agrees, returning to his overly happy self as if he hadn't just growled at his client.

I'm not sure what to think of him. His quick mood swings would annoy me, but I guess he's good at promoting Blake and managing his career. Blake certainly has a vast array of sponsors paying him top dollar.

Fausto interrupts my thoughts when he arrives at the table with tiramisu. Blake and I excuse ourselves, deciding to skip dessert. But the others stay behind to enjoy it.

As I'm walking upstairs, I text Fausto.

> Me.: Let me know if you hear anything interesting.

Fausto: Will do.

We reach the top of the stairs, but I linger when he turns toward his room. Between my body's reaction to him and my concern for his well-being, I'm not ready to part ways yet, I have a burning need to help him after watching his team ignore his stress.

Racking my brain for an excuse to chat, I come up with what's likely a weak question. It's all I've got, so I go with it.

"Blake, what's your evening routine now that the tournament has started?"

"I follow a fairly standard ritual," he says, continuing to stare at his phone as he walks toward his bedroom door.

Before he can escape, I follow up. "What's standard for you? I'm always looking for ideas to improve my routine."

He finally looks my way and walks back toward me. "I like to spend some time alone in the evening."

"Maybe you should listen to some soothing music tonight. You seemed extra tense at dinner. I'm worried about you."

He reaches out, places his palm on my cheek while searching my eyes. "How did you know? I tried to hide it."

"You overreacted to the food situation. You almost tore your napkin in half. And your jaw clenched so tightly, I feared you would break your teeth."

"You're quite observant. I'm sorry about being so harsh about the food. I'll apologize to Fausto in the morning. It's not an excuse, but I'm not handling the stress of Wimbledon well."

Taking a half step closer, I place my hand on his upper arm, offering my support. "I want to help. Is there something I can do?"

He leans his forehead against mine with a sigh, whispering, "Thank you, but you need to go to your room before I cross the line and kiss you."

My breath grows ragged at the thought of his lips against mine. I manage to murmur, "I'd probably let you even though it's a bad idea."

"That's why I'm going to tell you goodnight now. Sweet dreams."

He kisses my forehead and quickly retreats to his room for the alone time he said he needs the night before a match.

As I enter my room, a guilty twinge passes over me as I remember all the listening devices and cameras planted in his room. He won't be as alone as he thinks. God, I hope he never finds out.

---

As I'm toweling my hair dry after a hot shower, my phone dings.

Fausto: Didn't Natalie say that she just met Noah?

Me: Yes.

Fausto: Then why did Noah ask Natalie if things are on schedule?

Me: I assume it relates to coaching.

Fausto: They're talking about sponsor events at Wimbledon and which ones Blake needs to attend. Noah is fuming that Blake is pushing back on meeting the sponsors' requests for the shoes and racquets. He called him an unappreciative twat.

Me: There's clearly tension between them. What about Josh? Is he part of the conversation?

Fausto: Josh expressed his frustration that Blake isn't going along with his plan either. It wasn't clear what that meant though. I'll keep listening.

Me: Interesting. Keep me updated.

Fausto: Will do.

# 13

## BLAKE

I've never reacted this hard to someone's mere presence. It took every ounce of self-control to walk away from Bri tonight.

She was right—my stress is sky-high. Tomorrow I'll play my first match at Wimbledon, the tournament where things always unravel for me. I've already been forced into doubles. Now I'm bracing for the next disaster.

That's why I knew it would be tough this evening. My plan had been to eat quickly and then seclude myself in my room for the rest of the evening. That way if my nerves got the better of me, no one would know.

What I hadn't expected was that sitting so close to Bri during dinner would put my nerves further on edge. Without seeming to try, she sends warmth through me. It started with her smile. Next it was her touch when our limbs brushed at the table and then her breath kissed my cheek when we leaned close to talk.

Between the chemistry brewing between us and my anxiety over tennis, I feared a panic attack would hit me during dinner. Luckily the food arrived, giving me something else to focus on, which helped.

Upstairs she stopped me with real concern. She saw straight through the façade and asked how she could help. No one's shown me that kind of empathy in years.

I rake a hand through my already tousled hair, grappling with my confusion. Being near her is somehow comforting, torturous, and arousing all at once. It's time for a shower.

Stripping off my clothes, I walk into my bathroom and turn on the shower faucet. My cock is furious with me for denying it the pleasure of a night with Bri, so I set the water to the coldest setting. Stepping under the raining streams of water droplets, I remind myself that she never actually offered to assist in that way.

When she asked how she could help me, I almost lost it. I couldn't tell her what thoughts came to mind. I wanted to wrap her in my arms, kiss her luscious lips, and carry her to my bed to ravish her for the rest of the night. Instead, I gave her forehead a chaste kiss and walked away.

Unfortunately, the water is room temperature and does little to tame my arousal. Taking matters into my right hand, I lean forward and place my other hand against the shower wall. I close my eyes, and visions of the lovely Bri play out like a movie in my head.

She walks into my bathroom and slowly strips off her clothes. Playfully, she steps into the shower, running her index finger down my chest. I start to say something, but she puts her finger to my lips, signaling me to stay silent and let her take over. Slowly, she drops to her knees in front of me, taking me into her mouth. I almost lose it right then.

She swiftly creates a rhythm with her mouth and tongue that has me rocking back and forth, groaning with pleasure. I pull her head toward me, thrusting deeper until she takes all of me and pushes me over the edge with an intensity that causes me to shudder as I find my release.

I'm breathing heavily, and my chest is pounding. I probably shouldn't have done that to thoughts of Bri. Now, I'm going to want her even more. Shite. Take control of yourself, man.

When my pulse rate returns to normal, I finish my shower. Toweling off, I resolve to put aside thoughts of my sexy housemate and bury myself in my standard routine for the night before matches.

Normally, I'd look forward to this time alone the night before a match. The set routine has always been calming. Tonight, I'm not so sure how well it's going to work. But with nothing to lose, I watch videos of my opponent to make sure I remember his tendencies. That done, I make notes to read right before the match tomorrow.

Now it's time to wind down the evening with stretches. I start with my upper body and work my way down to my legs and ankles. The stretches keep me limber and help to prevent injuries. They also allow me to enter an almost meditative state, which is a welcome sleep aid the night before an important match. And if I ever needed that type of help, it's tonight.

When I've run out of muscles and tendons to stretch, I crawl under the covers and turn on my favorite playlist. I set the timer for one hour, knowing I should be in a sound sleep by the time the music turns off.

Closing my eyes, I concentrate on the familiar, hoping to drift off quickly. Something strange happens instead. An image of Bri appears, which is even more comforting than the music. What's up with that?

*If I'm not careful, I could fall for the beautiful princess.*

# 14

## BRIANNA

I hear a door creak open, followed by footsteps on the stairs.

Blake calls out, "Josh, let's go. I want extra time to warm up before my noon match."

Excellent. With Blake out of the house, it gives me a chance to sneak back into his room to plant the trackers and copy the contents of his laptop.

I pull on a pair of gloves, grab my cosmetics bag with the electronics, and quietly sneak into his room. This time, I start with the walk-in closet, flipping on the light switch. I select the clothes he's most likely to wear during his free time.

Those will be the best locations for the trackers, which are our insurance. We can already follow him using his smartphone, but these devices will work if he forgets his phone or turns it off.

It's cool in the evenings, so I tuck a tracker into each of his two jackets assuming he'll wear one of them if he goes out. I skip the hats because he's prone to handing those out to fans. Instead, I plant the rest in his trousers.

Task accomplished, I turn off the closet light and sit at his desk. Opening his laptop, it wakes without a password, which is lucky for me. I insert a USB drive, which will collect data and install software to track keystrokes and create a hidden login account.

Just as I'm about to leave, a trophy catches my eye—likely the one his sponsor requested for the photos. Curious, I pick it up. Could someone hide a coin in this? Holding it up to the light, I turn it in my hands, inspecting it from all angles. Looking underneath, the bottom is covered with felt, and one edge lifts slightly. I peel it back and find a dark, hollow compartment.

There's something inside. My pulse quickens. Have I found the hiding place for the coins?

Using my finger, I slide my discovery toward the opening. The corner of a piece of paper emerges. Grasping it between my thumb and forefinger, I ease it out, being careful not to tear it.

The paper is folded into a square about the size of . . . oh, no! The missing denarius coin would fit perfectly within the square of paper.

This would be the perfect way to sneak the coin across the border. It wouldn't show up on an X-ray at an airport because the base is metal. And if someone lifted the trophy, the paper would prevent the coin from making noise rattling around in the base. No one would ever notice it.

My stomach sinks as I unfold the paper. I've known Blake was a suspect, but I've inwardly hoped there's another explanation. Now, for the first time, I'm forced to seriously consider that Blake may be involved. Does this mean his coach is also part of the smuggling?

Nothing is wrapped inside the paper, but there is writing on it. I quickly read the note. It says:

**Stay the course. It will keep paying off.**

As I'm contemplating the note's meaning, my phone vibrates in my pocket. It's my alarm signaling it's time to head over to the Wimbledon grounds to watch Blake's match.

I quickly snap a photo of the writing and of the bottom of the trophy. Not wanting Blake to notice anyone found the hiding place,

I stuff the paper back into the hollow base, pressing the felt into place. Returning the trophy to its place on the dresser, I take another look around the room to make sure there's no evidence of my visit.

Reassured that Blake will never suspect I've been here, I peer out the door freezing when a pair of eyes lock onto mine. I let out of sigh of relief when I realize they belong to Erin. She gives me a nod.

As we meet in the hallway between rooms, I whisper, "You gave me a scare."

"We're the only ones here. Blake's team left for his match, and Fausto is at the market. I was looking for you because it's time to leave."

"I know. Let me grab my things."

"Okay. I assume I don't need to know why you were in Blake's room."

"You're right."

"Understood. But if I can help, you know I'm here," she says, following me into my room.

I pick up my Louis Vuitton purse as I say, "It's frustrating not to be able to share details of my mission with you. At the next opportunity, I'm going to revisit the edict that I can't. As my missions become more complex, it doesn't make sense to keep you in the dark. But I've taken an oath that I must uphold. For now, this is how it must be."

"I admire what you're doing, so don't worry about me. We'll make this work. My only concern is keeping you safe. Let's hurry though. You don't want to miss Blake's match."

"You're right. Let's go."

---

Entering the Centre Court stands, I find my seat while Erin locates a nearby vantage point where she can keep an eye on the crowd.

The match just started, but Blake is already dominating his

opponent. For me, it's an excellent chance to study Blake's game, spot patterns, and figure out how to adapt for doubles with him.

Before long, I'm spending less time evaluating Blake's game and more time staring at him. Everything about Blake makes me hunger for a repeat of two years ago. The sweat dripping from his brow reminds me of the heat between us that night. When he flexes his forearms to serve and his biceps bulge, I almost swoon. I can make out every defined muscle in his legs as he lunges for balls with outstretched arms. I could use another drink of that man.

When the game ends, I scan the Royal Box. Stephen is wearing a purple tie—our signal to meet. He catches my eye and nods. I was going to text him the photos, but talking in-person is even better.

As play resumes, I smile watching Blake drill the ball across the net and past his opponent. He's brilliant.

It's hard watching him shoulder so much weight. Winning this tournament could change his life. A loss may destroy him. The stress is impacting more than just his tennis. He's taking it out on everyone around him. He was in a better place when we first met—even after losing Wimbledon. Now he's different. Sure, there are moments when the charming guy I first met makes an appearance, but those are rare.

It makes me wonder whether having someone special in his life would fill the void for him. Would that make the losses more bearable? With the chemistry sizzling between us, I wouldn't mind finding out. My desires go beyond a mere wish for another night with him.

He's one of the few men who doesn't seem to care that I'm a princess. He's not pushing me to do anything for him. He has enough of his own money not to need mine. And he agreed to play doubles with me despite his concerns that it would hurt his chances of winning.

No, he's likely only tolerating the doubles matches for the money. He can't afford to lose his contract with the sponsor. He has plenty of money though. He could afford to lose the sponsor or change sponsors.

If only he weren't involved in this international drama, I'd be tempted to rethink my stance on what could be between us.

I sigh. Again, we've met at the wrong time. I'm not the one who can help him, and we can't be a couple. If he's involved in the smuggling, he has even more to worry about. I wonder whether that's the difference in him between two years ago and now. If guilt or fear of being caught is hanging over his head in addition to the pressure to win, that would explain his attitude and behavior.

No wonder he hired Natalie. I'm not sure a sports psychologist can fix all his problems though.

I'm sad thinking about what may lie ahead for Blake, but the cheering crowd returns my focus to the present. Blake swiftly closes out the match with an easy win.

As I stand to leave, a Wimbledon staff member approaches, saying, "Your Highness, you've been invited to the clubhouse. Would you like to follow me?"

"Thank you. Of course."

Prince Stephen and I definitely need to talk.

---

IN THE CLUBHOUSE, STEPHEN GREETS ME WITH A FORMAL SMILE.

"I've arranged for tea. Would you care to join me?"

"I'd be delighted. That's very kind of you," I say.

Stephen and I suppress grins as we go through these formalities. They're expected when two royals from different countries meet in public. As far as anyone knows, we haven't seen each other recently. They can't know we dined together a few nights ago.

He gestures for me to join him in a private room in the clubhouse where we can talk unobserved.

"It's good to see you again. Are you doing okay?" he says, pulling me into a hug.

"It's only been a few days, but they've been busy ones."

"Any issues?"

"It's been difficult not being able to directly communicate with you and the rest of the team. Secure texts don't work for everything. It's also challenging to do my job without revealing any details to Erin. It would be much easier if she knew what's going on." My frustration shows in my tone.

Stephen nods as he guides me toward a pair of upholstered, cream-colored swivel chairs next to a low table set with a fine-china tea service and a tiered cake stand with cakes and pastries. I immediately notice the omission of the traditional finger sandwiches. That makes me smile. We've shared enough teas and meals during training that he and Adrian know I love sweets but skip the mayonnaise-laden sandwiches every time.

He motions for me to sit in the chair on our left. I do as prompted, assuming my proper princess pose with closed knees, crossed ankles, and hands lightly clasped in my lap. While I'd love to relax and lean back in my comfortable chair, there's a chance someone might walk in on us and wonder why a royal greeting had turned so casual.

Stephen takes the other chair, mirroring my formality, while saying, "I know. My guards don't know the details of my covert life either. It can be frustrating at times. Can't you talk with Fausto though?"

I shrug, palms up. "Not really. He's only partially informed about our mission. And we're being extremely careful to keep up the ruse that he doesn't speak English. Besides, it would be strange if anyone caught me having extended conversations with our temperamental chef."

Stephen chuckles. "I gather he's playing the role well then. Does that mean he can actually cook too?"

I nod, amused at Stephen's mirth. He's usually all business. Adrian's usually the one who finds lightness in the serious moments.

"Fausto is playing his part to perfection, and his Italian food is quite delicious. But I know our time here is short, and we need to talk about the more important aspects of the situation. I planted all the devices in Blake's room. Have you heard or seen anything useful yet?"

I don't share that I've been horribly curious and even contemplated listening to the audio and watching video feeds myself. Ultimately, I couldn't do it. It would have been too personal given our history and recent flirting.

Stephen's face grows serious, his brows knitted. "Blake doesn't spend much time in his room, so there's nothing of interest so far. The team continues to monitor him though. It's a bit frustrating that we haven't made more progress. We need a breakthrough soon."

"What about his phone?"

"He listens to music, watches dog videos, and sends texts to Josh and Natalie about meetings. Our people did overhear one conversation between Blake and Noah that suggests Blake isn't particularly happy with his manager. Do you know anything about that?" he asks, raising his eyebrows hopefully.

I nod. "That's consistent with other tidbits I've picked up. I haven't been able to learn any details, though. Why is Blake dissatisfied with Noah?"

I lean forward expectantly, anxious to learn the details.

"Our agents think it's related to his sponsors and income. There's more to the story that we don't know. It's up to you to find out. It's important."

I close my eyes, wondering how I can possibly accomplish this. The last thing he'll want to discuss is something else that's causing him angst.

Throwing up my hands, I groan. "I know it's important, but it won't be easy. Blake is stressed to the hilt. He won't want to talk about something upsetting."

"But he trusts you. You'll find a way. I have another question. When you planted the electronic devices, did you have time to search Blake's room?"

Twirling the ring on my right hand, I sigh. "I did. From what I found, it's possible that Blake is involved in smuggling the coins. Also, his coach, Josh, is probably part of it. Maybe Noah too."

I'm bothered that my answer implicates Blake when my gut tells me he wouldn't be involved.

"And you're just now mentioning this? Why didn't you text? Never mind. Start at the beginning. What did you find?" Stephen looks at me in shock.

"Didn't I tell you it was difficult not being able to communicate directly. I thought this info was too sensitive to text. That's why we've set up ways to meet. Remember? Oh well, we're here now. Forgive my frustration. I'll explain."

I share how I found the hollow trophy with a folded piece of paper inside, omitting that I'd hoped to find evidence to exonerate Blake. "At first, I thought a coin might be wrapped in the paper. It was the perfect size to hold one. Instead, it was a note telling Blake to listen to his coach and proceed as planned for the payoff he wants."

"It sounds like his coach is the one in contact with the leader of the smuggling operation."

"It does. To me, the note sounds like a warning to Blake. I wonder if he's been threatening to abandon the operation."

I have to hope that Blake isn't willingly participating in something illegal. Otherwise, my judgment is off.

Rubbing his chin, deep in thought, Stephen softly says, "Perhaps."

He doesn't look convinced though.

Duty bound, I share another theory. "I also wonder whether there was a coin folded up in the note. Blake may have been instructed to remove the coin from the trophy and move it to another place. By writing the note on the paper surrounding the coin, they made sure he would see the writing."

He slaps his knee, saying, "Excellent deduction. If the coins are hidden in trophies, that would also explain how they escape detection at the borders. An X-ray wouldn't detect a coin inside the metal base of a trophy."

Stephen's earlier frustration has turned to enthusiasm at the prospect that we may actually be making progress in our investigation. I, on the other hand, am not at all happy with the direction we're headed. If there isn't a change of course soon, my prior one-night stand will be arrested for smuggling and who knows what other crimes.

Sullenly, I nod slowly. "Agreed. I also sent you photos of a hidden key I found. Have the experts determined what type of lock it opens?"

"I haven't heard anything yet. How do you know the key is his?"

"Technically, I don't, but it was in an envelope with a preprinted return address for a Paris hotel. I Googled the hotel. It's less than two kilometers from Roland Garros where Blake just played in the French Open last month."

Stephen's brows furrow. "I see. I gather you couldn't remove the key so we can duplicate it."

"I decided it was too risky. If you can't make a copy from my photo and tracing, then I'll *borrow* the key on a day that Blake has a match. You can send a delivery to me. Some red roses would do nicely. I'll pass the key to the delivery person. Someone else can return it later in the day along with a tin of chocolate biscuits from an admiring fan," I smile, proud of myself for placing an order for two of my favorite things.

I need something to cheer me up, and it's fun to poke at Stephen, trying to get a rise out of him or at least a slight smile. He obliges, with a half-smile.

"You're very clever, my dear. We get the key, and you receive flowers and sweets."

"Yes, it's the perfect trade, don't you think?" I taunt with a toss of my hair and wide grin.

"Of course. We'll text if we need the key," he says, with a shake of his head.

"Perfect. I really hope you'll need that key," I tease.

"You know you could just order the flowers and biscuits, right?"

"It's so much more fun to receive deliveries from secret admirers, even if they are fake ones," I muse.

"You're too much. Have you learned anything else?"

"Only one other thing that I haven't already passed along. We know Natalie and Josh met before, because Blake said Josh recommended her when he wanted to add a sports psychologist to his team. However, Natalie says she met Noah for the first time yesterday. That's inconsistent with what Fausto overheard. Fausto is fairly certain that Natalie and Noah have a history too. It probably doesn't matter, but why would she lie?"

Stephen shrugs. "Maybe they've spoken on the phone before, but they met in person for the first time yesterday. It could be as simple as that."

"I'll check with Fausto to see if that would explain what he heard."

"Or it's possible they were romantically involved and don't want anyone to know."

"She's married now. I think her wife's name is Cecilia."

"Yes, that's in the dossier from her background check. She hasn't been married long though. It's possible she knew Noah before her marriage. But I'll pass along the information. As a precaution, the team can take another look at her prior connections with both Josh and Noah."

"Good. Is there anything else that I need to know?"

"Yes. We have new intel indicating the coins haven't been handed off yet. The information we intercepted confirms the exchange will occur at Wimbledon. We hope to have more details soon."

"Is the handoff supposed to take place during a match or at a specific event?"

"We don't know. That's the problem. For all we know, it could happen when a fan asks for an autograph or takes a selfie. The coins are so small, it would be trivial to hand them off."

"That makes it almost impossible to prevent. What's the plan?"

"We need you to learn everything about Blake's schedule. Has he mentioned any events he'll be attending"

"He has a sponsor event later this week. That's the only thing they've discussed other than his matches."

"Find an excuse to go with him."

"Will do."

"We're watching the cameras you planted. We should see if he takes anything unusual with him. But if you can, take another look in his room. The coin may be hidden there."

"I searched it thoroughly. The only thing I haven't checked is his tennis bag. He almost always has it with him. I'll see if I can manufacture an excuse to go through it tonight."

"Excellent. It's possible he's keeping the coins with him until it's time to hand them off."

"What about the other player you mentioned? Any news about his involvement in the smuggling?"

"Nothing yet, but we have eyes on him."

"You're still not going to tell me who he is, are you?"

"It's better if you don't know. We have no reason to think he's dangerous, so we're not worried about you running into him. And if you do, this way you'll be completely natural."

"I don't like it, but I understand."

"We're supposed to be having tea, so we should quickly drink up and enjoy the cakes. Otherwise, the staff will wonder what we've been doing in here." He smirks.

"If they only knew you're like a brother to me."

"And you're the sister I never had. You know our parents had hoped for a love match when we were younger."

"I know, but they seem to have figured out that wasn't meant to be," I say, taking one of the cakes from the three-tiered tray as Stephen pours tea for us.

Twenty minutes later, we've finished two cups of tea and enough food to justify the time we've spent together.

Parting ways, I'm left wondering how we're going to intercept the coins, given they would easily fit in someone's pocket along with regular change. We're looking for a needle in a haystack as they say. Nothing short of strip-searching every attendee as they leave Wimbledon would work. I bite my lip so as not to laugh out loud at that thought. I can't imagine the uproar that would cause the British sensibilities.

Talk about tough tasks. Now I must convince Blake to open up to me about his troubles with his manager while devising an excuse to rifle through his tennis bag.

Hell. Why did my first real mission have to be an impossible one?

# 15
## BRIANNA

During the ride back to our rental house, Erin sits in silence, sensing that I need time to think. Finally, an idea for coaxing Blake to talk clicks into place, but I'll need a little help.

"Erin, I'd like some time alone with Blake tonight. We need to build some rapport if we're going to have any chemistry on the court. Could you persuade Josh and Natalie to take you out for dinner and drinks?"

"I can try. What about security?"

"Fausto can handle it."

"I could say I'm craving something other than Italian food and want to try a local pub."

"Perfect."

"I'll text them now."

A few minutes later, her phone dings.

"They want to know if we should invite you and Blake."

"Tell them it's your night off, and you could use a break. Besides, Blake won't touch pub fare during a tournament."

"That should work." She fires off another message.

I watch as she exchanges more texts.

"Done. They're looking forward to a night away from the tension Blake brings to the dinner."

"Good job. While you're out, see if you can learn more about them, particularly Josh's finances. Is he short on money? Or is he living a richer lifestyle than you would expect. I'm interested in anything unexpected that you may learn about him."

"Okay, but it would help if I knew why."

"Unfortunately, I can't explain. Just know it would be extremely helpful to my mission."

"Understood."

---

THE AROMA OF FAUSTO'S CREAMY LEMON RISOTTO WITH SHRIMP AND asparagus draws everyone toward the kitchen—everyone except one, that is.

"Where's Blake?" I ask.

Natalie points to the ceiling. "I heard water running when I left my room. He must be in the shower."

"Erin said you're eating out tonight. Where are you going?" I ask.

Josh answers, "Either the Rose & Crown or Fire Stables."

"If I'd known we were having shrimp for dinner, I'd be eating here," Natalie says, sounding disappointed.

With the mouth-watering aroma filling the kitchen, I worry they'll change their minds. Fausto raises two fingers and shakes his head, silently signaling that he's only cooked enough for two. I cringe and give him a warning look, hoping they don't notice he understood English. When they still don't budge, he shoos them out. Step one of my plan is accomplished.

A couple of minutes later Blake appears, brows knitted in confusion. "Where is everyone? Does this mean dinner is delayed?"

His tone tells me tonight will not be easy.

"Since we don't have matches tomorrow and don't need their help tonight, they apparently wanted an evening at a pub."

"Oh. Why didn't you join them?"

"Have you lost your mind? Can you imagine the scene it would make for a royal to turn up at a random pub? I don't need that stress any more than you do."

Rubbing his chin, he nods. "A quiet dinner at home sounds much better to me too. Please tell me that Fausto didn't decide that pizza is the new version of healthy eating. I'll scream if he says the wheat he used to make crust is a vegetable."

I laugh. "Don't worry. I spoke with him again. I think we're having shrimp. It smells wonderful."

Fausto gestures for us to sit at the table adjacent to the kitchen and hurries over with a beautifully arranged antipasto platter. My stomach grumbles at the display of thinly sliced meats, cheese, olives, pickled red peppers, and fig jam along with a few crispy crackers and baguette slices.

Why isn't this guy a full-time chef? He's incredibly talented even if food for athletes isn't his specialty. When this is over, I'm going to ask him about his background and if he'd rather be working in the palace kitchen or running his own restaurant in Catalinius.

I place cheese and meat on a cracker as I say, "You played extremely well today. I loved watching the match. I don't know about you, but I always feel so much relief after winning the first match of a tournament."

"I do. Today went well. My next opponent will be tougher, but I have a good record against him."

"Martina texted that she and Josh arranged for us to have a short practice tomorrow. I'm excited to get back on the court with you."

"Mmm-hmm," he replies, munching on an olive.

Pulling conversation from Blake is like trying to make a palace guard laugh. It's strange given that two years ago we talked easily. Now the weight of the tournament is crushing him. It's too bad he swore off alcohol during Wimbledon—a glass of wine might help.

As I'm contemplating what sort of alcohol or sex might loosen him up, Fausto approaches, saying, "*Vorresti un risotto al limone con gamberi o un pesce alla griglia con asparagi?*"

"He's asking if you prefer the risotto with shrimp or the grilled fish with asparagus." I explain.

"Fish, please."

"*Blake vorrebbe il pesce. Il risotto per me, per favore,*" I translate for Fausto.

"Thanks for convincing him to offer a healthier option," Blake says with a smile.

"He's talented. I think it's just his first time cooking for athletes."

"That's probably it," Blakes agrees.

"Did you see the hot tub out back?" I ask.

"Josh pointed it out," he says without enthusiasm.

"My muscles could use the warmth, but palace rules say I can't be in hot tubs alone. With Erin out, would you keep me company?"

He does a double take, nearly choking on a bit of food. His gaze drifts from my hair to my lap as though imagining me in a bikini, relaxing in the steaming water. Heat rises in my cheeks.

Tension and excitement threaten to overshadow the goals of my mission.

In a low gravelly voice he says, "I can't imagine how stifling it is to have all those rules to follow. I'd be in trouble all the time—for breaking them."

I work to keep my voice steady. "It's tempting to break them, and I sometimes do. But Erin would have to report the breach in security. She'd be in trouble. So—will you join me for a short soak?"

"Sure. If it's not too long."

As Fausto clears our plates he asks, "*Ho preparato un dolce ad alto contenuto proteico. Vorresti una porzione?*"

"He made a high protein dessert. Would you like to try it?" I ask.

"High protein? What is it?" Blakes eyes scrunch.

"*Qual è il dessert?*"

"Crème brûlée."

Blake and I burst out laughing. Fausto stares at us in confusion.

Catching my breath, I say, "I guess eggs and cream count as protein."

"True, but based on his description, I was expecting something less decadent—maybe cottage cheese topped with fresh fruit."

"Exactly. I love crème brûlée, but I'm going to pass. What about you?" I ask.

"None for me."

I owe Fausto for making Blake laugh.

"I'll tell Fausto to share the dessert with Josh, Natalie, and Erin when they return."

"Good idea. I need to make a couple of calls. When do you want to meet at the hot tub?" he asks as he stands and walks toward the doorway.

"Would an hour from now work?"

He nods, turning back and locking his eyes with mine. I gulp at the heat radiating from him.

In an even lower voice than usual, he says, "You've invited me to the hot tub to protect you, Princess. But who's going to protect *me* from *you*? I'll be defenseless again just like the last time you invited me over." His teasing wink is accompanied by a devastating smile as he knocks on the door frame before disappearing upstairs.

I'm left staring after him, open-mouthed, my body trembling and heating in unfathomable ways. I wrap my arms around myself to steady the sensations. Suddenly, my hot tub idea feels like the worst decision ever. But sometimes bad decisions can lead to excellent results.

Knowing Blake is still within earshot, I turn to Fausto, saying, "*Grazie per la deliziosa cena. Niente dessert stasera. Josh, Natalie ed Erin gusteranno la crème brûlée.*"

When Blake's footsteps fade, I add another request that raises Fausto's eyebrows, but he nods.

With that assurance, I go to my room to change clothes and go over my strategy.

*Let's hope my plan works.*

# 16

## BLAKE

Have I lost my mind? Not only did I agree to more alone time with a half-dressed princess in a hot tub, but I also couldn't leave it at that. I had to taunt her with reminders of our infamous night together. Then I practically invited her to a repeat. That can't happen.

Bloody hell! I'm a freaking idiot.

It's as if she's a temptress who put a spell on me. I can't stay away.

If she were anyone other than the princess, I'd suggest we sleep together to get it out of our systems. But we already did that, so I know better. It wouldn't be enough.

For weeks after we were together, thoughts of her haunted me at night. I wondered why we were both so adamant that it was a one-time thing. I contemplated revisiting the subject with her the next time we met at a tournament, but our paths didn't happen to cross. That shouldn't have surprised me, given the lack of overlap between the men's and women's tournaments. Except for the Grand Slam events and a few others, we're usually in different cities.

Maybe that was for the best. We share common frustrations and goals, so we could easily have been drawn into something we didn't have time for. Besides, long distance relationships are time sinks. They're full of heartache and loneliness when you're apart. I tried that once and learned my lesson. Never again.

During my meetings with Nicole, I've sensed she's noticed the tension between Bri and me. She hasn't brought it up though. And so far, I haven't raised the issue.

Talking to her about it might help, but it would feel like I'm betraying Bri. We swore that we'd never disclose our prior connection, and there's part of me that wants to protect it. I like that we're the only two who know, other than her guards from that night.

Somehow, keeping our secret seems even more important now. Since we've become playing partners and housemates, our connection has grown from merely physical attraction to something more. Being around Bri makes me smile. She brings a calmness to me that's a welcome escape from my stress. We even understand each other without the need for long explanations. And we cheer for each other as we each pursue our dreams.

No woman has ever had this effect on me before. It feels warm and comforting. But there's a major problem. It's temporary. That means I can't let myself be drawn into her more than I already am. The last thing I need is a painful breakup when Wimbledon is over and we part ways.

As with my panic attacks, I can learn to manage this situation. It'll be fine. I'll keep my interactions with Bri professional. We can be supportive friends. That should work.

But how am I going to manage sitting in the hot tub with Bri without wanting her? My body needs to get the message that intimacy is off limits.

I'll focus the conversation on tennis strategy for our matches.

And I'll take a cold shower before going downstairs to meet her.

# 17

## BRIANNA

Fifteen minutes early, I slip quietly out of my room and head downstairs to make sure everything is ready for step two of my plan.

As I step onto the patio, the scene stops me in my tracks. It's beautiful, peaceful, and secluded. I wish we had more time to enjoy this place, but at least Blake and I will make use of it tonight.

Soft music plays in the background as I follow a candlelit path to the bubbling hot tub. A woven basket is filled with rolled, plush white towels. A small table holds a silver tray of chocolate-covered strawberries. Two champagne flutes sit beside a wine chiller. The only thing missing is champagne. Instead, a bottle of sparkling water is nestled into the ice.

The scene is perfect—actually, it's too perfect.

I asked Fausto for a spa-like setup, but he clearly misunderstood. This looks less like a relaxation spot and more like a stage for seduction. No wonder Fausto raised an eyebrow when I made the request. He thinks I'm going to fuck Blake in the hot tub.

And when Blake sees this display and the skimpy red bikini I'm wearing, he's going to think the same thing.

Bloody hell, I've mucked this up. The goal was to relax Blake, not turn him on, or worse, scare him off.

As I try to think of last-minute changes, footsteps sound behind me. I turn just as Blake approaches. His arms are spread wide, and his gaze sweeps the area, silently questioning the setup. Finally, his hooded eyes land on me. "What's all this?" he asks with a knowing smirk.

Seeing him look at me that way makes me melt.

Heat radiates from his bare chest, and I can't help noticing the growing bulge in his swim trunks. I'd love to let him wrap his hard body around me and remind me of all the things his talented hands and cock can do.

Did I subconsciously want to send the wrong signal? How could I, knowing he may be a criminal. No, it's even worse. Based on what I found in his room, he's *likely* a criminal.

But my body just doesn't seem to care. I'm so screwed.

Mustering all the self-control possible, I say, "Fausto set this up for us. He felt bad about the crème brûlée and wanted us to celebrate your win today while relaxing."

That's technically true. I just left out the part where I asked for Fausto's help.

"Fausto's idea of a healthy, high protein dessert was rather funny," Blake chuckles.

I'm relieved at the lighter topic.

"When he first said high protein dessert, all I could picture was a steak covered in sugar."

We both laugh at the image. Soon I'm laughing so hard that tears are streaming down my face.

Finally, catching my breath, I wipe my face, saying, "It's not even that funny, but if we don't talk about something else, I'm never going to stop laughing."

"I know. I should be more upset about the challenges in communicating my food needs during the tournament, but I'm sure Fausto means well. Besides, having you around calms me," he says, closing the distance between us.

He stops so close to me that I feel his breath on my lips as I stare into his eyes. The sexual tension between us is palpable. I can't let him kiss me no matter how good it would feel.

I really can't.

Gathering my wits, I say, "I'm freezing. Let's get in the hot tub."

I step backward, drop my robe, and slide into the warm bubbles.

Blake pours two glasses of sparkling water and climbs in beside me. Our fingers brush as he hands me a glass, sending a tingling sensation up my arm. The mischievous sparkle in his eyes tells me he felt it too.

I'm playing with fire. Slowly, I shift along the seat to put some space between us.

Raising my glass, I say, "Let's toast. Here's to your win today and to many more to come."

"Thank you. I can only hope."

"The jets feel so good." I sigh, leaning my head against the side wall and closing my eyes.

"They do. This was a wonderful idea. The damp, cool weather here always factors into how fast my muscles recover after matches. This is the first time we've had a house with a hot tub."

"I'd insist on one every time if I were you. It's much better than vying for time in a hot tub at the gym."

"Agreed. And this one's co-ed. The view is much better," he smiles, tipping his glass in my direction.

"That's nice of you. I could say the same from where I'm sitting."

What am I doing? I need to cool things down, not heat them up more. I wonder if there's a way to turn the temperature down on the hot tub. Maybe that would help.

"Oh, I can assure you my thoughts are anything but nice." He grins.

I blush, hoping he'll chalk it up to the hot water.

This conversation is supposed to be about the mission. I need to redirect it before it's too late.

In a playful tone, I say, "Don't get any ideas. We're here to relax so we can play better tennis—nothing more."

"Unfortunately," he mumbles.

"I missed that. What did you say?"

"Nothing."

He bites his lip, clearly frustrated. He received the message. Still, I feel a flicker of disappointment. Maybe I'd hoped he wouldn't give up so easily.

Trying to stay focused, I say, "Oh. Okay. I'm glad we have time to chat. I need your advice."

He doesn't know that I spent all afternoon concocting this cover story. Hopefully, it sounds believable.

"About what?"

"I need to share a bit of background. For as long as I can remember, I've worked hard and driven myself to succeed at tennis. It's the only thing in my life that I've earned for myself. My title brought me the rest. That's why I value my tennis victories so highly. They weren't given to me because of my title, my parents, or our wealth."

"I hadn't thought of your situation that way."

My story so far is completely true, making it easy to tell with conviction and emotion. I'm proud of what I've done. Yes, my family's position gave me advantages, such as great coaches at an early age. But I put in the hard work. Day after day I'd wake at five in the morning to practice regardless of the weather or my mood. It meant that much to me.

"Most people don't. It's particularly annoying when I'm accused of playing tennis for fun to get out of *real* royal work."

EVEN AT MY LEVEL OF TENNIS, I DEAL WITH A NUMBER OF ISSUES THAT MY critics don't know about or understand. Like you, I've made sacrifices to pursue my passion. He nods as I tick off my list that includes injuries, early morning practices, strict diets, no relationships, and missed events with friends and family. Tennis is far from all fun.

Blake's eyes widen in astonishment. He reaches out and squeezes my shoulder. "That's infuriating. Do they even understand how hard it is to play at this level? I bet your royal duties are easier."

"No kidding. I love tennis or else I wouldn't put myself through the training. But I also push myself to help my country. That brings me to the reason I need advice. As you probably know, my parents have never allowed me to have sponsors or accept prize money from tennis tournaments."

"No, I didn't realize that. I thought we shared the same clothing sponsor. Isn't that why we're playing mixed doubles together?"

"I'm only allowed to wear their logo for this tournament. It's the first exception the palace has made. I'm hoping there will be more now that it's my brother's decision going forward."

"Is that because your parents stepped down and Xander is now king?"

"Exactly. And Xander is more likely to let me cut back on my duties and play in more tournaments. If that happens, I'll be able to earn money for the foundation that I'd like to start. That's why I need your advice. If this change occurs, I'm going to need a manager. Do you know of anyone?"

"Not that I can think of. I've been quietly keeping my ears open for a new one myself."

"Why? Hasn't Noah been your manager for years? From what I've heard, he negotiates extremely favorable contracts for you."

His jaw clenches as he shakes his head.

"Noah's been my manager forever. For a long time, I thought he was the best in tennis. More recently, he's made some financial decisions that were major mistakes. He also wants me to sign up with sponsors that would be terrible choices."

I'm dumbfounded. "He can't make you do that, can he?"

"Not technically, but when I object, he becomes impatient. I'm no longer that naïve young player he needs to boss around. I want even more say in the business side of my career, and my manager should support me. Unfortunately, at times, Noah seems to have forgotten that I'm the client. After much consideration, I've finally decided to find a different manager after this tournament and start over."

We drift closer, and I rest a hand on his arm. He leans into my touch.

"Thanks for warning me about Noah. Otherwise, I might have considered hiring him when you have a new manager."

"He may be fine for someone else, just not me. He's like a parent who still thinks of me as his child. He might treat you differently though."

Despite their problems, Blake is hesitant to completely destroy Noah's reputation. That speaks to Blake's character and loyalty that comes from a long relationship. My guess is that his decision to part ways with Noah has been a particularly difficult one.

We need more information, so I push forward. "I hate to pry, but you mentioned he made some business mistakes. Would you be willing to share the details? It would help me decide whether to keep him on my list of possibilities."

"I don't like talking about it, but for you I will under one condition. You must promise not to repeat the information to anyone else," he says solemnly, taking my hand from his arm and intertwining our fingers.

"Of course."

I'll try to keep my promise, but my team may need the information. Right now, I hate my job. Deceiving someone I'm growing closer to is tearing me up inside.

"He invested a significant amount of my money in a start-up company. The start-up went bankrupt within six months. I lost millions of pounds."

"Did he have permission to make the investment?"

"Technically, he did. He's been working with my financial advisors since early in my career. I'd given him authority to make investments back when I didn't have any experience in those matters. However, he typically mentioned his plans to me. This time he didn't, so I didn't have a chance to prevent the calamity."

"Had you known his plans, would you have stopped him or is it just hindsight that makes you realize it was a bad idea?"

"Under no circumstances would I have agreed to the investment," he states with an unquestionable conviction.

"May I ask what the startup did?"

He sighs. "You won't believe it. They made ugly tennis sweatshirts."

"You must be joking!" I laugh.

"The only joke was on me. They managed to lose all the money Noah invested for me in mere months. When they went bankrupt, they shipped me twelve cases of the unsold sweatshirts. They were the ugliest, lowest quality sweatshirts I'd ever seen. They were so bad, I was embarrassed to donate them to charity."

"Why would Noah invest your money in something like that?"

"He'd read that people were making millions in ugly Christmas shirts and sweatshirts, so he thought it was a certain winner."

"No wonder you question his judgment now. He puts you in a terrible position. I've heard athletes often find themselves in financial trouble due to poor investments by their managers. Have you recovered—financially, I mean?"

"I'm not broke if that's what you're worried about. I don't want to discuss it. It's painful."

"My apologies. I didn't mean to pry."

"The more I think about it, I'm changing my advice. Instead of hiring a manager, you should avoid the headaches of dealing with sponsors and managers. Doesn't your family have enough money to fund your foundation?"

"They do, but I want to use my passion for tennis to benefit the people in my country. That's not the case now. Instead, I'm spending my family's money to fund my tennis. It doesn't seem right. If I'm allowed to have sponsors and accept prize money, I could change that."

"In the beginning, I relied on my family to be able to play tennis. The circumstances were different, but I suspect we feel similar guilt."

"When we . . . umm . . . spent time together two years ago, you mentioned that your parents had sacrificed everything for you to play tennis."

"They did. My dad took a second job on weekends. We didn't go on family vacations. My parents drove old cars, put off repairs on their small house, and bought our clothes from thrift stores. Every extra bit of money went to send me to tennis events and pay for occasional coaching. I owe them everything."

"They must love you very much. I'm sure they're incredibly proud of you."

"They're wonderful parents. That's one reason I work so hard. I don't want to disappoint them. I never want them to have regrets or think they wasted their money on me."

That explains Blake's reputation for being laser focused on his game. He's trying to honor his parents' sacrifices. If he cares so much about them being proud of him, why would he put that at risk by doing anything illegal?

There's only one reason I can think of. Maybe he needs more money to take care of his family after he lost so much in the bad investment.

Deciding to test my theory, I say, "I'm sure you've more than made it up to them since you've had so much success."

"I've tried. I bought them a home and insisted they retire early."

"They must be grateful for your generosity."

"They are. They deserve so much more though."

"Do they come to any of your tennis tournaments?"

"Yes. They want to be here now, but I've asked them not to come unless I make it to the finals."

"I can understand that. My parents won't be here either unless we somehow end up in the finals for mixed doubles. Can you imagine the tabloids if our parents were to meet then? They would have us married before the end of the match."

"Good god. The tabloids are horrible. But from what you said the night we ... umm ..."

"Wait a minute. Why are we both being so awkward about that night? We fucked. Let's own it. It was fantastic—at least for me—but it's not something we have to dance around. Can we agree on that?"

"Agreed. I just wasn't sure if you had regrets or were trying to avoid the F-word since you're a princess," he says.

"I'm not a porcelain doll from the 1800s. Please treat me like a normal person, at least when we're alone."

He releases my hand and wraps his arm around my shoulder, pulling me even closer. Being near Blake has a soothing effect. Without thinking, I lean my head against his shoulder and absorb more of the peaceful feeling.

"Your wish is my command. Now back to my question. The night we ... umm ... fucked, all you would tell me was that we couldn't let the tabloids find us together. Why would that have been such a big deal? Was it because I'm a commoner?"

"Of course, not. My brothers both married commoners. That's not a big deal in my country. But a princess having a one-night stand is."

"Didn't your brothers have a number of—what should I call them—short-term girlfriends?"

"They did, but there's a double standard when it comes to women. A prince is seen as showing off his prowess or doing what men do. However, the tabloids christened me the 'Promiscuous Princess' when I was seen leaving a man's room in the middle of the night."

"That's not fair. I'd have thought in today's world we would have moved past such demeaning comments."

"We should have. The real stinger is that I hadn't even slept with the man. I was merely helping a friend with a project. We lost track of time, so I didn't leave until the middle of the night. If I was going to take the wrath of the press, I should have at least gotten the benefit of the deal." I laugh.

"Is there no way to stop them from printing lies?" he asks, as his free hand pushes a lock of hair off my face.

"Not when you can't prove what they printed was false. It was better to let the story die over time. There was no way to prove that nothing happened, and regardless, it was none of their business even if it had."

"I see. So that's why you're so careful about the press."

"That's one reason. After that instance, they took to following me and making up ridiculous tales of my *adventures*—very little of what they printed was true. More recently, I've avoided being seen alone with men."

"Will staying at this rental house with me cause problems?"

The concern in his voice is sincere.

"Since they don't know about our prior night together and there are so many people here, it should be okay. However, it wouldn't surprise me if they start saying we're dating. If that's all they print, I'll be happy."

"Or we could give them something to talk about," he says as his toes brush mine under the water.

"What are you doing?"

"Tickling your toes. I seem to remember you like that."

"You do, huh?"

"I do," he says, pulling me onto his lap.

"We can't do this."

"Why not? We're alone. We're adults. And I can't stare at your plump red lips for another second without tasting them," he says, placing his hand at the back of my head and pulling me in for a tender kiss.

Instead of pushing him away, I lean in, entranced by his musky scent and loving that he's taking control. He's finally showing me that he longs for me as much as I do for him.

Desire heats between my legs as Blake deepens the kiss, and we press our bodies against each other, seeking more. His kisses are even better than I remember. His soft lips are warm, and their pressure is firm and purposeful. And I feel his hard reaction to me.

There's no longer any doubt. We want, no we need, each other. I should stop this, but it's hard to fight the attraction.

When the kiss finally ends, we search each other's eyes for answers.

"Blake, I—" Before I can finish, he presses the tip of a chocolate-covered strawberry against my lips.

"I bet you can take the whole thing," he says with a teasing grin.

Damn. He's trouble.

As I consume the fruit, chocolate sticks to my lips and juice runs down my chin. Blake kisses each spot and murmurs sounds of pleasure.

I arch my neck upward, hoping he'll kiss the sensitive skin there.

He takes the hint, pushes my hair behind my ear to gain better access as he works his way from the front of my neck toward my ear.

"Oh my god, Blake. Your kisses make me want so much more."

"I'm going to give you everything you want but be patient. That will make it better, love," he says as he reaches between my legs, pushing aside the small triangle of my bikini. His finger explores as I wriggle on his lap, nudging him in the direction I want.

"You're a needy little princess, aren't you," he teases.

"If you only knew," I whisper in a breathy moment of truth.

I wouldn't want to admit to Blake how long it's been since someone brought me pleasure. I've been relying on my electronic assistant for too long.

He whispers in my ear, "Do you want to come now or with me inside you?"

"Do you have a condom? I'm not on birth control."

"Not with me. Let's go upstairs to my room."

The click of the patio door opening brings me to my senses as Natalie calls out, "Is there room for all of us in the hot tub?"

I sink under the water to straighten my bathing suit and reemerge across from Blake, creating a respectable space between us.

Between the unfulfilled need for Blake and almost being caught, I'm shaking all over despite the heat of the water.

What the hell was I thinking?

As I'm composing myself, Blake covers for us. "There's room."

Leaning toward me he asks, "Are you okay?"

"Yes, just a tad embarrassed."

"They couldn't see anything from the doorway. We could leave, but I'm the one who would be embarrassed if I stood up. We're stuck here for now."

"It's for the best. I shouldn't have let things go that far. We need to concentrate on tennis," I lament.

"I know. I know. It wasn't your fault. It was mine," he says as Josh and Natalie join us.

We offer them the strawberries, and I retreat into silence, too drained to make conversation. I close my eyes and try to untangle what just happened.

Out of the corner of my eye, I glance at Blake. He looks so composed—like nothing happened. Meanwhile my stomach twists itself into knots. I'd hoped he'd say it meant something, even if he thought it was a mistake. Instead, he quickly agreed it was nothing. That stings more than expected.

If I weren't already drawn to him, I never would have picked such a romantic setting to ask questions. But deep down, was I secretly hoping we'd reconnect? The problem is that I had an ulterior motive: the mission.

I'm sick over the fact that I let things get intimate when he's the subject of my mission. Was I trying to use sex as leverage? I swore I'd never do that. Or am I using the mission as an excuse to get closer to someone I've fantasized about for two years? Is the possibility of Blake being a criminal making him even more irresistible, sending our chemistry off the charts?

How did I twist myself into this tangle?

# 18

## BLAKE

Josh and Natalie just pulled the ultimate cock block—without even realizing it. I'm not sure if I'm relieved or upset—probably both. Mentally, I know the last thing I need is to start something with the princess, but the rest of my body strongly disagrees.

It could never work between us. We come from completely different worlds. I grew up in one of the few poorer areas of Surrey. My father managed a small hotel, and my mother worked in a restaurant. Bri, on the other hand, grew up in a freaking palace.

She trained with the best tennis players and coaches from a young age. I only learned because the owner of my dad's hotel invited me to join his kids on the court after school. I fell in love with the game almost instantly, even if I didn't exactly fit in with my secondhand clothes and worn-out sneakers. Luckily, they had a coach and kept inviting me back, despite my situation.

Eventually, the coach noticed how quickly I was improving. He suggested to my dad that I apply to a local tennis organization that supports children who can't afford to pursue the sport. I applied, and they selected me.

Thanks to that opportunity, my family's sacrifices, and years of intense training, I was able to go on tour when I turned eighteen. That was the start of what's turned into a successful career.

Ironically, that same path from poverty to professional tennis also led to meeting Bri. Every time I'm in her presence, I'm drawn to her. I crave her. I want to hold her. I just want her.

If only it were possible. Even if it were, it wouldn't make sense. We had it right two years ago. It was one wonderful night not meant to be repeated.

*It's time to let my desire for her go.*

# 19

## BRIANNA

Butterflies are fluttering in my stomach this morning, which isn't a surprise. Our first doubles match is today.

I'm both nervous and excited. Part of me wants the clock to speed up so we can start playing, while the other part wants to savor every second of the day.

We can do this. We have to. I want to win my first match at Wimbledon. I also need to win for the mission. If we lose, I have no reason to stay. That would be a problem.

Blake and I manage our stress differently, so we each stick to our pre-game routines. He has breakfast alone in his room while I prefer to eat with my housemates.

As I pack my tennis gear, I remind myself we're as prepared as possible. Blake's second-round singles match was yesterday morning. He won easily, so we were able to practice together in the afternoon. Then we met with our coaches to view videos of our opponents and go over strategies.

On the ride to the All England Club, the playful energy we shared in the hot tub is gone. Blake's all business. He's in full competition mode. I wish he were more talkative, but I'm relieved to see he's taking our match seriously. I was worried he wouldn't. To break the silence, I say, "Don't forget to use the hand signals Martina and Josh suggested. It will really help me to know which direction you plan to move when I'm serving."

He nods, but I doubt he'll use them.

"How long before the match do you want to warm up in the workout area?"

"Forty-five minutes."

"That works for me. I'll be in the locker room until then. Text me if anything changes."

Another nod.

"Are you always this quiet before a match?" I ask.

I expect another nod, but he surprises me by shaking his head. "Sorry, it's just my routine. I'm not used to having a partner. On the ride to a match, I think through my strategy and go over the points Josh has told me about my opponent. When someone says something to me, it's usually just information for me to take in, so I nod and continue with my mental prep. I didn't mean to be rude. I should have asked if you wanted to talk through those things with me. Did you want to discuss strategy?"

"No worries. This is a new partnership for both of us. I'd love to discuss our strategy."

For the rest of the ride, we talk comfortably, exchanging our thoughts and ideas. It's like he's a different person now that he's sharing what's in his head. What a relief.

---

An hour after arriving, we meet in the practice area to warm up with stretches, footwork drills, and exercise bikes. Blake teases me about my favorite stretches I learned in yoga. I make him try one and snap a photo when he ends up twisted into an impossible position. We're focused but having fun.

When our coaches give us a fifteen-minute warning until court time, butterflies flutter in my stomach, reminding me this is real. We gather our tennis bags and follow the coaches to the tunnel for Centre Court. They wish us luck and go to take their seats.

Once we're alone, Blake turns to me, takes my hand, and gives it a gentle squeeze. "Enjoy every moment. Play each point like it's the most important one. When the point is over, forget it and focus on the next one. Results will follow. We've got this."

"Is that what you do?"

"It is."

Before I can reply, a coordinator signals for us to head down the tunnel. A camera person records us as we move forward. When we're three feet from the exit, they stop us.

A booming voice announces, "Please welcome Blake Knight, current No. 2 in the world, and Her Royal Highness, Princess Brianna of Catalinius."

The crowd erupts. It's overwhelming and humbling.

Blake gives my hand one last squeeze and lets go.

Oh no! They've been filming us holding hands. That will make the news. It's too late to worry about that, though.

"Let's have some fun," Blake says, as we walk out of the tunnel.

"Absolutely."

I take my first step onto the sacred Centre Court grass at Wimbledon. I'm awestruck. Sacred is an odd word to use when the crowd is roaring enthusiastically, but Wimbledon is steeped in so much tradition that it seems appropriate.

This must be how commoners feel walking into the throne room to meet the king. I never understood it before. I do now. It's surreal— a once-in-a-lifetime moment for most.

Walking toward our benches, we wave to the fans returning their smiles. It's an honor to play in front of them. Hopefully, we won't disappoint.

Blake nudges me. "Princes Stephen and Adrian are in the Royal Box."

I glance at the box. Adrian is wearing a green tie. Stephen is straightening his purple one, clearly wanting me to notice. It looks like we'll be talking later. It's strange he didn't send a heads-up text. We're using the backup communication plan more than expected.

Despite trying to savor every moment, time flies. I'm pleasantly surprised that Blake is calm and seems to be enjoying himself, which helps my nerves. He's even complimenting me, using hand signals, and talking strategy. Anyone watching would think we'd played together many times before.

I'm not sure what changed his attitude and caused him to fully engage today. There's a part of me that hopes it's because he doesn't want to let me down. But his motive doesn't really matter as long as we're playing as a team.

And we are.

In a heartbeat, it's match point.

Blake serves. I'm on my toes at the net in case the other team returns the ball in my direction. Sure enough, I see the ball coming, lunge right, and with a quick punch of my racquet, drill the ball down the center of the court. It bounces past both opponents untouched.

We've won.

The crowd jumps to their feet, cheering and clapping. Blake runs to me, lifts me off the ground, and spins me in a circle. Returning me to the grass, he kisses me on the cheek, saying, "You were amazing!"

I nod, stunned at both the win and his praise.

Still dazed, we shake hands with our opponents and return to the bench. I take a breath, soaking in the win. Blake and I made it to the next round. I'll be here to continue my mission, and my dream of playing at Wimbledon continues.

Tears of joy and relief threaten to fall, but I press a fingernail into my palm to stop them. My nanny taught me that trick. It comes in handy. I don't need the press twisting the facts and printing a front-page photo of a crying princess.

Blake nudges me, signaling it's time to pack my gear.

That done, we sign autographs and take selfies with fans leaning over the stadium railing. A few minutes later, an official escorts us to the on-court interview.

Adriana, a former tennis-star-turned-reporter, greets us with a cheery, "Congratulations!"

"Thank you. It was such an honor to play before this wonderful crowd," I say, waving to the fans.

As I'm talking, Blake slips an arm around my shoulders, giving me a gentle squeeze.

Adriana grins. "That was a stunning performance, particularly given it was your first tournament match as doubles partners. What makes you two play so well together? Have you been practicing in secret?"

We both laugh. If she only knew how little we've practiced, she wouldn't believe it.

"Brianna is an excellent player. I've watched her play for years now. That made it easy to mesh our games," Blake says, beaming with pride as our eyes meet.

"Blake's a fantastic partner. Who wouldn't play well with one of the top players in the world?" I add.

"Your Highness, what was it like to play at Wimbledon for the first time?"

"It's a dream come true. I'm afraid I'll wake up and it won't be real."

"I promise that you aren't dreaming. You played and won your first match at Wimbledon. Do you plan to play singles here in the future?"

"If I'm invited, I'd love to. For now, I'm concentrating on making it as far into the tournament as possible in mixed doubles. I'm leaving the singles to Blake this year."

Turning to Blake, Adriana says, "Blake, you don't normally play doubles. What's different this year?"

"This is my first opportunity to play doubles with Bri. I wasn't going to pass up that chance."

That's not exactly true. In fact, he tried to talk me out of it. At least he's playing the role of loyal partner for the press.

Adriana asks, "Are you concerned this will take away from your chance to finally win Wimbledon singles this year?"

"Of course not. Being around Bri brings out the best in me. You saw how we played today. That will only help me in singles."

I'm shocked. Does he mean it? Or is he just hiding his real feelings from the press?

Turning back to me, Adriana says, "You two seem to have joined each other's fan clubs. I'm sure everyone here wants me to ask you this question. Are you two dating?"

I cough. Her question surprised me but it shouldn't have. She probably saw the video of us holding hands in the tunnel.

"No. We're only tennis partners," I say. But with Blake's possessive arm around me, it probably wasn't very convincing.

I can only imagine how this will escalate speculation by the tabloids.

Blake adds, "While I'd be lucky if she saw me as dating material, I'm sure there's a long line of more suitable bachelors looking to gain her attention."

Ariana says, "We'll leave it at that. Congratulations again. We'll see you in Round 2."

Wow. What makes him think he's not dating material? He's hot as sin. He's a multimillionaire. Our chemistry is off the charts. Is his statement further proof that he's a criminal and knows I could never date someone who breaks the law? Or was everything he said merely for show?

---

WE'RE APPROACHED BY A STAFF MEMBER AS WE EXIT THE COURT AND ENTER the tunnel.

"Excuse me, His Royal Highness Prince Adrian requests you join him so he can congratulate the two of you personally."

"Both of us? I'm sure he only invited Princess Brianna," Blake asks.

"No, sir. The invitation was for both of you. Please follow me," the staff member says.

Blake shrugs and, looking at me, says, "Lead the way,"

It's a short walk to the members' area where Prince Adrian is standing.

Blake bows his head to show respect for his country's prince.

Adrian reaches out to shake Blake's hand, signaling a more relaxed greeting. Turning to me, he kisses my cheek. We're both royals and have known each other for so long, we're like family. And given that our royal ancestors are all related if you go back a few generations, we actually are family.

"Congratulations. You played wonderfully today." Adrian says.

"It was an incredible day for us," I say.

"It's an honor that you were here to watch us," Blake adds.

"It was entirely my pleasure. My brother had other commitments after your match today, so he sends his apologies for not congratulating you personally."

"Please thank him for us," I say.

"We're proud to support our highest-rated British player and our childhood friend from Catalinius. At least one of us will be at your matches. We hope you'll keep winning so there will be several more matches to watch."

"We'll do our best," Blake says.

"I'm sure you will. I'm sure you two have other places to be now, so I won't keep you," Adrian says as he lightly sandwiches my hand between his two hands, passing a folded paper into my palm.

I discreetly slip the note into the hidden pocket in my tennis skirt that's designed to hold a ball. It will be safe there until I can read it in private.

"Thank you. We look forward to seeing you in the Royal Box," I say.

Prince Adrian departs. As we walk toward our locker rooms for much needed showers, I ask, "Have you met the prince before?"

"No. I've met his parents and brother, but not him. On the rare times that I'm introduced to royalty, it's awkward. I never know what to say."

"You don't seem that way with me," I tease.

"That's different. We met through tennis, so we have that in common. I've only known them as the royals we bow to. Meeting them is rather daunting."

"The UK's royal family are big tennis fans, so I'm sure they are just as awed by you."

"I doubt that. But we have something else to discuss now."

"What?"

"How are we going to celebrate your first win at Wimbledon?"

Really? He wants to celebrate? That's incredibly exciting and decidedly unexpected coming from Mr. Serious.

"What a wonderful idea! But don't you have a singles match tomorrow?"

"I do, but there's time for a small celebration."

He's so sweet and thoughtful. I can't believe he's making celebrating with me a priority. "Count me in. What do you suggest we do?"

"Leave it to me. I'll surprise you."

"I like this version of you. Not that I'm complaining, but what happened to Grumpy Blake?"

"He's taking a break. Our schedules are different for the rest of the day. I'll find you at the house at six tonight. Does that work?"

He's opening up to me more and more. I suspect that not many people see this side of Blake's personality. It makes me feel guilty that I'm investigating him. I really hope he's innocent and that he never finds out what I've been doing.

"I can't wait. I love surprises—if they're good ones. Be sure to clear it with Erin though. Otherwise, she might veto it over security concerns."

"Will do."

We part ways. I walk to my locker room, my lips upturned in a wide smile.

What a day! I still can't believe we won.

When I reach to straighten my tennis skirt, my smile disappears when I remember the note from Adrian. It must be important, but I can't read it until I'm somewhere private.

With that thought, I walk faster.

# 20

## BLAKE

I should be spending the rest of the day prepping for my match tomorrow afternoon. Instead, I'm planning a special dinner for Bri.

I don't know why I blurted out the idea of celebrating tonight, but there's no going back. I promised Brianna a surprise, and she deserves one—she played phenomenal tennis today.

My idea seemed simple enough until I remembered that I don't have Fausto's number, and I don't speak Italian. Fortunately, Natalie was watching our match. I caught up with her before she headed back to our house, so I sent instructions with her. Hopefully, the online translator on her phone will work to relay my message to Fausto. If all goes well, he will have things ready for tonight.

With that problem solved, I focus on recovery, starting with time on a stationary bike. My cool down is running late due to Prince Adrian's invitation. Surprisingly, I'm not stressed, thanks to Bri. Playing doubles with her left me uncharacteristically calm. I hope this feeling lasts.

When I finish my post-match workout, Josh and I climb into an

SUV for the ride to the house. Settling into the black leather seat, he asks, "What time do you want to meet tonight to prep?"

"We need to reschedule our meeting to tomorrow morning. I have plans for tonight."

"Huh? We always meet the night before a match."

"Not this time. Bri and I are celebrating our win over dinner. Then I want time alone to think through tomorrow's match."

"Oh. I see. You want time *alone*," he says, wiggling his eyebrows.

"Don't get any ideas. It's not like that. A little change in routine will help my game. It makes sense to celebrate Bri's first win at Wimbledon."

"Of course, it does. A little celebrating could do you good." He chuckles.

I wave him off, not bothering to deny his innuendos. He wouldn't believe me even though I'm telling the truth.

It's just dinner with a friend. She is a hot, sexy friend that I've slept with before, but it's clear that won't happen again.

Flashbacks of our time in the hot tub invade my thoughts. Vivid memories of her in that tiny scarlet red bikini have my mouth watering. My eyes followed the water droplets disappearing into her cleavage. She tasted like strawberries, chocolate, and desire. She moaned like an angel. Suddenly, I'm not so sure it won't happen again. My cock certainly is hoping it will.

Maybe another cold shower is in order.

---

At six, I cross the hall to knock on Bri's door. It feels like I'm showing up at a girl's home to pick her up for our first date. I'm a tad nervous but excited.

Bri opens the door. She's stunning in her casual dress and bright red lipstick. But it's the sparkle in her eyes that utterly captivates me.

"Are you ready to celebrate your big win?"

"You mean our big win. And, yes, I'm absolutely ready. What are we doing?"

"Give me your hand and close your eyes."

She looks unsure.

"Come on. I won't let you fall. Trust me."

She finally offers me her hand.

Taking it, I place my other hand on the small of her back. "Eyes closed. No peeking. I'm going to turn you in the right direction, and we're going to take a few steps forward."

"Okay, but warn me when we reach the stairs."

"Don't worry. I'll take care of you."

Her body is stiff, but she follows my directions. Instead of helping her downstairs as she expects, I guide her toward the double doors at the end of the hallway.

"Stop here. I need to open a door."

"Okay. Where are we? Aren't we going downstairs?"

"Be patient. You'll see. We're crossing the threshold of a door, so step across it and open your eyes."

Her hands fly to her face, covering her mouth in surprise. "Oh! How did you plan this?"

"With a little help. Do you like it?"

"Who wouldn't?"

The candlelit balcony has a table for two with a white tablecloth, sparkling crystal, and fresh flowers. Soft music is playing in the background.

"I debated whether to plan an evening out or a quiet one here. But if we went out, fans would swarm us, and security would be extremely difficult. I decided time alone to enjoy our win would be better. I hope this was the right choice."

After she shared what playing at Wimbledon means to her, I want tonight to be a special celebration. I won't burst her bubble by pointing out that the next round will be much more difficult. But it's likely this will be her only win at Wimbledon this year.

"It's absolutely perfect. I can't believe you went to so much trouble."

She rises on her tiptoes and kisses my cheek, sending warmth down my body.

"I had help from Erin, Natalie, and Fausto," I admit.

Her eyes go wide, and mouth drops in shock.

"How did you communicate with Fausto? I didn't think anyone else in the house speaks Italian."

Proud of myself, I answer, "We don't, but Google translate saved the day."

She laughs a little awkwardly. "I should have thought of that sooner."

"Me too. I could have given my menu requests to him directly."

"True."

For some reason, a worried look crosses her face.

"What's wrong?"

She hesitates. Turning to face her, I place my hands on her shoulders and look into her eyes. "Bri, please tell me. Why do you look so worried?"

She sighs. "You shouldn't be taking the evening off tonight. I want you to be ready for your match tomorrow."

She's right, but nothing could stop me from making tonight special for Bri. She played and won her first Wimbledon match. That's a once-in-a-lifetime event. She doesn't hang out with her coach socially, so it's up to me to make tonight memorable for her.

I smile and kiss her forehead. "Is that all? Don't give it a second thought. A calm evening with you is exactly what I need."

She relaxes. "Okay. Let's enjoy the evening. Can you believe we won today? We barely had a chance to practice together."

"Of course we won. We both played well." Hopefully, my words don't betray the concern and guilt I felt earlier. Walking onto the court, I worried it was a mistake to have skipped practicing with Bri.

She looks at me like I'm from another planet, clearly doubting the inevitability of today's win. "Blake, you know two people can play well individually and still lose if they aren't working together. I was surprised that we were so in sync today."

She's smart and no pushover. I love that she analyzes her game even when we're celebrating a victory.

"We clicked the moment we met, so it comes naturally. If I were a fan of doubles, you'd be the perfect partner for me. Our chemistry works.

"It certainly did today." She studies me, clearly still second-guessing our lack of prep.

"It's time to celebrate. Let's start with a toast."

I pop the cork on a bottle of champagne, which elicits an adorable tilt of her head and twinkle in her eyes.

Taking her glass from me, she says, "Wow! Who conjured the light-hearted, fun-loving version of the man I first met? What happened to the laser-focused, fun-avoiding Blake who's been living here for the past week?"

I chuckle. "It was you . . . along with some reflection."

"I don't understand."

"Let's sit. You've been incredibly patient with my mood swings and rudeness. I owe you an apology and an explanation."

I motion toward the cozy rattan sofa for two. We sit and our knees touch, but neither of us shifts apart.

She sips her champagne. "I started to think you were two different people."

"I've been dealing with . . . a lot. I've handled it poorly. I'm sorry."

"Is it more than your problem with Noah?" she asks gently.

I exhale slowly. "Yes. I didn't want anyone to know for fear the press would find out. They would roast me on the front page of every tabloid. From what you've said, you understand how the press can make your life miserable."

"I do. But don't worry. Anything you share with me will be safe. I won't tell anyone," she says, pressing her free hand against her chest.

"I trust you with my secret. That's not why I'm hesitating. When I organized this dinner for you, it didn't include baring my troubles.

It's supposed to be a celebration. We can discuss this another time. I don't want to ruin tonight."

Resting her hand on my leg, she looks at me with sincere concern. "You won't spoil anything. I've been walking on eggshells trying to figure out what was wrong. It's a relief to talk. Please tell me what's wrong."

"Okay. Give me a minute to organize my thoughts and decide where to start."

"Don't they say it's always best to start at the beginning?"

"They do. I remember telling you two years ago that I felt tremendous pressure to win Wimbledon because I'm from the UK."

"You did."

"It's more than just the need to win for my country though. It's the one Grand Slam I haven't won. People are saying I choke. I'm getting older and running out of chances with the younger players who are drilling their serves and playing like seasoned veterans in their early twenties."

"But you're still at the top of your game. Those younger players fear you on the court."

"They do, but they might not fear me as much if they hear the rest of my story."

"What do you mean?"

Her gaze turns darker and so sad. What must she be thinking?

"Oh, no. It's not that. I'm not dying." I push a lock of her hair behind her ear, incredibly moved by her concern.

She exhales audibly. "That's a relief. Before I think of more devastating possibilities, please tell me what's going on."

"Okay. Sit back. This will take a while to explain. You see, I have a history of injuries, falling ill to viruses, and a slew of other disasters at Wimbledon. Every year there's been some reason things haven't worked out for me here. In the beginning, I was young and knew I had many more chances to win, so I didn't think much about it. Hell, the first few years, I didn't even expect to win. Then more years passed, and I still hadn't won. With each passing attempt, the pressure increases."

"You still have plenty of time," she reassures with a squeeze to my forearm.

"That's what I told myself every year. But this year felt different in a bad way. A couple of months ago, I started dreading Wimbledon for fear something horrible would happen again. The worry and fear that I would never achieve my dream and remove this weight off my shoulders started to weigh me down. It consumed my thoughts."

"I can see how that would happen."

"It became worse though. One day my heart raced, my chest tightened, and I broke out in a sweat. I knew I was having a heart attack and rushed to the doctor."

"Oh, my god. How bad was it?"

She leans forward grasping my arm with both her hands, the color draining from her face.

"Fortunately, my heart was fine. It was my first panic attack. It turns out the symptoms are very similar to a heart attack."

"At least it wasn't a heart attack. But you said it was the *first* one. Have there been more?"

"Yes."

"You must have been so frightened."

"I was. I still am, if I'm honest. They can happen at any time. And the fear that the press would learn about it and tell everyone that I panic over my tennis matches made it even worse. I couldn't talk to anyone."

I'm shocked that I'm talking about this so freely with anyone other than my therapist. It's cathartic to be able to share this with someone I haven't paid to listen. Bri makes me feel so comfortable and safe.

"I can't imagine how hard that was. Is that why you hired Natalie?" she asks softly.

"Yes. Eventually, Josh figured out what was going on and recommended her. She's been helping me learn to deal with this."

"Are there drugs that can help?"

"I opted not to go on medication. Some drugs are approved for athletes, but there have been several scandals lately with tennis players testing positive for unauthorized substances. The list of banned drugs changes regularly, so I didn't want to take the risk that something I took could come back to haunt me the next time there's an update."

"That makes sense. How are you managing?"

"Doc taught me techniques for getting through an attack when one happens. We also decided that I'd change my routine for the tournament. I arrived earlier than usual to have time to settle in. I promised myself I'd focus solely on practicing and not let myself be distracted."

She clasps her hands over her mouth. "Oh, no! Then I arrived to play doubles with you. No wonder you tried to talk me out of it. The distraction must have freaked you out."

"You have no idea. Then you said it would be your only way to play at Wimbledon and fulfill your dream. I couldn't let you down. I knew how much it was killing me to have an unfulfilled need to win here. I couldn't be responsible for that happening to you."

"I had no idea. Agreeing to partner with me was so incredibly generous and unselfish of you. You truly understood what I was feeling."

I nod and squeeze her hand. "I did. That's why, with Natalie's help, I became determined to make it work. I could spare a few hours to practice and play matches with you. Josh and Natalie helped me think of our doubles as extra practice time."

"That makes sense, but I'm so sorry. I never would have intentionally put you in that position. I didn't know."

"Please don't apologize. It turned out to be the best thing that could have happened for me."

"How's that?"

She looks mystified. It's a cute look on her. Doesn't she know how incredible she is?

"I'd been waiting for something bad to happen. I assumed that being forced to play doubles was that *bad* thing. But I'd found a way to handle it and turn it into a positive. At that point, I thought things were under control, and I could still win."

"You have a great team. I'm glad they were there for you."

"I know."

"Thank you for sharing. I understand why you're so focused on tennis. It also explains why you haven't been much fun to be around most of the time. What changed tonight?"

"In the last day or two, I realized that I wanted to help you win. That led to some self-reflection. I slowly started seeing what was happening. Despite my dread of failing, I had moments with you on the practice court and in the hot tub where I felt like my happy self again despite things not going to plan here. After our night in the hot tub, I remembered that the tournaments I've won were ones where I was relaxed and felt good about life and my game. I've never felt that way here before. I vowed to change that going forward."

"Is that why you're happier tonight?"

"Yesterday, I saw you in the stands during my match. It made me smile to know you had taken the time to be there even if it was only to prep for our matches. I played great. It was a relief. Then today, it felt like we were having fun on the court. I wanted to be there with you. I'm sorry to say I hadn't expected that. I hope my honesty doesn't hurt your feelings too much."

"Of course not. I'm thrilled you had fun today. It was a fantastic feeling to play together. My adrenaline was pumping. In fact, I've never played better."

"We brought out the best in each other. After we won, it was like a ray of sunshine washed away the dark clouds that had been hovering over me. I can never thank you enough for that."

"I don't know what to say, except I'm happy for you."

"Don't say anything. Let me kiss you."

I bend toward her luscious lips, hesitating ever so slightly to give her a chance to push me away. When she doesn't, I press my mouth firmly against hers and begin to show Bri exactly how much I appreciate her.

My lips tingle as my hands roam down her back, pressing her against me. I want Bri to know what she does to my body and how much I want her.

She moans, "You feel sooo good."

"I can't get enough of you. We should go to my room."

She jerks her head back, eyes wide, "No! We can't."

"I'm sorry. I thought you wanted this too."

"Oh. I do. That's not it. We need to go to my bedroom. Erin will panic if my room is empty tonight."

At least I hadn't totally misread the situation. "I'm not sure I like the idea of her walking in on us though."

"She won't if she knows I'm safely inside. I'll text her. Let's go."

She takes my hand, and we hurry to her room.

I should take this slow and savor each moment tonight. But we both have so much pent-up sexual energy, it's not possible. Instead, we shed our clothes the minute Bri's bedroom door is locked and fall onto her bed facing each other.

We kiss and explore each other with our hands. Our bodies mold perfectly to each other. As we intertwine our legs, all the memories from two years ago come flooding back. I remember she loves when I nibble her ear and kiss her neck, so I quickly move to do just that.

She immediately shivers with delight and nuzzles her neck against my face, begging for more. I happily comply.

Her fingernails gently skim down my back sending sensations of pleasure straight to my cock. Good god, she remembers.

"You're a goddess! Do that again."

"I need you inside me," she begs as her fingernails skim up my back, making me squirm.

"Are you ready for me, love?" I ask, reaching my hand between her legs, finding her drenched for me.

"Past ready. Please. Now," she groans in needy frustration.

"Hold on, let me grab a condom." Fortunately, I remembered to throw my wallet onto the nightstand when we stripped. After the hot tub, I've vowed never to be without a condom again any time there was a chance Bri might say yes.

She grabs the foil wrapper from me, rips it open with her teeth, and slowly rolls the condom onto me in a move that almost causes me to lose it. "Your hands are magic," I groan.

I trace my cock over her wet folds. Positioning myself at her entrance, I ease in, letting her adjust to my size. She arches into me, and I slide in with a moan of pleasure. "You are so perfect. Are you okay?"

"I'm so far past okay."

We move in sync as I thrust in and out. I reach under her, grabbing each of her ass cheeks, tilting them upward to hit her magic spot.

"Yes, oh my god, yes! Don't you dare stop. I'm almost there," she screams.

Feeling her pulsing around me, I find my release that's more amazing than ever before as white lights flash under my closed eyelids.

We remain still and silent except for our heavy breathing as we gradually come down from the natural high.

When our breathing returns to normal, I excuse myself to dispose of the condom

Returning, I help her clean up and then spoon her against me and it occurs to me that this was different than two years ago. We now know each other better. We shared personal details in the hot tub. We truly are a team on the tennis court now and work well together. When I look at her, I want to make her happy. It makes me wonder if there could be a future for us.

# 21

## BRIANNA

Morning light filters through the window coverings, nudging me to wake. I groan, not ready to leave the comfort of bed. I've never been a morning person, but today, I'm cocooned in the security of a tightly wrapped blanket. I smile and stretch.

Wait.

That's not just a blanket. Blake's arm is around my waist. And his leg is tangled with mine.

He never left.

Memories of last night rush in. The balcony celebration he planned was perfect. He trusted me with the issues and fears he's facing. Then when we could no longer resist our attraction, he treated me with an unexpected tenderness, practically worshipping my body.

He was perfect.

As the morning brain fog clears, reality sets in. My body may automatically crave Blake, but he's still a suspect. Last night I let my personal feelings interfere with the mission.

How do I fix this?

Then again, it may help me gain his trust. But that thought makes me sick to my stomach. I wouldn't trick Blake, or anyone, with sex. He'll think I'm a horrible person if he ever finds out about my role as a Covert Royal. I'd never convince him that last night was about us, not my mission.

Of course, there's no reason for him to find out.

What's done is done. Besides, it's not like we hadn't done the same thing before. He wasn't a suspect then. And he'll never learn about my secret life. No one knows—not even my brothers.

I'm overreacting. Some alone time will clear my head and refocus my attention on the end goal.

There's only one problem—Blake's sound asleep and wrapped around me. I'm captive and have no desire to move. Waking up, snuggled tightly in his arms is pure heaven. I could lie here in his warm embrace all day and be completely contented.

Maybe it would be okay to rest here a little longer. I smile, closing my eyes, and drift back to sleep.

---

SOMETHING IS NIBBLING ON MY EARLOBE. MY PARENTS' YORKIE MUST HAVE snuck into my palace apartment again.

Wait.

That's impossible. I'm at Wimbledon in London.

A deep voice whispers, "Love, you need to wake up. Breakfast will be ready soon." The nibbling resumes.

"Mmm. Maybe later."

A hand slips between my thighs. "Fausto will be here with breakfast any minute. You might want to put clothes on."

I bolt upright. "Did you say Fausto is bringing breakfast? No! He can't know we slept together. This is a disaster."

Blake laughs. "He's just the chef. Why do you care if he knows we were together last night?"

I can't tell him that I'm worried it will get back to the other members of the Covert Royal team.

"I try to keep my personal life from anyone other than Erin. It'll make things awkward with Fausto."

"Then you'll be glad to know I was teasing. Breakfast is downstairs as usual."

I playfully smack his shoulder. "That was mean."

"I tried other more friendly ways to wake you first. When those didn't work, I went for the shock factor."

I yawn, stretching my arms above my head. "Now you know my secret. I'm not much of a morning person even after all the years of early practices."

"I could tell," he chuckles, rolling onto his back and sinking onto his pillow.

Somehow, he keeps his leg draped over mine as if he's afraid I'll try to escape.

"What about you? Do you prefer mornings or evenings?" I ask, as I rub my eyes, yawning.

"With my travel schedule, I cross so many continents and time zones, my body is always confused. Besides, our matches are sometimes in the morning and other times they don't start until ten o'clock at night. At this point, I've forgotten if I ever had a preference."

"If you were on holiday for three weeks, would you wake up early and go sightseeing or sleep in and party into the night?"

"I'd sleep for the first three days and then figure it out," he grins.

Rolling onto my side, I curl into him, nestling my head into the crook of his shoulder and draping my free leg over his. "That was a dumb question on my part. With tennis tournaments back-to-back all year, I'm guessing you don't get many extended holidays."

"I don't. A week off is a rare treat."

"Have you thought about skipping a few of the lower-level tournaments and taking some time for yourself?" I ask, slowly tracing my finger along the contours of his chest and abs.

"Not really. My career will likely end in five to seven years. I've always assumed there would be time to rest and do what I want then."

"We live strange lives, don't we? There's rarely any free time. I'm not playing tennis year-round like you, but when I'm not on tour, my royal duties fill my days."

"What's that like?"

That's my cue. He's given me the perfect opening to turn back to the mission even if it is a mood killer.

I close my eyes, not wanting to betray my feelings, explaining, "When I'm in Catalinius, it's impossible to go anywhere and not be known. But I can't complain too much. My oldest brother has it even worse. Since he took the throne as king, his photo is now on all the coins and paper money. Even the people on day trips to the island would recognize him."

"Why doesn't Catalinius use the Euro?"

"It may become our currency someday, but that hasn't happened yet. I've heard that a number of people are collecting our coins in hopes they'll be valuable if we eventually change to the Euro."

"I can see that. My grandfather collects coins. I usually take foreign coins to him from my travels."

My pulse skips a beat. Is this the proof our team has been looking for? Is Blake doing this for his grandfather? That doesn't make sense though. He could just buy collectible coins and give them as gifts. Why resort to crime?

I press on. "Did you collect any for him from recent tournaments?"

I'm internally dreading his answer.

"A few. Nothing too special."

"If you picked up any local coins when you played in the Catalinius tournament, I'd love to see them. Our coins capture the history of my family. I could share what I know. Then you could pass it along to your grandfather."

"That would've been great. But I always mail the coins to him before I leave the country. It's too much hassle to carry them around with me."

Huh? That doesn't match our intel. There's supposed to be a handoff here.

"Oh. I see." But I don't really. I'm more confused than ever.

He kisses the top of my head and carefully disentangles us. "As much as I love lounging in bed with you and enjoying your slow morning routine, I need to have a quick breakfast and leave for my match."

"Of course. I'd rather no one come looking for us anyway. I was thinking about watching you play again today. Would you mind?" I ask.

"That would be fantastic. You were a calming force for my first match. I'd love to have you at this one too. You can be my good luck charm."

Blake kisses me on the cheek, pulls on his boxer briefs, and gathers the rest of his clothing. He peeks into the hallway, then quickly hurries to his room.

Finally, I'm alone and my thoughts are racing around my head.

Why would he admit to collecting coins for his grandfather. He must assume that I'm not aware of the laws. He didn't admit knowing that certain coins were illegal to possess outside their home country.

More importantly, is our intel completely wrong? Does that mean the exchange is not happening at Wimbledon. Is he simply putting the coins in an envelope and mailing them to his grandfather to get them out of the various countries? If that's the case, then am I completely off base looking for hiding places in trophies?

Someone needs to check out Blake's grandfather. I'll send an encrypted text to Princes Stephen and Adrian.

Me: Grandfather is a collector. Receives items by mail.

Team: Will follow up.

Me: Thanks.

Now for the next part of my plan.

# 22

## BLAKE

Josh and I arrive at Wimbledon two hours before my second-round match. Even though it's my opponent's first-time here, I can't take winning for granted. When someone has nothing to lose, they often play their best and take risks that can lead to an upset. It's important for me to stay focused and stick to my standard pre-match warmup routine.

As we walk to the practice court, Josh asks, "What's different today?"

"What do you mean?"

"Man, you're humming and smiling. I'd swear there's an extra bounce in your step."

Was I really humming? Whenever a random thought from last night pops into my head, I can't help smiling. I knew another night with Bri wouldn't be enough. It just fueled my craving for her. But I can't share that with Josh.

Instead, I simply say, "I'm feeling good about today after Bri and I won yesterday. That's all."

"If you say so. Don't be overconfident though. You'll need to concentrate. This new guy is solid."

"Don't worry. I'm here to win. I'm ready to warm up with groundstrokes."

After 45 minutes practicing my ground strokes and volleys, I work on my serve.

Josh says, "Your serve is on fire today. Don't forget to kick a few wide. Geoff tends to lean toward the center and won't move fast enough to reach those."

"Will do."

Josh says, "That's enough court time for now. Let's move to the outdoor workout area."

"Great. Let me grab a granola bar from my bag to eat while we walk and discuss strategy."

After taking several gulps of a sports drink, I tear open the foil on my snack and sling my bag onto my shoulder.

As we walk off the court, I say, "I haven't watched Geoff play much. He's new to the higher-level tournaments. What else should I keep in mind?"

"He rarely comes to the net, so well-placed drop shots could earn you easy points. And his second serve needs work. Be ready to pounce on it and slam it back."

"Got it."

As we keep walking, I visualize shot sequences that will force Geoff into tough positions that I can exploit. By the time I've worked through several scenarios, we arrive at the outdoor exercise facility.

I head straight for the stationary bikes, put on my headphones, and hop on to keep my muscles warm. This is the relaxing part of my routine—I listen to the same seven songs every time. Like most pros, I'm superstitious, and changing my routine stresses me out.

The final song, *Don't Stop Believin'*, begins playing. It's a classic reminder of where my head needs to be.

When it ends, I signal Josh, and he hands me the resistance bands. I go through mobility and core exercises—leg swings, arms circles, and torso twists to loosen up and prevent injury. Given my history of injuries at Wimbledon, I'm taking all the precautions I can.

During my stretches, Josh and I chat about who's making coaching changes, whose injuries are holding them back, and which players are dating each other. The rather mindless conversation calms my nerves.

A loud buzzing from Josh's smartwatch signals it's time to move to the next phase of my warmup.

First, I take a short break to chat with the other players who are standing around. Marco boasts about how great he's feeling. Another top player, Thomas, complains that he's sick of the rain delays.

"At least the rain—" I start, but Marco interrupts.

"Hey, Oliver! Bring some of those samples over here."

A guy carrying a tray of cups joins us.

"Everyone, this is Oliver. His company makes amazing sports drinks. You should try them," Marco says.

"Nice to meet you, Oliver. I'm always looking for new drink options."

Thomas asks, "Are those the herbal-tea ones that I've been hearing about?"

"They are. It's an herbal tea blend infused with horseradish. It opens your airways, which improve oxygen levels. There's nothing else like it on the market. I brought samples for everyone."

We each take a cup as Oliver continues, "It's like a shot. Drink it in one sip for maximum benefit."

Thomas says, "Okay. Bottoms up."

I'm skeptical, but with two endorsements, why not.

As soon as the muddy brown liquid hits the back of my throat, I feel a vicious burn, and my eyes water. Oliver was right—my airways clear as if I've inhaled menthol. It must be the horseradish.

When the burn fades, I say, "Oliver, I'll admit it opens things up, but it tastes awful. No wonder you told us to down it in one sip."

Thomas says, "It wasn't that bad."

Marcos adds, "Agreed. The benefits are worth a little unpleasantness."

"Maybe," I say.

"Thanks for trying it. We'll be reaching out to your managers with more information about sponsorship opportunities. Good luck in your matches," Oliver says, then walks away.

I shake my head and grab my water bottle to rinse away the taste. That drink was disgusting. I understand the benefit, but yuck.

Rejoining Josh, I begin the final part of my warmup—jumps, sprints, and medicine ball throws—to further raise my energy level. My pulse rises quickly, and sweat beads on my forehead. I'm ready for battle.

I double-check the contents of my tennis bag.

Six racquets. Check.

Extra sweat bands. Check.

An extra shirt. Check.

Trail mix and drink bottles. Check.

Until this year, I assumed my coach properly packed my bag. Then one of my friends showed up on court without his racquets. We haven't let him forget it. Since then, I've personally checked my own bag.

Hoisting my gear onto my shoulder, Josh and I walk down the tunnel toward the court. Along the way, fear rises. What if I have a panic attack? I quietly do the breathing exercises that Doc prescribed.

Suddenly, an image of Bri pops into my head. I smile. She promised to be here. I need to see her. Somehow, I know that will calm me.

At the end of the tunnel, I pause. When my name is called, I step onto the sunlit court. I wave to the crowd and search the section where Bri will be sitting. My heart sinks. She's not there.

She's probably just running late.

I unpack my drink bottles and set them in front of my bench. As I pull a racquet from my bag, I look again—still no Bri.

There's a pit in my stomach, but I shake it off. She'll be here. At least, I hope she will.

During warmups, I force myself not to glance at the stands. When the umpire signals the start of the match, I allow myself one last look.

Her bright smiling face locks on mine. I exhale. She's here. That helps me even more than my breathing exercises.

The match begins, and soon I confirm that Josh was right. Geoff doesn't like coming to the net. Taking advantage of that knowledge, I easily win the first game. During the break before the next game, I munch on a handful of trail mix to tame my grumbling stomach. Tennis burns a lot of calories.

Fifteen minutes later, I win the first set. But something is off. My energy is fading too fast. My stomach isn't just growling—it's queasy. It must be the heat. I need to hydrate better if I'm going to win two more sets.

Geoff's first serve of the second set whizzes by me in a blur. I shake my head. What's wrong with me? It wasn't any faster than his prior serves. I shake my head, but that makes it worse. I'm overcome with dizziness, and a stomach cramp doubles me over.

Bloody hell. Don't tell me I picked up a stomach bug at Wimbledon again.

I have to push through. I can't fail again.

My palms sweat and heart rate soars. No! Not the fuck now. I can't be having a panic attack too.

Barely catching my breath, I signal the umpire to call for a trainer to come. At the end of this game, they should be able to give me something for my stomach ache. That will get me through the match.

At the baseline, I try to focus on Geoff's movements while attempting to block out the pain. I just have to last a couple more points.

Mustering every ounce of remaining strength, I return Geoff's serve and dash across the court. Seeing the blurry ball cross the net, I stretch, barely getting my racquet on the ball. It skims across the net, dropping just out of Geoff's reach.

As my body falls to the ground, the crowd erupts.

I try to stand but can't. The pain is unbearable, and the dizziness is worse than any hangover.

I'm screwed.

The last thing I hear is the sound of fast-paced footsteps.

Darkness envelops me.

# 23

## BRIANNA

Blake makes the shot of the match.

I jump to my feet, cheering as loudly as anyone in the crowd. He threw his whole body into it, losing his balance but winning the point. It was a spectacular shot—almost superhuman.

But he's still on the ground. Why doesn't he get up?

"No!" I clasp my hands over my mouth. He's writhing in pain.

I stare as people rush to his aid. He drank a lot of liquid between games. It could be muscle cramps from dehydration. Or he may have sprained an ankle.

The crowd is eerily quiet. All eyes are on Blake. He's not moving.

I glance toward the Royal Box where the princes were. Their seats are empty.

Minutes pass. Medics surround Blake. They're not tending to a twisted ankle or helping him to his feet. My concern soars.

Helplessness washes over me. I want to go to him, but I'm not allowed on the court. I could go to the tunnel waiting area. My player's ID card will get me that far. He'll have to pass through there when he leaves.

Picking up my bag, I turn to leave, but a collective gasp ripples through the crowd. My head swings back to the court where everyone is pointing. Medics are wheeling out a gurney.

I've never seen an injury require this level of attention at a tennis match. He must have hit his head or broken a bone. I have to go now.

Moving to the aisle, Erin joins me. She's been watching from a standing area a few rows behind where I was sitting.

She says, "This woman has a message for you."

I turn to the woman wearing an official Wimbledon staff shirt. She says, "Your Royal Highness, please follow me. Arrangements have been made for you to travel to the hospital where they are taking Mr. Knight."

Erin clears the way for us to follow. We're led to a private exit where a royal vehicle is waiting.

"Please take a seat inside with his Royal Highness," Adrian's driver says, motioning for Erin and me to join Prince Adrian in the back.

As soon as the door shuts, I ask, "What's going on? Do you know what happened to Blake? Did he break something?"

My stomach churns. My hands won't stop shaking. He has to be okay.

"They haven't said yet. But he's on the way to hospital. I assumed you would want to be there. We've arranged for a private waiting room."

"Thank you. That's exactly where I need to be. I couldn't tell what happened. He went for the tough shot and fell, but it didn't look like he hit his head. It just doesn't make sense."

"I'm sure he will be fine. They're probably taking him to hospital as a precaution. The local hospitals are excellent."

"That's reassuring. But I'm not family. They won't tell me anything about his condition."

"Don't worry. I'll take care of that. I'm known to have a little influence in this country," he grins, lightening the tension.

"Touché."

How did I not remember he'd just pull his prince card?

———

Thanks to Adrian, we enter through a private door and are led to a small room, avoiding the press at the main entrance. It's bleak and sterile with a white table, four plastic chairs, and a wall clock with giant red numbers.

We wait. And wait.

It's been an hour and four minutes. I've watched every single second tick by. So far, no news.

Josh, Noah, and Natalie arrived half an hour ago but are stuck in the main waiting room. For security reasons, Erin and Adrian's bodyguard insisted we wait here. I wanted Blake's team to join us, but there's not enough space.

Unfortunately, we can't discuss our mission because there are cameras everywhere—even in this tiny waiting room. The last thing we need is a nosy security guard reading our lips and selling the story to the tabloids.

So, we sit in silence, sipping tea Erin managed to find while Adrian's guard stands watch.

Another forty-five minutes pass before a sharp knock startles me.

Adrian says, "Come in."

The door opens with authority, and an older man, wearing an expensive suit under a white coat, steps in.

"Your Royal Highnesses, I'm Dr. Shepard. I've been asked to provide you with an update on Blake Knight's condition."

"Thank you, Dr. Shepard. Please have a seat."

Adrian and I sit across from him.

"Is Blake okay? What happened?" I ask, my voice shaking.

"Mr. Knight's condition is serious. But he's strong and in excellent physical condition. That will help his chances."

"What's wrong with him? Did he tear a muscle? Break ribs? What do you mean by 'help his chances'?" I ask. My voice trembles as my panic skyrockets.

"No. It wasn't a physical injury of that nature. We believe he was poisoned."

"Poisoned?" Adrian asks.

"You mean he had an allergic reaction to something?" I suggest, unwilling to believe the worst.

"No. I mean he was poisoned. It could have been accidental or on purpose."

My jaw drops in shock and horror. How could that have happened? My thoughts race through possibilities. Could it be related to our investigation?

"What was the poison?" Adrian asks in an unexpectedly calm tone.

"We need to verify it with further tests, but we believe the poison came from an oleander plant."

"I didn't know that oleanders are poisonous," I manage to utter as my body shakes and my voice quivers.

"They are. All parts of an oleander plant are extremely poisonous, even the flowers and roots. In fact, a small dose can be fatal."

"Are you saying Blake will die?" I ask as a tear escapes and trails down my cheek. I can't bear the thought of losing him.

"We hope not. If it was a mild exposure, he will pull through. We need to watch him closely overnight."

"When will you know if he's going to be okay?" Adrian asks.

"This is a strange poison. He'll either be fine in one to three days or . . . not."

I gulp, my worst fears realized. He could die.

"Can we see him?" I ask.

"Not until tomorrow. But you can help. We need to find out how he was exposed to the poison. We don't want anyone else to accidentally ingest it. And if he recovers, we can't risk another exposure. It could be fatal."

"There's an oleander bush in the backyard of the house where we're staying. Could that be it? Would touching a leaf or smelling a flower have been enough to poison him?" I ask.

"That's possible, but he may have ingested it."

"How could that have happened?" Adrian asks.

"Ask the people who were around him what they saw him eat or drink. Then when he feels up to answering questions, we may learn more."

"Based on when he collapsed, can you estimate when he would have ingested the poison? That might help us narrow the possible sources," I say.

"Usually, I would say two to four hours before he fell ill. But given his level of exertion, I suspect the poison acted faster than that. My best guess is it was in something he ate or drank one to two hours before he passed out."

"That's helpful. We'll make sure to have this checked out quickly," Adrian says.

"Very well. I need to get back to my patients," Dr. Shepard says as he stands.

"We'll leave contact information. Please let us know if there is any change in Blake's condition," Adrian says.

"We will," Dr. Shepard promises as he leaves.

"Let's go," Adrian says.

I nod, knowing we need to find somewhere to talk away from the cameras.

As we walk to the waiting car, my thoughts swirl. Was this a freak accident or a targeted attack? Is there trouble between thieves? Was there a double-cross?

And why did I let myself fall for the target? Should I come clean to Adrian or pretend nothing happened between Blake and me? If they find out, will they kick me out of the Convert Royals? If I'd trusted the evidence pointing to Blake, I wouldn't be in this mess.

Worse—if I'd stayed focused on the mission, I might have seen the threat. Maybe, I could have protected him. If he dies, I'll never forgive myself. He doesn't deserve that fate, even if he's guilty of smuggling.

As we reach the car, Adrian says, "I've arranged for our guards to follow in a separate vehicle so we can talk."

"Okay," I say, sliding into the back of the car.

He joins me, and the car pulls away.

"Do you know if this was an accident or intentional?" I ask.

"We received intel that there was a threat to Blake, so we believe it was intentional."

"And you didn't think to tell me? What the bloody hell?"

"Calm down. We weren't sure the threat was credible."

"What if I'd been poisoned too? How would you explain to my parents that you didn't think it was important to share such critical information with me."

"We had someone watching him. What's important is that we determine when he was poisoned."

"We'll revisit your strategy when this mission ends. But based on the doctor's estimate of the timing, Blake must have ingested the poison during his pre-match warm up."

"Agreed."

"Josh is the one who would know what Blake consumed before his match."

"Yes, but Josh could be the one who poisoned Blake, so we need to be careful. Whoever did this to Blake expected him to die. They won't be happy if he survives and may make another attempt on his life."

"True. We have to tell Erin and Fausto what's going on. We need their help to protect Blake."

"I agree. I'll check with Deputy Harrington for clearance to read them in."

"Thanks. It doesn't make sense having trained guards and not using them when someone's life is in danger."

"You don't have to convince me."

"What's next?"

"It depends on how Blake is doing tomorrow."

What he really means is it depends on whether Blake lives.

# 24

## BLAKE

I wake up chilled. My head is throbbing, and there's an incessant beeping that won't stop. It's impossible to focus on tennis when I can't get a good night's sleep. I try to roll over and bury my head under the pillow, but something tugs at my arm.

I yank harder, determined to escape the incessant beeping.

"Ouch," I yell.

The beeping grows faster and louder.

Doors fly open. Lights flood my eyes.

"What the bloody hell?"

A stern voice says, "Mr. Knight, calm down. Please stop moving. You pulled your IV out."

My pulse spikes. The beeping escalates. What's happening? Am I dreaming? Is this a panic attack? Is it possible to have one while I'm asleep?

I finally manage to call out, "Who are you? Why are you in my bedroom? What IV? Where am I?"

"You're in hospital. I'm Nurse Beasley. Do you remember what happened yesterday?"

"Huh? Hospital? Yesterday?"

"You're okay. Try to take a deep breath. Then tell me what you remember."

If I'm okay, why am I in a hospital? My head is pounding. It hurts to think—but I try.

Slowly, I say, "I remember playing the match. My stomach started hurting. I felt dizzy."

"That's right. You collapsed on the court." Her voice softens.

"Did I catch a virus? Was it food poisoning?"

I must be in the Wimbledon medical facility, hooked up to an IV for rehydration.

"The good news is that you're improving. I'll let Dr. Shepard explain the rest—he's coming in now," she says, stepping back.

An older male voice says, "Hello, I'm Dr. Shepard. Welcome back to the living, Mr. Knight. How do you feel this morning?"

Morning? But my match was in the afternoon. Wait—someone asked me about yesterday. I'm so confused.

"My head hurts like someone took a hammer to it."

"That should subside in the next few hours. Are you nauseous?"

Hours? I don't have hours. Medical timeouts only last ten minutes. My brain is so foggy. Nothing's making sense.

"No, not really. I'm thirsty though. And my arm hurts. I need to hurry and get back out on court."

"We'll get you water and fix your arm where you yanked out the IV. Now that you're awake, you shouldn't need it anyway. But you won't be going back onto the court. Your match is over. It was yesterday. You've been unconscious for more than fifteen hours."

"What do you mean? Is this stomach virus or food poisoning that serious?"

"It wasn't a virus or food poisoning. As shocking as this will sound, you were poisoned."

"Huh? You mean Bri's chef served me something spoiled and gave me food poisoning?"

"No. That would have been much simpler. Unfortunately, we believe you ingested a poisonous substance from an oleander plant.

You were lucky. It could have killed you. Do you know how that could have happened."

"What? Poison? No way."

"Think about yesterday. What did you eat and drink during the four hours before the match? We want to make sure you don't accidentally consume the same thing again."

"Believe me, I never want to go anywhere near anything related to oleanders again. I have no idea how I was poisoned though. I've either eaten at our house or had prepackaged food and drinks."

"Then the answer may be as simple as a leaf falling into your cup of tea. We'll probably never know. But if there are any oleanders in the yard where you're staying, be careful to avoid them."

I'm no plant expert. I'll have to look for a photo on Google.

"I won't go near one of them ever again. How long before I'm back to normal?"

"You should be feeling fairly well by tomorrow."

"That's good news. Do you know if I won my match before I collapsed? I can't remember."

"You were ahead but didn't finish the match. I'm sorry."

Is he saying I'm out of Wimbledon singles? How can that be?

"That means I forfeited. Again."

"What's important is that you're alive and can leave the hospital this afternoon. You should rest for another twenty-four hours though."

I nod, clenching my jaw as my blood boils. I white-knuckle the bedsheets and bite my lip to keep from screaming.

I'm grateful to be alive, but my dream is dead. I won't be holding up the Wimbledon trophy this year—maybe not ever. Why does this keep happening to me? It's like I'm jinxed.

Dr. Shepard pats my shoulder "One more thing. Princess Brianna is waiting outside. I'm told you have a doubles match with her in a couple of days. There's a good chance you'll recover enough to play. Should I send her in so you two can make plans?"

He's patronizing me. There's no way I'll be playing at Wimbledon again in two days. For fuck's sake, I'm lying in a hospital bed, recovering from being poisoned. Does he think I'm a fool?

Through gritted teeth, I say, "I'm not sure that's a good idea."

"She's been extremely worried about you. Perhaps you could let her see that you're on the mend before I send her away."

"Sure." I mutter.

The doctor walks to the door and opens it. "Your Royal Highness, you may come in. Blake is very tired, so just a quick hello. Then he needs rest."

"Of course," she replies.

She hurries to my bedside, reaching for my hand. "Blake, how are you feeling? I've been so worried."

"I'll be fine. No need to worry," I say, sharper than I intend. I'm still fuming.

"Do you need anything? Would you like me to sit with you?"

"No. There's nothing you can do."

"There must be something."

"No. You don't understand. I need to be alone. Thank you for stopping by."

She looks at me like a puppy who doesn't understand why she's been scolded. I turn my head away, hoping she'll take the hint.

"You need rest. I'll check on you again later. I'm glad you're doing better."

She gives my hand a gentle squeeze, then releases it. I hear her footsteps fade but don't watch her leave.

I'm mad at the world. And I'm especially furious with her eccentric chef. I'd bet money that he's the one who poisoned me. Who knows what he put in that fresh pesto? He probably chopped up random leaves from the garden. It's just my bad Wimbledon luck that they turned out to be toxic.

I knew playing doubles would ruin my chance to win. If I hadn't agreed, Bri and Fausto wouldn't be at my house. And I knew better than to let my guard down. I don't even believe in relationships. Why did I let myself get close to Bri? This is all my fault.

A twinge of guilt reminds me of Bri's dream—playing at Wimbledon. She needs me to make it a reality.

But I brush that worry aside.

I held up my end of the bargain. We played a match. We won. She's fulfilled her dream, unlike me.

I don't owe her anything more.

I'm done.

# 25

## BRIANNA

After visiting Blake at the hospital this morning, I've spent the rest of the day trying to understand what happened. No matter how many times I replay our conversation, it still doesn't make sense.

When Dr. Shepard said I could see Blake, I felt a huge weight lift from my shoulders. I was excited—relieved, even—to see with my own eyes that he was okay.

I thought he'd be happy to see me. He wasn't. He didn't even want me there. That stung. I told myself he was just weak and needed rest. But if I'm being honest, I'm not sure that's the only reason he pushed me away. Something else felt . . . off. I've racked my brain for an explanation. Still nothing makes sense.

The good news is that Blake is being released. Josh is on his way to the hospital to bring him home. They should be here after dinner. It's hard to believe that only twenty-four hours ago we weren't sure Blake would survive.

I'm relieved he's recovering quickly, but I don't know what to expect after this morning's frosty reception. What if he still doesn't want me around? How am I supposed to continue investigating him if he shuts me out completely? Not to mention—it's a blow to my ego. A princess is rarely unwelcome company.

Steeling myself, I walk into the kitchen. Fausto is preparing a salad while Erin and Natalie chat nearby.

Plastering on a smile, I ask, "Should we ask Fausto to make some comfort food for dinner while we wait for Josh to return with Blake?"

"That would be great. I'm starving," Natalie says.

"Sounds good," Erin agrees.

I turn to Fausto and ask, "*Potresti cucinare spaghetti alla marinara con pane all'aglio, per favore?*"

"*Sì, naturalmente,*" he replies.

Following up, I tell him that we want him to share the spaghetti marinara and garlic bread with us.

He nods, already humming as he scurries around the kitchen gathering ingredients. I smile. The request clearly made his day.

---

AN HOUR LATER, THE SMELL OF BUTTER, GARLIC, TOASTED BREAD, AND simmering tomato sauce draws me back to the kitchen. Natalie and Erin are standing at the kitchen island across from Fausto. I'm jealous when I see that they're tasting slices of garlic bread while they watch our chef cook.

"Hey! That's not fair. Where's my garlic bread?" I ask, pretending to pout.

Erin slides a breadbasket toward me, stealing another piece for herself in the process. Between bites, she says, "This is the best garlic bread I've ever had. You need to tell him to make more." She winks at me, knowing that Fausto understands her English fine.

"Let me try it." I take a bite. "Mmm. Erin, you're right. This is fantastic. Fausto, *questo pane all'aglio è delizioso. Pane extra, per favore.*"

Remembering to translate everything is tedious, but I grew up speaking French, Italian, and English, so it's not difficult.

"Sì," he says with a satisfied nod.

"I need to check in with my superiors. I'll be back in a few minutes."

"Okay, but you better hurry if you want any more garlic bread," I call after her.

This is the perfect opportunity for me to learn more about Blake's doctor, so I ask, "Natalie, do you work for Blake full time?"

"Yes, at least for now. He's hired me to be available full time though Wimbledon. I'm not sure what he'll need afterward."

"It's wonderful that you were able to do that for him. Did you have to refer your other clients to other doctors?"

"I typically only work with one player at a time. It allows me to give them the best experience."

"Oh. That's interesting. Is that common?"

"More common than you would think. Most of us who work with top-level players only have one to three players at a time."

"I didn't realize that. You and Josh make a good team for Blake. Have you worked together before?"

"Not really. I've worked with Thomas before, and Josh is good friends with his coach. That's how we met."

"It's a small world, isn't it?

"Definitely."

"It seems that Noah is well connected. Blake is lucky to have him too."

"Hopefully, Blake appreciates him. They've been butting heads lately, so I'm not sure."

"Really. Why's that?"

"Who knows. You've seen how testy Blake is. He's stressed."

"Don't I know that. He was annoyed I showed up at the hospital this morning. What's up with that?"

"As a doctor, I can't share what he's dealing with. I just hope he doesn't introduce more change into his life."

"Do you mean like hiring a new manager?"

"I do. He's under enough pressure without making major

changes in his team. In my professional opinion, that wouldn't be healthy for him."

"Change can be difficult, particularly if one already has stress," I agree.

"It can. I told him that. If you have any influence with Blake, maybe you can help steer him in a steady direction. Sometimes advice is more convincing when it comes from a friend."

"We'll see."

Erin returns just as Fausto starts plating dinner. We're all starving, so we decide to eat at the kitchen island.

While we wait, I think about what Natalie said. I understand her hesitation about Blake making changes while under stress. But didn't Blake say she recommended changing his Wimbledon routine this year to calm his fear that something bad would happen? Why is changing managers different?

As soon as Fausto places a bowl of pasta in front of me, I twirl a forkful of spaghetti and raise it to my lips.

The tangy tomato sauce and perfectly *al dente* noodles nearly make me moan. Pasta has always been my comfort food—and that's exactly what I need tonight.

We're enjoying the calm quietness that accompanies a satisfying meal.

Then—bang. The front door slams against the wall.

Jarred by the sudden noise, my fork clatters against my pasta bowl.

We all jump to our feet and rush toward the front of the house to welcome Blake home.

Blake looks pale except for the dark circles under his eyes. He's uncharacteristically hunched over. He's clearly been through hell. I don't know what's hitting him harder: the physical trauma or another emotional Wimbledon loss. All I know is that he's broken.

Josh says, "The doctor said you should eat a small meal tonight. I'll have Fausto make something bland."

But Blake snaps, "No way! I'm not eating anything else he

cooks. He poisoned me. Bring me an unopened bottle of water and a new box of energy bars. I'm not taking any chances. I'll be in my room."

I cringe. Did he just accuse Fausto of poisoning him? How dare he?

"Be reasonable, Blake. Fausto didn't poison you. We all ate his food. Everyone else is fine. You need a real meal tonight."

"I said no. Do as I asked—or leave."

Wow. Talk about storming in under a dark cloud of negativity.

"Blake, I know you've been through quite an ordeal, but I can assure you that Fausto didn't poison your food. I'm sure the authorities will determine who did this to you. Please don't worry about Fausto's cooking though," I say as calmly as possible under the circumstances.

"You can't tell me not to worry. You aren't the one who almost died. Feel free to eat whatever you want to, but I'm not eating another thing from this house that isn't from a sealed package. Period."

"But you need your strength for our match in two days. That requires real food, not just energy bars," I say.

"You know that's not happening. I didn't want to play doubles in the first place. Now, I can't play."

"When I spoke with Dr. Shepard this morning, he said you will be fine to play," I say.

"He doesn't know what he's talking about. I'm going to bed."

Blake's being bloody stubborn. To say his mood is morose would be an understatement.

We can only hope Blake cools down by tomorrow.

After that exchange, I've lost my appetite entirely, so I retreat to my room to send a message to the princes.

> Me: My time here may be coming to a premature end.

> CR: Not acceptable.

Me: It's not my choice.

CR: Make it work. Be creative.

Me: I'm not a magician.

CR: You are now. No choice. Improvise.

Me: Understood.

How am I supposed to convince a man who almost died—and now wants nothing to do with me—to play a match in two days?

Given his attitude, I don't really want to be around him either. He's letting *me* down. He doesn't care about my Wimbledon dream. He's not any different than all the other men who pretended to care about me. All he really cares about is himself.

A familiar knock-pause-knock-knock at my door announces Erin. "Come in."

"Are you okay?" Erin asks as she enters and shuts the door behind her.

"I'm fuming and hurt. I can't believe that Blake said the things he did. Fausto would never poison someone. And why is Blake brushing me off so harshly? I know he's upset that he lost his chance to win this year, but it's not my fault or Fausto's. I thought Blake and I were friends."

"Is that all you thought you were?"

"I made a mistake letting myself believe there might be a chance for us when this is all over. Apparently, I was wrong. I can't think about that now."

"Don't give up yet. I suspect he's lashing out at everyone. After you came up to your room, Blake stormed off to his room. The rest of us stayed in the kitchen to chat. Josh shared that Blake was a pain in the arse the whole ride back from the hospital. I don't think it has anything to do with you or even Fausto. He's mad at the universe. He'll calm down by morning."

"If I weren't on a covert mission, I'd tell him that I'm fed up with his selfishness, and then I'd move out of the house tonight. But I can't. I'm stuck. Even worse, now I have to beg him to play our match in two days. If I can't convince him, it will compromise the mission."

I don't share that if he leaves Wimbledon now, we'll lose the opportunity to learn whether he's involved in the smuggling, and I'm still holding onto the hope that he could be innocent.

"I suspected as much. How are you going to talk him into playing?"

"Didn't you know I'm a magician? Just call me *Bri the Brilliant.*"

"Huh?"

"Never mind. I'm going to talk to him now."

"Don't you want to give him more time to cool off?"

"I've got to deal with him now. Wish me luck."

"You've got this."

I cross the hall to Blake's room. I hesitate. Should I knock? If I do, he might turn me away. I can't risk that. I knock and simultaneously turn the doorknob.

The room is pitch black. As my eyes adjust, I spot a human-shaped lump splayed across the bed.

I listen carefully, trying to detect his breathing pattern. If he's sleeping, I'll come back later. Fortunately, his breathing isn't that regular, so I quietly venture closer to his bed.

He's lying on his stomach unable to see it's me, but he's not asleep.

I whisper, "Blake, I'd like to talk."

"Not now," he grunts.

With him just home from the hospital, the timing is terrible, but I must have this conversation now. Otherwise, the mission will be at risk. In what I hope is a conciliatory tone, I say, "I'm truly sorry, but this can't wait."

"Say what you must and then leave. I need rest."

"First, I can't let you ruin Fausto's reputation. We all ate the food he prepared. He didn't poison you. When you're feeling better, please apologize to him. Will you do that?"

"Ugh. He doesn't speak English, so he doesn't know what I said."

"Whether someone could understand you isn't the issue. You unfairly slandered him in front of others. Besides, anyone would have understood the gist of your rant. It's important to his reputation and to me that you let everyone know it wasn't Fausto's fault. I'll be happy to translate an apology for you. He doesn't deserve to be treated that way."

"Fine. Now leave."

"I'll leave, but I need to clear up one more thing. I know your dream has been delayed again. You'll have another chance next year. On the other hand, I probably won't. I'm asking you to stay here and play our second-round doubles match in two days. Your doctor said you're able to play, so you don't have a real excuse to quit. In addition, it would mean the world to me."

"I almost died. Someone poisoned me. Why would I put myself in danger again?"

"It was probably an accident. Why would anyone want to harm you?"

I can't share that he was likely poisoned on purpose. Besides, it wouldn't do him any good to know that. While I feel guilty lying to him, I have no choice. There's too much at stake.

"Maybe they wanted to make sure I didn't win."

"It's hard to believe one of your competitors attempted to kill you merely to keep you from winning. Even if that were true, then you're safe now. They would want you out of singles, not our matches. No one pays nearly as much attention to doubles, much less mixed doubles."

"You've played here now. It's not as if we had a chance of winning. As you said, I'm not an experienced doubles player."

Mr. Grumpy is here in full force again. I understand his disappointment. He's also dealing with the fact he just faced his mortality firsthand. I'm not sure how I would feel in his situation, but I certainly hope I wouldn't be rude and obstinate with the people I'm close to.

"I know we don't have a real chance at winning the tournament, but we played well as a team. And this is my one chance. Whatever happens, it should be decided on the court, not by us walking away. If we lose, I can accept that. But it's important to me that my time at Wimbledon lasts as long as possible. I need you to do this for me."

He closes his eyes, wiping them with his fingers. In a soft voice, he admits, "I don't know if I can. I'm not ready to go back out there."

I should have known. He's afraid he'll have a panic attack on the court. I feel like a heel, forcing him to do something that could crush him. Yet again, my mission and my heart are at odds.

"At least think about it, and let's talk again in the morning. Good night."

I walk out of his room, softly closing the door.

I'm conflicted. I wanted to tell him that this isn't my fault. I'm not his enemy. But if he's guilty of smuggling, then technically, we *are* on opposite sides.

I also wanted to call him selfish for not wanting to play, but am I the selfish one? I'm demanding he fulfill my dream when his was crushed.

I remind myself that the mission requires me to encourage him to stay, but I also want to continue competing. What kind of person am I to push someone who almost died to go back on the court in two days?

I reassure myself that his medical doctor signed off, and his sports psychologist actually recommended that he keep playing. But they aren't the ones guilting him into continuing. I am.

This is the first time a mission has made me face this type of dilemma. Prior to this one, I merely collected information for our intelligence officers or passed something for them. This is an entirely different experience. Our training didn't prepare me for the ethical and emotional tradeoffs I'm encountering. It makes me wonder if I'm really cut out for the Covert Royals.

In addition, I thought Blake cared for me. He's the only guy I've given a real chance to in a long time. That's over though. He's made it clear that he doesn't want me in his support system. Even worse, he's willing to trample my feelings without a second thought.

From here on, the only things that matter are my country's interests and my tennis career.

Why does that hurt so much?

# 26

## BLAKE

I wake from a nightmare, drenched in sweat. My memory is hazy. In my dream, I think I collapsed on the tennis court, woke up in the hospital, and forfeited my Wimbledon match. What a colossal disaster. Thank goodness it was just a bad dream.

Wiping my forehead with my hand, something sharp grazes my face. I pull my hand away and freeze. I'm staring at a hospital wristband.

No. no, no. It wasn't a dream.

I was released from the hospital last night. And just like that, the memories of the last two days come flooding in.

Shite. I'm hit with the sickening realization that I was a complete arse to Bri, at the hospital and again when I got home last night. I was grumpy and snapping at everyone, wanting them to share my misery.

If I'm honest with myself, I've been frustrated and difficult since I pulled out of the quarterfinals at Wimbledon last year due to a torn hamstring. The people around me have tolerated my behavior, probably because I pay them salaries well above what they would make elsewhere.

But I don't pay Bri. And she's the one I treated the worst. I was another level of arsehole to her. It's a miracle she hasn't already left. She must really want to play. Otherwise, she'd have told me to shove my attitude and walked out.

She didn't deserve my wrath.

I toss the blankets aside and stumble to the bathroom to splash cold water on my face. As I reach for my toothbrush, I stare at my reflection, assessing the damage. Surprisingly, I look better than expected. If I didn't know what had happened, I'd think this is just the beginning of another day to gear up for my next match.

A knock on the door interrupts my thoughts.

"Come in."

"Good morning, Blake. How are you doing?" Natalie asks.

What kind of question is that? I almost died. How the hell does she think I am?

But attempting civility, I respond, "I'm alive. I guess that's not too bad given the circumstances."

"Excellent. I wanted to discuss your plans for the rest of the tournament."

"There is no rest of the tournament. I forfeited the match by collapsing."

She has lost her mind. Didn't she see what happened? If not, they're replaying it on every news channel. She can watch me collapse on court and be carted off on a gurney.

"I mean the mixed doubles with Brianna."

"After the way I treated her yesterday, I doubt she's speaking to me, much less wanting to play as a team."

"She understands you went through a frightening experience. While I'd suggest apologizing for your rude, cold behavior toward her, I know she wants to continue playing doubles with you. And you need to play a match at Wimbledon again as soon as possible to work past any lingering fears. The worst thing you could do is wait until next year to play on these courts again."

After the way I treated Bri, it's hard to believe she could forgive me, even if I offered to play tennis with her.

"Really? You think she wants to play. Even if she does, I'm not sure I should? I was in hospital yesterday. How can we expect to win after that? Won't losing be more fodder for the press? The headlines will say I even choke in doubles at this tournament."

I don't mention my concern about having a panic attack on court.

"Are you kidding? The press is singing your praises based on the rumors you plan to continue playing after being poisoned. When you show up and play with Brianna, they'll crown you as the new Superman. You have nothing to lose, which also means that you're unlikely to suffer a panic attack during the match. Am I correct that's what you're really worried about?"

"You know me too well, but I guess that's your job. I hadn't thought of it like that. And I don't really want to let Bri down. I've been feeling guilty about planning to walk away. Her dream would die with mine."

"That's yet another reason you need to play tomorrow."

"You're right. Where's Bri? We need to talk."

"You do. I think she's in the study."

I nod. I'm not sure I can fix things with Bri, but it's worth a shot. After all, she told me to think it over last night as she left my room. Let's hope that means she'll give me another chance even if it's just for the sake of playing our match.

---

THIRTY MINUTES LATER, I'M SHOWERED, SHAVED, AND DRESSED. I FEEL almost normal—at least physically. Mentally, I'm struggling. There's nothing like facing my own mortality, failing to win Wimbledon yet again, and realizing what a jerk I've been to the people who care about me.

I need to find Bri. It's time to repair the damage I've done to her, if that's possible.

I slowly make my way downstairs, rehearsing my apology.

Peering into the study, I see Bri sitting on the sofa, staring at her tablet. I hesitate to interrupt her, particularly when I haven't come up with any magic words to make things right.

But waiting won't make it easier, so I force myself forward. "Bri, can we talk?" I ask tentatively.

She looks up. "Sure. Have a seat."

"Thanks."

As I sit in the chair across from her, I search her face for any sign of hope. All I see are her sad eyes and her lips pressed into a tight line. Clearly, she's not eager for this conversation. I can't blame her.

"Did you think about what we discussed last night?" she asks.

"Yes, and much more. First, I'd like to apologize. I'm so sorry for how I treated you yesterday and the horrendous things I said. There's no excuse. You've been such a wonderful person. I've even wondered if there could be more between us. And now, I'm not sure what to say other than to express my sincere desire to make this up to you."

"Does that mean you'll play our next match?"

"It does. And I'd like your help with apologizing to Fausto. I had these wild ideas that he picked leaves from the garden to prepare his sauces. But any trained chef would know not to cook with oleander. I just wasn't thinking clearly. I know he isn't the person who poisoned me."

"I'd be happy to translate. He deserves at least that," she says with a neutral expression.

I suspect that her true emotions are hiding behind this practiced princess pose. The dig is there though, and I can't argue with her. I'll also let the rest of our housemates know that I don't blame Fausto. His reputation shouldn't suffer because of my outburst.

As for patching things up with Bri, all I can do is share my truth.

"Understood. And as for us. . ." I pause. "Last night, you called me out for being a selfish prick. I can't say you were wrong. I've been difficult at best, and yesterday the way I treated you was unforgivable. I don't want to make excuses, but there are things I should have shared with you sooner. If you're willing to listen, I'd like to remedy that now."

Bri's shoulders relax slightly, but she also frowns. "This sounds serious. What didn't you tell me?"

"I've been going through a very stressful time. It started after Wimbledon two years ago. You know what happened there."

Bri nods. "Yes, go on."

"Soon after that, my manager, Noah, made some unexplainable business decisions that resulted in me losing quite a bit of money. I told you about the ugly sweatshirts, but that wasn't his only misstep. He also signed me up with a couple of new sponsors without discussing it with me. I threatened to fire him, but he assured me it wouldn't happen again and argued the new sponsorships were great deals for me. He begged for a second chance, which I granted out of respect for our long-time working relationship. I've been trying to monitor my business dealings closely since then, but I'm always on edge."

"I can see how that would be stressful. How are your finances now, if you don't mind me asking? All you said before was that you aren't broke."

"Stable. And my portfolio is growing. But I'll never have the same level of trust in Noah. That's the reason I plan to make a change."

"I don't blame you."

"Thanks for understanding. There's more though. Several months ago, mysterious emails began showing up in my inbox. They revealed various . . . umm . . . let's call them *indiscretions* by my prior coach. At first, I didn't believe the accusations. I assumed someone was either trying to disrupt my training or wanted to steal my coach."

"That's horrible," she says, her eyes wide with worried surprise.

I was mortified at the time because he put my career at risk. Remembering the situation still makes me shudder.

"It was, and it got worse. Each subsequent email came with more direct proof."

"What exactly were his indiscretions?"

"I guess there's no harm telling you. He was running a side business selling marijuana. Not only did he put himself at risk of arrest, but the authorities could also have thought I was involved. Even worse, I found out that he'd been using it himself. Not that I care what he personally does, but he put me at risk of testing positive if I'd accidentally consumed one of his food products or inhaled vapors. Others have been suspended from tennis for years after failing drug tests."

"Why in the world would a pro tennis coach do something that carried so much risk?" she asks, placing her hand over mine.

"I gather he started using it to manage pain from an old shoulder injury, and then he grew it into a business. Selling to others like himself made it profitable."

Her eyes narrow. "But how did he transport it across borders and through all the airport security inspections?"

"He always insisted on bringing along his favorite blend of coffee. It was the only kind he would drink. Apparently, he hid the marijuana in the coffee."

"Clever. I guess the coffee tricked the drug-sniffing dogs. You're lucky that someone alerted you about the problem. What did you do about it?"

"I told Noah, and we confronted him. He admitted that it was all true. I fired him on the spot."

I don't share that at the time, I couldn't believe my coach had betrayed me so profoundly. Now, it's hard to trust anyone who works for me, except Doc. At least she took an oath to do right by her patients.

Bri's eyes gleam with approval as she nods. "I would have done the same. Is that when you hired Josh?"

"It is. I hired him in December so I'd have a coach at the Australian Open in January. Changing coaches at the beginning of the season wasn't easy, but I had no choice."

"You didn't. Did you ever learn who sent you the emails? I'm guessing you'd like to thank them."

I throw my hands up in frustration. "No, I still don't know who it was, and I'm not sure they have my best interests at heart. You see the emails didn't stop when I fired my old coach."

"That's strange. What happened next?"

"During an interview, I was asked if it was a relief to have a good team back in place. I said it was. Then the interviewer commented that my team must be happy to know they have job security. I responded with an off-the-cuff remark."

"What did you say?"

"I said that I've learned we're all replaceable and circumstances can change without notice. I didn't mean for my comment to cause waves, but it triggered another anonymous email."

She squints and wrinkles her nose, asking, "Really? That's odd. What did it say?"

"I memorized it. It said, 'You should appreciate the good people who are trying to help you. Their jobs should be secure.'"

"That's weird and a little creepy." She briefly shudders, wrapping her arms around herself.

"That's what I thought. I started wondering if someone on my team was the one sending the emails. I have a large team when you also count the people who don't travel with me. It could have been any of them. I didn't know whether to confront each one or ignore the email. Ultimately, I decided to wait. I assumed more emails would arrive if the sender had more to say."

"Did you try to trace the emails?"

"No. I was in a tough spot. Noah checked and couldn't figure it out. I didn't know who else could help. The emails weren't threatening, so I let it drop. The only problem was it left me not really knowing if I could trust anyone on my team. As a result, I started shutting down and keeping more to myself."

"I'm guessing that was lonely and frustrating." Concern clouds her features as she reaches to stroke my arm.

She has no idea how right she is. I place my hand over hers and let her warmth and support flow through me as I admit, "It was. I'm sure you're wondering why I'm sharing these things but being poisoned was a wake-up call. It made me reflect on how and when my grumpiness emerged in full force. I'm convinced it began when doubts crept in about my team. Before that, I was stressed at the thought of never winning Wimbledon, but I wasn't miserable and didn't lash out at others."

Her eyes flicker with understanding. "How awful. A tennis player's team is like their family. It would be crushing not to be able to trust your family."

"It has been. Add to that the panic attacks I told you about, and it's been a lot."

I haven't told anyone that it was also terrifying to know that I couldn't trust anyone. I lived in fear that there was some even more sinister plan that I didn't know about.

"You didn't say when the first panic attack happened."

"In early March, I started having nightmares about being an old tennis player still struggling to win Wimbledon while the fans and commentators pitied me. I'd wake up drained and sweating after the dreams. Not long after, I had what I thought was a heart attack."

"So you've been dealing with this issue for several months now, right?"

"Yes. Apparently, the initial panic attack was triggered by the struggles with my team combined with the increased pressure as Wimbledon drew near."

"I would've panicked waiting to see if another attack occurred."

"Exactly. They assured me the attacks aren't life-threatening. That helped. But after the second attack, I hired Natalie."

"Who else knows what you've been going through?"

"Only Josh and Natalie know about the panic attacks. At least, I hope they haven't told anyone else. As we discussed, it could cause me problems if it became publicly known."

"I won't tell anyone, but there's nothing to be ashamed about. Panic attacks are more common than you realize. In fact, at some point you may want to share your situation. You could help others know it's okay to get help."

"I'm not ashamed, and I would like to help others at some point. I'm not there yet. Hopefully, I will be in the near future. I'm still struggling myself. I fear my opponents would see me as weak. Even worse, the press would comment on my mental health and inability to win."

"You aren't weak, and the press should be ashamed of themselves if they did that. However, I understand your feelings about the press. You don't trust them nor would I."

"Thanks for your support. I shared all this hoping that it would help you understand that nothing I said or did was about you. I've been fighting myself and trying to figure out how to move forward. I've accepted that I won't win men's singles this year, and I haven't had a panic attack. I'm making progress. I'm also ready to play doubles with you tomorrow if you'll still have me as your partner."

"It means the world to me that you've taken me into your confidence. It helps me understand. You've been dealing with so much. The problems with Noah and the panic attacks were plenty. But you've also received strange emails, are working with a new coach, are suspicious about the rest of your team, and now you've been poisoned. With all you've been through, the last thing I can ask of you is to play tennis tomorrow. There's no need. Your health and mental well-being come first. I'll be fine."

"Natalie says playing will help me work through my fears. And, even more important, your dream will continue. It will be best for both of us."

"Are you only doing this because Natalie is forcing you to?" she asks, her face scrunched.

I'd thought she would be jubilant, not guarded, and certainly not challenging my motivation. I take a moment to consider my thoughts.

"That's an unexpected question. Before now, I hadn't parsed my feelings that precisely. Natalie did help me reach the decision. But no, she's not forcing me. I'm offering to play because I want to. Do you?"

Her face relaxes into an easy smile as she nods and enthusiastically says, "Yes."

"Excellent. Dare I ask you to consider forgiving me?"

"Probably. Let's see how things go." There's a hint of teasing in her voice that's reassuring.

"That's a start."

As we're standing to leave, Josh walks in with a big grin.

"What has you so happy?" I ask.

He says, "You'll never believe what just happened?"

"I'd believe almost anything at this point. I just hope your smile means it's good news this time," I say.

"Your second-round opponents just dropped out. You have a walkover. That means the two of you are advancing directly to the mixed doubles quarterfinals! Congrats!"

Excitement lights up Bri's face, as she says, "You must be joking. Are you sure?"

"Absolutely sure. One of them sprained their ankle and can't play. You two celebrate. I'll call Martina and arrange practice times for you two."

I don't wish anyone harm, but that's the best news I've heard. I'll have an extra day or two to recover.

Without warning, I embrace Bri, lift her off the ground, and twirl her in a circle as if we've won another match. Her surprised giggle is a welcome sign she's not objecting. Setting her back on her feet, I take her cheeks in my hands and stare directly into her gleaming green eyes. "Bri, let's do this the right way. I'll be there for you. We'll work together as a true team. Is it a deal?

"Deal," she murmurs in a soft, husky voice.

We seal it with a toe-tingling kiss.

*Progress. Major progress.*

I cross my fingers that we're past the hardest part.

# 27
## BLAKE

After all that's happened, my expectations for this match are low. I suspect Bri's are too. Knowing that makes it easier as we step onto the court.

We smile and wave to the crowd.

I'm surprised and thrilled at the full stands. A doubles match never attracts a crowd. Occasionally, fans arrive early if the next match is an important one. But these people are clearly here for us.

They're all on their feet, clapping and cheering as we walk to the bench. Natalie was right. People are excited to see Bri and me back on the court. I chuckle when I hear someone in the crowd yell, "Blake, you're proof that we Brits are a hardy bunch."

Someone else calls out, "Why didn't you team up with the princess sooner?"

My heart is full at the outpouring of support. This is a special moment for me, but even more so for Bri.

I flash a thumbs up, which triggers another wave of applause. Their cheers are the perfect motivation and reminder. I'm fighting not just for me, or even Bri, but for my country and our fans. No matter what the outcome is today, Bri and I will give it everything we can and fight until the end.

The match starts, and we quickly take the lead. We're playing spectacular tennis—making shots that we'd normally miss. With expectations so low, we're free to relax, go for every shot, take extra chances, and generally have fun. I'd love to bottle the unusual combination of inner calmness and outward excitement. It's incredibly powerful.

It's also a recipe for success because an hour and a half later, Bri slams the ball past one of our opponents to seal the win. We've won our match with relative ease.

I throw my racquet down and pick her up, twirling her in a circle and planting a kiss on her forehead.

"Bri, you were amazing!" I say, settling her feet back onto the grass but keeping my arms around her.

"Thanks, so were you. But you're not really supposed to be manhandling a princess in public. Not that I mind but the palace might be calling to reprimand us once they see the photos." She laughs.

I quickly step back, whispering, "I'll try to keep my manhandling to private locales. Perhaps there's somewhere around here that wouldn't have so many prying eyes?"

"You're so bad, and I love it. But that's for later."

That's what she thinks. I have another idea.

# 28

## BRIANNA

As we walk off the court, I ask, "Do you still have your sponsor's event tonight?"

"I do. We'll handle some business, and then they want me to pose for photos."

"Is there any chance I could tag along? I'm not familiar with how to deal with sponsors and would love to observe."

"Absolutely."

That was easier than expected. I'll let Stephen and Adrian know I've secured the invitation. Secretly, I wanted to spend the evening with Blake anyway.

"Are you sure they wouldn't mind?"

"Of course not. They'd probably pay me to bring royalty to their party." I laugh.

"You're going to think I'm kidding, but sometimes I forget about my title when I'm playing tennis."

"When I'm in the zone, I forget things too."

"By the way, I assumed your sponsor's event is a party. Why would you be doing business at a social event? What's that all about?"

"It is a party, but I also need to deliver some stuff they want. It's what Noah and Josh were talking about at dinner the other night. That part shouldn't take long. Afterward, we can have dinner together. How does that sound?"

"Perfect. I have time to shower and change in the locker room. Can you meet me outside there when you're ready?"

"Not so fast. We have another stop to make first," he whispers into my ear.

I shudder as his warm breath tickles my neck.

"What are you talking about?"

"Follow me."

With a gentle hand on my back, he guides me through the underground tunnels. We stop when we reach the training areas, and he looks around. At this time of day, it's not too busy.

"What are you doing?"

"It's clear, come on," he says, as he urges me into one of the private massage rooms.

The room is stark. The walls are white. The floor is white. There's a counter with supplies along one wall, a chair in the corner, and a basket for used towels and linens. Everything is white, except the massage table in the middle of the room. In sharp contrast to the rest of the room, the table is black with metal legs.

"Did you clear this detour with Erin?" I ask.

He nods and drops his bag on the floor. Taking mine off my shoulder, he drops it near his.

Putting his arms around me, he pulls me toward him, pressing his lips against mine.

I melt into him, moaning at the chills he sends down my spine.

As he pulls away, he says, "Do you know how hot it was to watch you win that last point? All I could think about was getting you alone to celebrate."

"Really?"

"Absolutely."

"Would you like to kiss me again?" I playfully smile, tilting my head.

He laughs and pulls me against him, practically growling, "That's not all I want to do."

"Mmm. I'm liking this version of you much better."

"Good. Consider this the next step in my apology to you."

"What do you have in mind?"

"It'll be easier to show you. Do you trust me to take care of you?"

"I do."

He picks me up, carrying me to the massage table where he gently places me near one end with my legs dangling off. Without further words, he gently pushes my shoulders until my back is against the table.

Peeling my tennis skirt down my legs, he moans, "You are so beautiful and already so wet for me. I can't wait to taste you."

In seconds, he raises each of my legs to rest on his shoulders, spreading me for him. I close my eyes in anticipation of his mouth connecting with me. But instead, he starts by kissing each of my ankles and slowly . . . oh so agonizingly slow . . . he works his way up my calf until he reaches the back of my knee. He pauses there, nipping, kissing, and licking the tender skin until I'm writhing in need.

"Please hurry. I can't wait," I beg, my breath rapid, as I lean forward to grab his head and move it to where I crave his lips.

He pulls back, saying, "Patience, my love. I promise it will be worth the wait."

He returns to his ministrations. I'd swear he's dragging it out even more as my desire for him skyrockets with each tender kiss and touch. His mouth moves to the inside of one of my thighs while his thumb caresses the other one. The sensations in two sensitive areas are too much.

I shout, "Now! Please! I really can't wait any longer."

"If you insist."

And his lips press against me in the most delicious way. His tongue flicks and licks, circling my swollen nub. As I arch into him, wanting even more pressure, he lets his teeth graze over me.

I moan, "Ohhh! That's so good. Don't you dare stop."

"No chance," he murmurs while maintaining his rhythm of kisses, tongue presses, licks, and nibbles that drive me insane.

I grab his hair, pulling his head tighter against me. When I think it can't get any better, he plunges a finger into me while sucking my nub. I crash over the top, throbbing against his lips. "Yes! Yes! Yes!"

He draws out my orgasm to the absolute finish and then pulls me into his arms, holding me against his chest until my breathing returns to normal.

Finally, he softly asks, "Will that do for an initial celebration of our win?"

"Absolutely. I can't wait to see what you have planned if we win again."

Who would have thought such a nondescript room would be the perfect place to enjoy our victory?

"If we pull off another win, I'll come up with something. We have to hurry now. My sponsor won't be happy if we're late."

"Okay. Can you meet me outside my locker room?"

"Sure. We should leave here separately. See you in 45 minutes," he says as he slips out the door.

I hate to admit it, but we make a wonderful team *on and off* the court.

# 29

## BRIANNA

Blake will be here any minute to walk me to his sponsor event.

For a long time, I've felt like Blake had two different versions of himself. Two years ago, he was friendly and fun to be around.

Then I arrived at Wimbledon this year and found him grumpy, frustrated, and somewhat of an arse most of the time. But lately, he's starting to resemble the man I first met—the one I've dreamed about on lonely evenings.

Ironically, I'm the one who's supposed to be wearing different hats. On the court, we're partners trying to win. Off the court, we can't keep our hands off each other. And on top of all that, I'm supposed to be investigating him.

I keep telling myself that there's a logical explanation for his involvement, and I'll be able to help him in the end. But I'm probably just kidding myself and will end up heartbroken and possibly embarrassed that I allowed myself to fall for a criminal.

Hearing footsteps, I look up. Blake's approaching, so it's time to learn what I can from the sponsor event tonight.

"Are you ready?" he asks.

"Yes. Where's the event?"

"It's in the giant white tent on the other side of Court No. 1."

"Let's go."

As we're walking, I ask, "Which of your sponsors is hosting this event?"

"It's ProLuxe, the travel company. They hold this VIP party for their clients every year. I'm expected to show up and let everyone take selfies. You know the drill."

"You must do a million of these meet-and-greets. Do you ever tire of the attention?"

"It can be tedious, but something tells me tonight will be more enjoyable."

"Are you flirting with me or are you excited about the business deal you're working on tonight?" I ask with a teasing nudge to his arm.

"It's not the business part I'm looking forward to."

"Oh. Why not let Noah handle it? Or can you no longer trust him even for minor business dealings?"

"No, that's not it. My sponsor has expectations that I don't like."

"Can you back out of the deal?"

"No. I'm under contract. I don't have a choice right now. It's not a big deal. Let's talk about something else like how wonderful you look tonight."

"That's a subject I like. You're rather handsome yourself."

If Blake and I didn't need to be at this event, I'd suggest we find a place where we could be alone for the rest of the evening.

As if reading my thoughts, he whispers, "I'd rather be in the back corner of a dimly lit restaurant seducing you right now."

"That's not far from what I had in mind. But maybe we order takeaway and head straight to bed."

"I like how you think. Do you like Thai?"

"Spicy would be perfect." I wink.

As we near the tent, Blake steers me behind an outdoor display.

Hidden in its shadow, he pulls me against his warm, hard body and melds our lips into a passionate kiss. His talented tongue slowly tantalizes and teases my mouth, utterly consuming me.

Eventually, he pulls his head back, studying my eyes. "I don't know what you've done to me, but I can't get enough of you."

"It's you who has mesmerized me." I don't add that I can't focus on anything other than him, including my mission.

"We should go inside now, but I plan to pick this up again later."

"I certainly hope so."

Before we enter the tent, someone draws Blake into a conversation. While they chat, I hear two men speaking Italian around the back corner of the structure, but I can't see their faces. Their voices are hushed. I only overhear snippets. They mention gold coins and perfect hiding places. Then I hear two familiar names, Josh and Thomas. I can't make out more details except I pick up the word "problem." The men also say something about Blake not having a choice. That's the last thing I hear before one man says they should go back inside the tent.

Interesting. Their words imply Blake is being coerced to do something they want, and it likely involves the gold coins. That would be consistent with Blake saying he has a problem with his sponsor's expectations.

If these things are all connected, there's a good chance those men work for Blake's sponsor. I need to identify the men and pass along this information to Stephen and Adrian.

I watch for two men to come around the corner, but no one has emerged from that direction. They must have entered the tent through another opening. Let's hope I recognize their voices because I didn't even get a glimpse of the men.

Blake says, "Bri, you're in deep thought. What about?"

"Oh, it's nothing. Are you ready to go inside?"

"I am. Let me introduce you to everyone."

We barely step inside when we're surrounded by people. Fortunately, Erin is never far away and keeps a small boundary around us.

Blake introduces me to David, the CEO of ProLuxe. David is thrilled to have me at his party. I can tell that he'll use our casual meeting as a conversation starter at all future cocktail parties.

Turning to Blake, he asks, "Do you have the trophy and racquets ready?"

"I have the trophy in my bag. I accidentally left the racquets at the house," Blake says.

The look on David's face is either horror or anger, I'm not sure which.

"You knew I needed them tonight," David chastises through gritted teeth.

Why the overreaction? It's not a big deal. It's just some racquets. Unless I was right and coins really are being passed in the handles. We need to check the racquets before Blake hands them off.

"We can do photos with the trophy. Come to our next doubles match. I'll give the racquets to you then," Blake says.

"That's a problem, but we'll talk about it later," David barks.

Blake and David excuse themselves to take photos, leaving me with Erin. I text Stephen and Adrian an update.

Turning to Erin, I tell her about overhearing two men talking and that I want to wander around to see if I can recognize who they were. Fortunately, there aren't too many speaking Italian, so I'm hopeful.

Eventually, Blake finds us and introduces me to more people.

By the end of the evening, I'm exhausted but fairly certain I've identified the two men I'd overheard. They're executives with ProLuxe.

That mystery solved, I still have one more thing to ask Blake when we're in private. The problem is I can't let him know why I'm asking. I don't want to risk him realizing what I've figured out.

Back in our Range Rover for the ride to the house, I finally have my opportunity.

"Blake, you said that your coach has been experimenting with different racquet weights."

"He has. Why?"

"Martina wanted me to add weight to the handle of my racquet. She suggested using weight strips under the grip tape. Is that what Josh does for you?"

If he says no, then I may have found a possible hiding spot.

"He tried that, but more recently he's having silicone injected into the end of the racquet under the cap. I'm happier with that solution, except when they put in too much weight. It's a fine balance."

Bingo. The weight of one of the missing coins is almost identical to the heaviest weight one would add to a racquet handle.

I nod. "Thanks, I'll tell her."

It's too late to arrange a meeting with Stephen and Adrian, but I can send a text.

> Me: Key aspects clear now. Handoff tomorrow soon after match. Need to meet.

> Princes: What is clear?

> Me: Too complicated. In person.

> Princes: Understood. Meet after your match.

> Me: That may be too late. Can we meet earlier?

> Princes: Not possible. Meet in tunnel.

> Me: Have someone follow Blake after the match. I think he's being forced to participate. Will there be an escort to take me to the meeting place as usual?

> Princes: Will handle Blake. Yes to escort.

> Me: Thanks.

I've done all I can for tonight. Let's hope it's enough. If not, tomorrow could be a disaster.

# 30

## BRIANNA

I'm not sure how to explain our recent tennis success. Perhaps, it's because there's no time for nerves with the investigation nearing a turning point. Or it could be that my suddenly supportive partner is raising my level of play.

Whatever the reason, today's win was a complete surprise. Our match was much tougher than the previous two. We split sets and were behind in the tiebreaker. Somehow, we came back and won. Now, Blake and I are headed to the championship round for mixed doubles.

It still hasn't sunk in. I should be elated. Instead, I'm disappointed that Blake and I won't have a chance to celebrate. The mission isn't over, but it may be in the next few hours. And unless I can prove Blake isn't a willing participant, he might be arrested along with the other smugglers.

I was worried about how I'd meet with Stephen or Adrian after the match. But the problem solved itself when Noah arranged an unscheduled interview for Blake. Hopefully, our Covert Royals team has someone following Blake in case the handoff takes place before we meet up again.

A staff member escorts me to the meeting I requested with one of the princes. Ironically, we're headed toward the same area of the tunnels where Blake and I had our private celebration yesterday.

At first, I was surprised they wanted to meet in the tunnels. But in hindsight, it makes sense. We couldn't keep using the clubhouse without drawing attention, and there are only so many private spaces at Wimbledon. Repurposing one of the private training rooms is an obvious choice.

As we walk, I organize my thoughts. There's so much to explain, and we're running out of time to prevent the handover of the coins. When the princes said we couldn't meet until after the match, I considered breaking protocol and calling them directly. In the end, I stuck with our plan and followed orders. Hopefully, I won't regret that decision.

Our escort turns to Erin, who is a few steps behind me. "I under-stand you will want to check out the meeting room before Her Royal Highness enters," he says, motioning to the middle door.

Erin nods and steps inside to do a security sweep. I wait with the guide near the room to our right.

Hearing a soft click, I turn my head and see the door opening on my right. Before I can utter a word or scream, the guide and one of the guards push me inside. My hands are yanked behind my back as a dark cloth covers my eyes.

My training kicks in automatically. I assess the situation, look for my captors' weaknesses, and prepare an escape plan. With a guide and three guards nearby, I need to wait for my opportunity. Fighting my way out at this point won't work.

Pressure on my shoulders forces me down as a gruff voice barks, "Sit."

The sound of duct tape being torn off a roll rips through the air. With the proficiency of professionals, they tape my mouth and begin securing me to a chair—binding my wrists and ankles. The room is soundproof. Screaming would be pointless.

The guide asks the gruff guard, "Do you need me to stay and help?"

"No. Go make sure her bodyguard is secured. We can't have her interfering. When we're through here, we're supposed to help with the other player."

"Okay."

The door opens and shuts again. That's one fewer person to fight off.

The sound of another door opening causes me to turn my head toward the far side of the room. Heavy footsteps approach, and a familiar voice says, "I never would have expected a princess to be involved. I guess you can't trust anyone these days."

"Noah," I say through clenched teeth. "It's you who can't be trusted."

"I'm very loyal. You're the one who infiltrated my business and have wreaked havoc. It's your fault that Blake won't be around to continue his successful career."

"What are you talking about? What have you done to Blake?"

"Nothing yet, but neither of you will be playing again. You'll disappear without a trace. Rumors will abound that two lovesick players eloped to an undisclosed paradise never to be seen again."

"No one will believe that."

"I don't care as long as it gives me enough time to clean up this mess."

"I assume you're referring to retrieving the racquets with the coins in the handles and giving them to David, the CEO of ProLuxe."

"You are quite clever aren't you."

"How did you talk Blake into going along with your plan?" I ask.

"Maybe you aren't as smart as I thought. Blake has no clue what's going on. He's merely a convenient courier. We hide the coins in his racquets. He carries the racquets across borders. Then he hands them off as gifts to the sponsors. And we don't even have to give him a cut of the proceeds. It was perfect until you came along and started interfering."

That's a relief. Blake's innocent. My instincts were right. If I can get out of this alive, maybe there is hope for us.

First things first though. I need to keep Noah talking, so I ask, "What about Marco and Thomas?"

"Thomas is a pain in the arse. He's almost as much trouble as you with all his questions to Marco about his recent lifestyle improvements. Marco's going to dump him as a doubles partner, so Thomas won't cause any more problems."

"I gather you have to give Marco a cut."

"Unfortunately, we do. You won't live long enough for my answers to matter, but that's enough questions. I'm out of patience."

"Indulge me in one more question. Why did you poison Blake?"

"I said no more questions. Now shut the fuck up."

Apparently, that's all I'm going to learn, but it's enough.

Unless something changes quickly, my life will end shortly.

I moan, leaning forward in my chair, writhing from side to side. "I'm going to be sick."

Footsteps walk past, toward the door behind me. "Just don't get it on me," Noah says with disdain.

He's such a jerk. I groan and continue moving, visibly in pain.

Speaking to the guard, Noah says, "She's not going to be a problem now. Go check on Blake. He'll put up more of a fight. I'll be there as soon as I confirm David received the coins and we've silenced the problem princess."

Using my teeth, I nick the duct tape on my wrists. I jerk my arms upward, freeing my hands. My loud groaning successfully masks the tape ripping.

Doubling over in apparent pain, I yank upward on leg zippers at the bottom of my sweatpants, cutting through the tape binding my ankles to the chair.

I slowly raise a corner of the blindfold. Noah's by the door with his back to me.

Perfect.

I toss the eye covering aside and yank off the mouth tape,

causing intense pain. My groans are real now. I cover my mouth, hoping he won't notice the difference.

In one swift move, I jump to my feet, pick up the chair, and slam it into the back of Noah's head. The wood makes a satisfying crack. Unfortunately, it doesn't knock him out.

He lunges at me. I duck, evading his hands and land a solid kick to his groin.

He screams, doubling over in pain.

The soundproof room works in my favor now. His guards don't hear him.

I lock my arms around him and flip him onto the floor. Freeing his belt from his trousers, I roll him onto his back and secure his hands.

Stripping off my sweatpants, I use one leg to bind his ankles and the other to secure him to the massage table that's bolted to the floor. He won't have a chance of reaching either door. For good measure, I gag his mouth with one of my wristbands.

It's time to find Blake. I grab my phone from my bag and open the tracking app. His phone and tennis bag are both nearby.

Cracking the door slightly, I see two guards. Softly re-closing the door, I lock it from the inside. Going to the back of the room, I check the other door.

I'm in luck. Slipping through the door into the adjoining room, I find Erin. She's tied up but working to free herself. Her eyes flash with relief when she sees me.

I hurry over, remove the gag from her mouth, and finish untying the ropes holding her captive. "I'm so sorry. I shouldn't have let them capture you. How did you get free so quickly?" Her words are filled with remorse, anger, and more self-blame than necessary.

"It wasn't your fault. They used duct tape on me instead of rope. They underestimated me. My bigger problem was Noah, but he's not going anywhere now."

"Excellent."

"We have to find Blake. They plan to kill him."

"Do you know where he is?"

"Yes. He's nearby. I'm tracking his phone. We have to get past the guards though. There are at least two out front."

"These rooms are all connected. We can move from room to room until we're past them. Then we'll slip out." She says as she pulls off her sneakers.

"What are you doing?"

"I have a few things hidden that will help."

She pulls a knife from underneath each insole in her shoes, hands me one, and quickly puts her shoes back on. She takes her jacket off and turns it inside out, revealing a Wimbledon volunteer logo.

Finally, she extracts two baseball caps from her jacket pockets, saying, "We can hide our hair under the caps. They won't be expecting us to escape, and they definitely won't be looking for two people with short hair."

"Good job. Have you been carrying these the whole time?"

"Of course. I'm always ready to sneak you out of crowds. I just never thought we'd be using them for this."

"Glad you're prepared. Let's go, but this time I'm taking the lead. You're my backup."

"I'm right behind you."

Thanks to Erin knowing the layout of this area, we sneak through four rooms. We startle a player in the last room who's mid-massage. We quickly apologize, grab a couple of towels to improve our disguise, and hurry out the door to the main hall. We quickly blend into a group of people passing by and distance ourselves from the unsuspecting guards.

I follow the tracking signal. Something's wrong. "Blake's tennis bag is moving but his phone isn't. Maybe we should split up."

"No way. You may be in charge, but I'm not leaving you."

"Okay, let's go to his phone first. It looks like it's in a room down that side wall," I say, pointing to our left.

"I don't see a guard. That's good."

"Or it means they've taken him somewhere else."

We hurry toward the door to the room. I knock loudly and quickly move to the side, my back to the wall. Erin mirrors my position on the other side of the door.

"Who's there?"

I recognize the gruff voice. It's the guard who tied me up.

In my deepest voice, I mumble, "Noah. Open the bloody door."

"What? Who is it?" he asks.

Instead of answering, I pound on the door again.

It swings open and he peeks out. Turning to see me, his eyes go wide in shock. As he reaches for me, Erin tosses a towel over his head and yanks it back while I give him a kick between his legs.

It works like a charm. I'll have to thank my Covert Royal instructors. That kick is turning out to be particularly effective. Of course, my follow-up chop across his shoulders finished the job.

A voice inside calls out, "Roger, what's going on out there?"

I've heard that voice before but can't place it.

I put my finger to my lips, signaling Erin to stay quiet.

Lowering my voice again, I mumble, "Nothing. Toilet."

"Good grief. Can't you hold it?"

Erin and I remain silent, waiting for the right moment to burst in.

"Never mind. Find a toilet and get back here. Blake, we're out of time. Drink this. They're going to be here any minute to interview you about the sponsorship for this new sports drink."

"None of this makes sense. Why aren't we in a regular interview room? Why wouldn't the sponsor want me to drink it while we speak?" Blake asks.

"Noah gave me the instructions. You know he has your best interests in mind."

"I'm not so sure about that anymore. Is this the same drink I tried the day someone poisoned me? If so, I'm not touching it."

"What are you talking about?"

"Marco and Thomas recommended some sports drink that day. It tasted like crap. Maybe that's how I was poisoned. I'm not drinking random shite again."

"You saw me open this can. What's the big deal?"

"Why do you care so much? What's your interest?"

"Noah said you need this deal to be able to keep paying me."

It's someone on his team that's working with Noah. No wonder the voice is familiar.

"Huh? That's bollocks. That's the last straw. Noah's fired, and I'm leaving."

"No, Blake. You're not going anywhere. Sit down and drink."

"Bloody hell! Why are you pointing a knife at me?"

I cover my mouth to stifle the impending gasp.

"Because you wouldn't cooperate willingly. You have two choices now: the drink or the knife. You pick."

I put my hand to hold Erin back. We don't know how close the knife is to Blake.

"Have you lost your mind? What's wrong with you? Why are you doing this?"

"All you had to do was play tennis and keep working with Noah. Your life would have been great. So would ours. But no, you had to start complaining about Noah, investigating his finances, and questioning his decisions. Now, you've teamed up with that nosy spy, Brianna."

And just like that, my cover's blown. Damn. There won't be any chance for us even if we survive this mess.

"Spy? She's not a spy. She's a princess."

"Don't play dumb with me. You had to know about her. Otherwise, you never would have agreed to play doubles."

"I'm playing because Noah said the sponsor made me. It's also Bri's dream."

"That's why she's sending encrypted messages to British Intelligence? I don't think so."

How the hell does she know that?

"You've lost your mind."

"Quit delaying. Now pick. You're dying one way or the other."

No, he's not! I'm not losing him that way.

Holding up three fingers, I signal Erin.

She nods, and we ready our knives.

Blake says, "Fine, Natalie. Get that knife away from me, and I'll swallow the drink."

Ignoring the countdown, we burst through the door. I slap the drink out of Blake's hand just as he's throwing it at Natalie's face.

Erin rushes to grab Natalie's arm and slices it. Natalie screams as the knife clatters to the floor, harmlessly.

I'm relieved when the footfalls of a fast-approaching mob turn out to be Stephen, Adrian, Deputy Harrington, and a slew of others.

Finally. Where have they been? Didn't they get my text last night?

Before I can ask, Blake pulls me in for a hug, asking, "What are you doing here? And why did Natalie say you're a spy?"

Instead of answering, I turn to Deputy Harrington. "Don't arrest Blake. He didn't know."

A look of horror and confusion crosses Blake's face. "Arrest me? Why would they do that? I'm one of the good guys. Bri, what's going on? Who are you anyway?"

Everything I'd feared is happening. Blake is going to hate me. I need him to let me explain. Even then, he may never speak to me again. At that thought, tears well in my eyes. But I can't let them fall. Not in front of my team. This is not the place.

Holding onto the last thread of my self-control, I manage to say, "We need to talk."

# 31

## BLAKE

Two hours later, I still don't have answers. Bri and I were whisked away in Range Rovers. The blacked-out windows hid us from outsiders, but we couldn't see out either. With all the twists and turns the driver took, I have no idea where we are. All I know is that I've been in this room with a silent guard for a long time. They even took my mobile phone, so I'm left with my own thoughts.

I start to worry another panic attack will hit, but at this point, I'm not even sure what the trigger would be. I've lost Wimbledon, and at least two members of my team turned out to be criminals. What's a guy to do when he can't trust his sports psychologist? And now, the woman I've been falling for may be a spy? I'm too confused to know what to be stressed about at this point.

I ask the guy standing in the corner, "Am I free to leave?"

He replies, "It wouldn't be safe."

"That wasn't my question?"

"That's all I can say."

"Can you tell me what time it is?"

"No, sir."

An eternity later, someone knocks on the door. It opens, and Deputy Harrington says, "It's time. Would you join us in the debriefing room?"

"Do I have a choice?"

"Always. But I'm assuming you'd like answers to your questions. I'm told you have a lengthy list."

"I do."

"Then follow me."

"Where's Bri?"

"She'll be there."

We walk down the hall and enter a small, windowless conference room. Bri is already waiting for us.

Harrington directs me to sit across from her while he takes the seat at the head of the table.

"I'm pleased to report that we have successfully broken up a smuggling ring, saved lives, and retrieved stolen property that was illegally removed from various European countries."

Bri says, "Do you finally believe me about Blake? He wasn't involved. Is that why he's here?"

"We know Blake is innocent. The whole story is complicated, though. You both played separate roles, along with other participants who will not be named here. When we finish this debriefing, you'll understand more."

Bri nods. I'm more confused than ever.

Harrington continues, "We now know the identities of everyone involved. Noah was running the smuggling operation. He recruited Marco when he couldn't hide enough coins in Blake's trophies and racquet handles."

"Originally, I thought Thomas was involved, too. Am I right that he wasn't?" Bri asks.

"Yes."

"There was a note in Blake's trophy that said 'Stay the course. It will keep paying off.' Was it Noah wanting to make sure Blake didn't replace him?" Bri asks.

"That's the one thing we haven't figured out, but that would be a reasonable assumption," Harrington answers.

Blake chimes in, "It would be wrong though. The note didn't have anything to do with the smuggling or my coach. The engraver for that tournament always puts a note of encouragement in the base of the winner's trophy. He was just reminding me that when you win, you must be doing things right and should stay the course. But I have another question. How does Natalie fit in? She was my doctor. It doesn't make sense. Is she even a sports psychologist?"

"The real Natalie is a licensed psychologist. The person you know as Natalie is actually CeCe Wright. She lost her license about five years ago. Then about two years ago she teamed up with Noah to assist him in his side business."

"What happened to the real Natalie?" I ask.

"She's off the grid in a remote area doing research."

"What about Josh? Was he involved?"

"No. He met the fake Natalie through Marco. Apparently, Noah had been worried that you would fire him. He wanted Natalie in place on your team to convince you not to make any changes."

"Why did I think she was helping me with my panic attacks?"

"She probably was. Until she lost her license for sleeping with several of her patients, she was a successful psychologist. Her goal was to keep you winning tournaments and working with Noah so they could use you to smuggle coins. They needed you to keep playing."

"What finally convinced you that Blake was innocent?" Bri asks.

Harrington says, "I have a confession. We knew at the beginning of the investigation that Blake wasn't guilty—at least it was unlikely he was willingly involved. We'd suspected Noah for a long time. And we knew someone else on Blake's team was working with him. Initially, we thought it was Blake until he reached out to a museum asking about a coin he found. He wanted to know if it was valuable. The museum contacted us, and we arranged to meet with Blake in private. It was then that we recruited Blake to help us."

Bri's jaw drops as she jumps to her feet. "How dare you keep that from me? You led me to believe he was likely guilty. You even had me bug his room when you knew he was innocent."

"You bugged my room? How could you invade my privacy that way? So you really are a spy?" I ask.

She doesn't deny it. Instead, her lips press together, and she looks at Harrington. That's all the answer I need.

I grimace. Everything with her has been a lie. She *is* a fucking spy. Did she watch—and hear—me moan her name in the shower? Did she sleep with me as part of her job? Of course she did. I was falling for her, but none of it was real. She used me.

"Please, both of you," Harrington says. "Let me explain. We wanted to keep you two safe and needed you to behave normally. Blake, your room had to be bugged so we could watch if anyone tampered with your equipment or tried to hide something. And Bri, we didn't want to risk you and Blake appearing to be working together or sneaking around for private conversations. Blake needed to react the way he normally would. He couldn't want to play doubles, and he couldn't be having suspicious conversations with you. It would have raised too many questions from Noah."

"So, instead, you lied to both of us," I say.

"No. I omitted information."

"You lied," Bri snaps. "You told me that Blake was a suspect."

"That wasn't an outright lie. We didn't *believe* he was a suspect, but there was a small chance that he showed up with the coin to misdirect us. We had to be certain."

"That's fucked up. Someone poisoned me. Do you know who that was?"

"It was Marcos. He wanted a bigger cut of the profits and thought with you out of the way, it would be better for him. He didn't know that you weren't receiving a share. Fortunately, we received intel that your life was in danger that day and were able to redirect events."

"What do you mean? I ended up in hospital. I could have died."

"Not exactly."

"What do you mean?"

"You weren't actually poisoned. Oliver, the representative for the sports drink, works for us. He switched out the poisoned drink for one that merely made you sick. That way, we protected you without exposing the mission."

What the bloody hell!

They *let* me think I nearly died? There's absolutely no one I can trust—British Intelligence, my therapist, and Noah all betrayed me. The hardest part is that even Bri lied to me.

Bri's brows furrow. "But Dr. Shepard said Blake was poisoned with oleander leaves. How do you explain that?" Bri protests.

Harrington calmly explains, "Dr. Shepard works for us. Marcos put oleander leaves in the drink that Blake was supposed to consume. Blake had to believe he was lucky to survive because he wouldn't have survived the original drink."

Bri is livid, her index finger jabbing toward Harrington. "I can't believe you let me think that Blake might die when you knew he would be perfectly fine. I worried needlessly and was made to look like a fool."

Apparently, Bri wasn't in that part of the plan. But that doesn't excuse the rest of her actions. However, I'll deal with Harrington first.

"I'm the one who should be furious. You destroyed my Wimbledon singles hopes. You made me ill. And you let me believe that I'd been poisoned and almost died. You did all those horrible things to me when I'm the one who clued you in on Noah's crimes and agreed to help you catch him. How can you possibly justify your actions?" My voice is almost shaking with fury as I glower at the intelligence officer and await whatever excuse he plans to offer.

Harrington's voice doesn't waver. "Again, it was critical to the mission that both of you reacted as if Marcos had been successful at poisoning Blake."

"You said it was Marcos who set out to poison me. Was he working with Natalie today to kill me?"

"No. That was Noah. He had figured out that Bri was working with the authorities. They overheard an earlier conversation and became suspicious. Natalie planted software on Bri's phone that intercepted Bri's more recent texts. That's how they arranged to capture her today. They couldn't risk Brianna making contact with us. And as for you, they planned to leave a suicide note blaming you for the smuggling. They hoped they would be long gone before anyone asked more questions."

"You mean you didn't get my text last night?" Bri grimaces.

"No, we didn't," Harrington says.

"Then how did you know to show up today?"

"You made the signal with your racquets at the beginning of your match today. We knew something was wrong when we sent someone to meet you. You were already gone. We would have been there sooner, but that caused a delay in tracking you."

"I see," she says.

Harrington follows up. "That raises another question. Why did you send the signal with the racquets if you thought we'd received your texts?"

"I almost didn't. It was a last-minute decision. I feared that I hadn't relayed the seriousness of the situation in my text. Something about the reply made me question it."

"What was that?" Harrington asks.

"I texted my contacts last night, asking to meet before our match today. I was clear that timing was critical. To my surprise, they replied that it wasn't possible. I had to make sure that we met today, so I did the racquet signal."

Harrington nods. "Well done. Your instincts are good. I believe that should answer most of your questions. Do not discuss these events with anyone outside this room. You're bound by our confidentiality agreements. I'll leave you alone now to discuss what I understand may be some . . . umm . . . personal issues between the two of you."

"I'm assuming you'll be listening," I snarl, debating whether I even want to be in the same room with the princess right now. I'm not sure I can believe anything she says at this point.

"I can assure you that we will not," Harrington says.

"Why should I believe you?" I question.

"You don't have to. You can leave and talk elsewhere," he says.

"No, what I have to say is short. Here will be fine," I bark, having decided that it's better to close this chapter today and be done.

Harrington nods and leaves.

The second the door closes behind him, Bri says, "I'm so sorry. I had no idea that you were working with Deputy Harrington. They kept me in the dark. I can't believe it. I trusted them."

I hold up a hand. She stops talking. "Forgive me, but that doesn't really matter now, does it? You lied to me and used me. You clearly are a spy, aren't you?"

She lowers her head, whispering, "I'm not at liberty to discuss my involvement in these events."

The veins in my neck are pulsing as my anger swells. "Right. You're a spy. Clearly, you aren't the person I thought you were. Bloody hell, you had sex with me to work your way into my life even while thinking I was a criminal. What does that say about you? And to think I was falling for you. I've thought other women were gold diggers or celebrity chasers, but you're worse than all of them. On top of that, you bugged my room and lied to me. You can't be trusted. I can't believe I fell for your act."

"Blake, you can't really believe what you're saying. Our emotional and physical connection was real. Please believe me," she pleads as her eyes flood with tears.

"Save it for the next time you need to manipulate a man. I don't want to hear more of your lies."

"It's not a lie. I was falling for you too, but I can't blame you. I wouldn't believe me either. I'd thought I could prove you were inno-cent. And I did. Harrington just already knew it."

She looks devastated. But I won't fall for her incredible acting skills again.

"I'm leaving. Don't bother to speak if our paths cross. I want nothing more to do with you."

She nods as she wipes tears from her eyes.

My heart aches with regret and disappointment. I'd started hoping there was a future for us. But I've had enough of her duplicity and lies. Shaking my head, I walk out the conference room door, slamming it behind me.

The heat rises in my face as I storm down the hallway and out of the building. I'm angry—at her, at my team, and at British Intelli-gence. Hell, I'm angry at myself for daring to let my guard down.

And I can't even call my therapist. She fucking tried to kill me today. How messed up is that?

But Bri was the worst. She's one hell of an actress. She betrayed me, but damn it if I didn't want to hug her and tell her it would be okay. For some inexplicable reason, my heart wanted to believe her even after the role she played in this cocked-up mess.

No wonder they recruited her to be a spy. She's damn good at her job.

# 32

## BRIANNA

Talk about awkward.

Blake and I are still living in the same house. There's nowhere else for me to stay during the final weekend of Wimbledon. Fausto, Erin, and Josh are coordinating schedules so that Blake and I don't cross paths.

I assumed Blake would move out, but British Intelligence is insisting that he play the final match with me. I'm not sure what they are holding over him, but it must be something. After what happened on this mission, I can't even pretend that I'm fully informed.

The only thing I've heard is that Harrington tried to convince Blake that playing will distance him from news of the arrests. I'm not sure Blake trusts anything anyone tells him at this point though. Who can blame him?

Harrington is also trying to appease the higher ups at Wimbledon. With Marco's arrest, he's out of singles, and Thomas had to withdraw from men's doubles. He couldn't play without his partner. Wimbledon won't be happy if Blake and I drop out too. That would cancel the mixed doubles championship match. I'd never be invited to play at Wimbledon again.

More importantly, I'm aching to my core, knowing that I hurt Blake by spying on him and doubting his innocence. It's been a hard lesson. Being a royal spy means it's virtually impossible to have a relationship with the people I'm around. It's too complicated. I need to close the door on that dream and stay focused on tennis, my duties to Catalinius, and on the Covert Royals. Love can't survive the secrets and lies my missions require.

The pain is killing me. One moment I want to cry, and the next I want to scream at Blake for the horrendous things he said and thinks about me. It's true I was part of a covert operation to break a smuggling ring, but nothing that happened between us was part of that mission. Hell, I tried to stay away from him, but the attraction between us was too great.

We were both victims of the situation. Had they trusted us to play our roles, we could have trusted each other.

In reality, I only have myself to blame. I signed up for the Covert Royals. I begged for more important missions. I knew I'd only be given the necessary information for my role. I just never expected they would *lie* to me. They crossed the line. And as far as I'm concerned, this was my last mission.

This raises other questions. Did Stephen and Adrian know about the lies? What about my parents? Did they know? If so, for how long?

My trust is shattered. Blake doesn't want anything to do with me. My tennis career is likely over. And I'm leaving the Covert Royals.

I'm left with a life of ribbon cutting at dedication ceremonies.

I flop across my bed, tears cascading onto my pillow. The bleak reality sinks in. Everything I care about is gone.

Sometime later, I hear Erin's distinctive knock.

"I need to be alone," I say, my voice hoarse.

"I'm sorry, but your parents and Blake's parents are downstairs.

Blake and Josh are nowhere to be found, so your parents suggested Fausto cook dinner for the five of you."

"No way. I can't sit through dinner tonight."

"I pulled your mother aside and attempted to explain the situation. It appears that Deputy Harrington already spoke with them. To quote your mother, she said to tell you that duty calls."

"No! Tell her that duty is on vacation."

"Brianna, I respect your privacy, but I have a key and am coming in."

The door opens and then quickly clicks shut. I roll over to face her, whispering, "I can't do this."

"You can. I'm going to help you. A little concealer and makeup will do wonders. I also brought you a flask of brandy. Take a gulp. It will help."

"Thanks, Erin. I never know what you'll pull from your jacket."

"Don't forget, I'm still your friend. We'll get through this."

"I'm not sure I'll ever recover from this disaster."

"You will. You have your family and me."

"I thought I could have Blake too."

"I know. I'm sorry."

"Me too. I'm not even sure he'll show up to play our match, no matter what his coach or Harrington says."

"Blake doesn't seem any happier than you. Josh took him out tonight to talk."

"He may not want to do anything for me, but I'd think he'd want to try for the title even if it's doubles instead of singles. Wouldn't you?"

"We can only hope."

# 33

## BLAKE

When I tell Josh that I'm done with Wimbledon, he insists we grab a drink at an out-of-the-way pub he knows. As far as I can tell, Josh is the only person who hasn't betrayed me in the last few months, so I grudgingly agree. It's better than sulking in my room, avoiding Bri.

The pub is small and dark with dingy wood paneling. Football plays on the TV. A few regulars sit at the bar munching on crisps and drinking beer. No one pays any attention to us as we claim the corner booth.

I've given up on my training for now, so I happily raise the pint he sets in front of me. Downing half the glass in one long pull, I feel a sense of relief. At this point, I seriously doubt things could get worse, but I might as well drown my sorrows tonight.

Josh says, "Mate, I can't believe the story you told me. It's obvious you've left out some details. What I don't understand is why you're mad at Brianna."

Fidgeting with the drink coaster, I assess whether I can share more with Josh. It would help to have someone to talk to about what Bri did, but I can't. "Unfortunately, the officials made me sign a confidentiality agreement. I can't say anything else. This whole situation is beyond comprehension."

"I respect that. But you said Brianna was faking her attraction to you. I just don't believe that. Have you seen the way she looks at you?" He flutters his eyelashes, pretending to mimic her.

I almost laugh at his abysmal imitation, but my mood is too dark. "You don't understand. She's a phenomenal actor."

"No one's that good," he says with confidence.

I smirk. "Apparently, she's been trained by the best."

I wonder if our encounter two years ago was part of a mission too. I don't even know how long she's been a spy.

Josh leans forward. "Blake, quit ripping up that poor coaster and look at me. Does it really matter what Bri did when you still have the chance to take home the Wimbledon mixed doubles title?"

Between clenched teeth, I explain, "I don't want to be anywhere near her. She'll screw me over again."

Truthfully, I'm not sure what else she could do now—other than try to convince me things between us were real. Is that what I'm afraid of—that I'll fall for her story again?

Resting his chin on his palm, Josh furrows his brows. "I see. Your plan is to screw her over first by not showing up."

"Exactly," I say, downing the rest of my pint, avoiding his stare.

His face hardens. "You two would probably lose anyway. But if you show up, you'd at least get the prize money. Otherwise, you're going to forfeit quite a bit."

I clench my fists. How dare he insinuate that we'd lose? We made a great doubles team. We're quite capable of winning this tournament. But I'll be damned if I'll defend Bri to Josh. Instead, I seize on the other half of what he said.

"Why does everyone think I need more money? I'm a multimillionaire."

Palms up, he says, "It's not about what you need. It's about business. Who would walk away from that kind of money over a disagreement with your partner. You're guaranteed the second-place money if you merely show up and play. You don't even have to talk to Brianna."

Hmm. I hadn't thought of that. I admit, "That's true. I could physically show up and ignore her. She can go fuck herself for all I care."

Josh slaps me on the shoulder. "That's the spirit."

Before I can respond, his phone dings with an incoming message. "Oh no!" he groans.

"What is it?"

"You'll never believe this. Your parents are having dinner with Bri and her parents. They're all at the house waiting for us to join them."

What a great time to be at the pub. I don't want any part of that shit show. "Let's order another round and pretend you didn't receive the message."

His face twists in disbelief. "Are you kidding? It's your parents, a former king and queen, and a princess. Are you really going to stand them up?"

*I only thought it couldn't get any worse.*

---

SOMEHOW, WE SURVIVED DINNER LAST NIGHT. I WAS ABLE TO AVOID TALKING to Bri by being particularly attentive to my parents.

I have no choice but to play today, now that all the parents are here to watch. There's no way I would disappoint my mom and dad. But it doesn't mean I have to play well.

And it doesn't mean I have to speak to Bri. To escape riding with her, Josh and I left the house four hours prior to the match. We spent the first two hours eating breakfast and lounging in the locker room.

I want to skip my normal gym warmup, but Josh is too bored to sit around for another two hours, so I give in. At least that fills the time and distracts my thoughts until it's time to play.

With fifteen minutes until the start of our match, I walk down the tunnel toward the court. Bri is standing at the end, looking around anxiously. When she sees me, relief washes over her face, but she doesn't have a smile for me today. Oddly, that bothers me. Of course, it's not as if I'm smiling at her either.

When I stop beside her, she says, "Thanks for being here."

I nod, refusing to look at her. Being so near to her is confusing. My anger is still smoldering, but part of me wishes there were an explanation that would wipe away the pain of her betrayal.

In a soft, hopeful voice, she whispers, "I know you're not speaking to me. Can we at least talk about strategy during the match?"

"Nope."

"I'm really sorry. I never meant to hurt you." Her voice is full of pain and resignation.

But she *did* hurt me. She destroyed my heart and my trust. I won't let her do it again.

Our names are called. Without thinking, I start reaching for her hand but pull back before making contact.

We walk onto the court to cheers and give quick waves to the crowd. But the joy I've felt the other times we've played is missing.

At least this will be over soon. I'll never have to spend another moment with Bri. That should be comforting, but it's not.

The match starts, and I let a few balls pass by that I could easily have returned. Bri's face crumples in disappointment.

She's slamming back every ball she can reach. I'm not sure if she's trying to win this match single-handedly or if she's taking her anger out on the balls. She's even running to my side of the court, attempting to return balls I should be hitting. She's playing nothing short of great.

We still lose the first set.

During the break, Bri says, "I know you want to hurt me, but be careful. To me, it looks like you're hurting yourself instead. No one expected me to win. Granted, losing will be hard on me, but we've done better than I'd ever hoped. I'll be okay. Ask yourself this question: If you purposefully lose this match, will *you* be okay?"

She's right. I'm a competitor. I thrive on winning. And I'm starting to wonder whether Bri was as much a victim as I was. Hell, my heart hurt listening to her sob last night. That wasn't an act.

In the first game of the second set, I start playing to win. I even exchange a few words with Bri. It works. We start talking even more in the next games and win the second set. A tiebreaker will determine the champions.

Before it begins, I tell Bri, "Let's win this. After all we've been through, we at least deserve to raise this trophy."

She gives me a quick smile, albeit a sad one.

We play our hearts out. It's close, but the final shot catches the line. We've won.

Instead of hugging her, I say, "Good job."

"Thank you. I know it's not what you wanted. But you finally won Wimbledon, even if it is a doubles trophy."

She's right. Unfortunately, I lost the prize I'd decided was more important.

---

AFTER THE AWARDS CEREMONY ON THE COURT, WE'RE INVITED TO MEET Princes Stephen and Adrian inside the All England Club. Bri's family and mine are invited as well. This will mean the world to my parents.

We take photos, chat with the royals, and accept congratulations. Now it's time for the famous pose on the balcony where crowds of tennis lovers stand below us, cheering. A chill runs down my spine. I've been waiting a lifetime for this moment.

As we turn to walk back into the club, Prince Adrian asks to speak with me privately. I can't imagine what he wants, but I can't turn down the invitation.

I follow him to the other side of the building, and we step onto a small, hidden balcony, away from the crowds. One of his guards stands watch at the door. Prince Adrian points toward the glass wall with a beautiful view of the ivy-covered buildings and bright-colored flowers adorning the paths.

The view reminds me of the first time Bri and I shared a moment alone on a Wimbledon patio two years ago. She turned a sad evening into a perfect one for me.

Unfortunately, Bri didn't turn out to be the person I thought she was. She's a spy. Seducing me was part of her job.

My mind understands. My heart doesn't. It aches to a level I never thought possible. I thought she was everything I could ever want. She filled me with love and comforted me. Our passion and chemistry were explosive. It was real to me. Unfortunately, it wasn't for her.

Prince Adrian says, "I'm know what happened here. But I doubt anyone shared the whole story with you."

With my best poker face, I say, "I'm not sure what you're talking about. I've merely played tennis here."

He chuckles. "I'm pleased to see you take your oath to our country seriously. So do I. I'm not asking you to share anything with me. And what I plan to tell you falls under the confidentiality agreement you signed with British Intelligence. Do you understand?"

Every time I think the worst is over, I'm wrong. He's probably going rip my life further apart, but I might as well get it over with, so I say, "I do."

"Good. I probably shouldn't tell you this. But someone I care about is truly miserable. From what I can see in your face, I suspect you aren't doing much better. I can't stand by without trying to fix this situation. I just need you to listen. Will you do that for me?"

What is he talking about? Surely, it's not Bri who's miserable? Regardless, I'm a loyal British subject. When someone in the royal family wants to share something with me, who am I not to listen. "Of course, Your Royal Highness."

"I'm now speaking as Adrian, not as a member of the royal family. Stephen and I were part of the intelligence team with Princess Brianna. She's also like a sister to me. She's a good person.

She believed in you and defended you from the beginning. One reason she worked so hard on her mission was to prove your innocence. At first, we didn't understand why. Then it became apparent that she had feelings for you—real feelings. I won't ask you to confirm it, but we suspect you two have some history. If we'd known sooner, she wouldn't have been assigned to this mission. In the end, it made her the perfect choice. She was determined to get to the truth. You may also recall that she's the one who saved your life."

"Thank you for telling me," I say, feigning indifference. Inside, my stomach is churning. I'm not sure how to process this. Did she really fight for me and believe in me? Is it possible that her feelings were as real as mine?

"You're welcome. You two make a great couple. I hope you'll give it a chance."

"I can't. She manipulated me and seduced me to gain information. I guess it was part of her job."

"Oh. I see. You don't think she actually cares about you. You think you were just part of a mission."

"She's always in the tabloids flitting from guy to guy. She probably uses her wiles in all her missions. The tabloids say she's the . . ."

"Have you done all the outlandish things the tabloids have printed about you? Of course not. The tabloids are trash. She's never become involved with anyone on her prior missions. If that's who you think she is, you don't deserve her."

Realization dawns. After the betrayals by my prior coach, Noah, and Natalie, I immediately assumed that Bri was untrustworthy too. But she's the one who fought for me, calmed me, encouraged me. Yes, she hid some things from me, but they weren't things that caused me harm. Ultimately, they helped me.

I stare at the sky. "I'm a bloody fool, aren't I?"

Adrian grins. "That's what I've been trying to tell you. You and Bri are both lovesick puppies that need to wake up before you lose the best thing that ever happened to either one of you."

My face falls when I remember my conversation with her after I learned she was a spy. "It's too late. You wouldn't believe what I said to her."

"We heard," he admits.

"Of course you did. Harrington lied when he said no one was listening, didn't he?"

Adrian waves off my comment. "That doesn't matter. She's here one more day. If you want to fix this, you better put a plan in place."

"I may need help."

"If you promise not to hurt her again, Stephen and I will help."

"Do I have any chance of fixing this?" I ask, hopefully.

"Have you heard the term *grand gesture*?" he asks with a smirk.

"Yes. Do you think that would work?"

He shakes his head. "No. Think bigger. You need a royal-worthy gesture."

"In other words, I need to apologize profusely or do something extreme to prove my feelings to her."

"You need to do both, and while you're at it, add in some groveling."

"Understood."

This isn't going to be easy, but a plan is quickly forming in my head. I need to hurry and set the plan into motion. The first step is to explain it to Adrian.

# 34

## BLAKE

Yesterday, I quickly shared my plan with Prince Adrian as we walked back inside from the balcony. He relayed word to Prince Stephen. I didn't want to scare Bri off with a sudden about-face in my attitude toward her, but I *did* want her to see my anger was gone. The princes helped by drawing me into a conversation with her.

Later, when we arrived home, I cornered Erin and Fausto to explain their part in my plan. At first, they were hesitant to help after hearing about my fallout with Bri, but eventually, I convinced them.

As planned, this morning Erin ensured Bri arrived in the kitchen at 9:00 a.m. for breakfast.

Ten minutes after I heard them go downstairs, I sneak down the steps and pause outside the kitchen doorway where Bri can't see me. She's sitting on a tall barstool at the island.

She's beautiful even with the dark circles under her sad eyes. How did I ever believe what we shared wasn't real? Neither of us would be this miserable if it hadn't meant something.

I'll make this right. I don't want to imagine life without her.

After a couple of minutes, I walk into the kitchen and stop at the side of the island, offering a cheery, "Good morning, everyone. Fausto, those crepes look amazing. It's too bad I have to meet my parents for breakfast today."

At my request, Fausto made Bri's favorite Nutella and fresh strawberry crepes. I'm hoping they will brighten her mood.

Fausto and Erin return my greeting. I almost laugh, remembering how Fausto spent two weeks pretending not to speak English. No wonder Bri was so mad when I accused Fausto of poisoning me. He understood my entire tirade. Fortunately, he's the forgiving type. We've worked things out.

That's not the case with Bri though. I catch her watching me from the corner of her eye, but she doesn't speak to me. She probably assumes I don't want to talk to her. I'd also bet that she's still mad at me for all the horrible things I said.

That's why my goal this morning is simple. If I can convince her to do one thing, it will be a success. I do my best to hide my nerves as I smile and ask, "Bri, would you be willing to ride with me to the dinner tonight?"

She scrunches her eyes and tilts her head, studying my face. I'm not sure if she thinks I've lost my mind or that I have a sinister plan for revenge. That's not good. I don't know what to say to make it better, so I remain silent, waiting for her response.

She turns back to her crepes. "That's not necessary. We can each arrive with our own parents."

My smile falters. "We *could*, but my parents were invited to go with yours if you ride with me. It would be incredibly special for my parents to arrive at the dinner with royalty. I know I'm asking a lot, but would you do it for them?"

Her eyes soften. "Of course. I didn't realize the situation. I wouldn't want to disappoint your parents."

Goal accomplished. I fight the urge to high-five Erin and Fausto. I'll thank them later.

"Bri, you don't know how much they will appreciate this. Thank you."

"Your parents are wonderful and so kind. I'm happy to do it for them." She gives me the first hint of a smile I've seen this morning. It's a start. We're also talking in full sentences, which gives me a little hope.

"I'm off to meet my parents for breakfast. I'll see everyone later."

I quickly leave the kitchen to work on the rest of my plan.

Tonight is the Wimbledon Champions Dinner. This year, Bri and I are attending as winners—not the singles champions, but winners all the same. If I'm lucky, I'll win even more tonight. It's a longshot, but I'm giving it my all.

I spend the rest of the day double-checking the arrangements for this evening. But with each passing hour, more doubt creeps in. What if my plan isn't grand enough? What if nothing I do will be? I have to press on. Living without Bri can't be my fate.

---

THIS IS THE FIRST TIME I'VE HAPPILY PUT ON MY TUXEDO FOR THE Champions Dinner. Bri and I earned our spots this year, so it feels different. Tonight will also be a major turning point in my life—either for the better or worse, depending on what happens with Bri.

As I step into the hallway with a bouquet of purple and white flowers for her, Bri's door opens.

She takes my breath away. Her mahogany hair drapes over her shoulders. The short, purple satin cocktail dress hugs her figure, showing off her long legs to perfection.

Her lips turn upwards as she gives my tux-clad body a slow perusal. Then she suddenly blanks her face as if remembering we're still at odds. Hopefully, that will end shortly.

"You're gorgeous, Bri."

"Thank you."

"These are for you. I'm told you love purple roses."

She lifts her eyebrows in surprise. "I do, but who told you that?"

I'm hoping she'll think it was Erin. I'm not ready to share that Adrian and Stephen helped me with the plans for tonight.

"Does it matter?" I ask casually.

She taps her cheek with her index finger, considering my question. "Probably not, but who knows. So many people have lied to me —either directly or through omission—I'm having trouble deciphering what matters."

"I understand. Why don't we call a truce? Let's promise not to lie to each other about anything? Can we do that?"

"Does this mean we're speaking again?"

"I hope so. I owe you an apology. I'm sorry for all the terrible things I said. I never truly believed them. I just felt tricked and manipulated. Like you, I didn't know whom to trust and lashed out at everyone. I'll never forgive myself for how I treated you."

"The things you said about me were incredibly hurtful. But I know I hurt you as well. I'm sorry for that. I like your idea of a truce."

The tension between us eases. A calmness washes over her face that I suspect mirrors mine.

"Excellent. I'm hoping you'll eventually be able to forgive me. Tonight, let's enjoy our well-earned invitations. How does that sound?"

"Yes. Let's celebrate. But at some point, I'd like to talk more."

"Me too."

Taking her hand, I lead her down the stairs and out to the waiting car. The fact she didn't pull away gives me a smidgeon of hope.

The short ride to the dinner starts out a little awkward, but gradually we're talking, laughing, and smiling. The occasional touch of our knees and brush of our hands gives me confidence that my plan could actually work.

As we approach the venue, a spectacular display of lights marks the entrance. A red carpet lines the walkway where dozens of photographers stand behind a rope vying for the best angles.

While we wait for the cars in front of us to unload passengers, Bri turns to me. Her eyes are moist. "Blake, thank you for playing mixed doubles with me. I'll never forget that you made my dream come true. And for us to walk in as champions tonight . . . It's more than I could've imagined. I'll be forever grateful no matter what happens . . ."

She doesn't finish her thought. This is an emotional night for both of us.

"But for you, I might not even be alive, much less a champion. I'm the one who is grateful. Again, I apologize for being such a wanker. Shite. I probably shouldn't use that language when talking with a princess. Can I pre-apologize for all future times I put my foot in my mouth?"

She laughs. "Just avoid it around my parents or in formal settings around my brothers. Even if they didn't really mind, Xander and Evan would give you a hard time. Otherwise, no need to apologize."

My minor *faux pas* lightened the mood.

"That's a relief."

Walking into the ballroom, it's as if I'm seeing the Champions Dinner for the first time. Sure, the décor changes every year, but it always seems about the same to me. However, tonight the lights shine brighter, the music is happier, and the words of congratulation ring true.

I'm not surprised when people sympathize about the poisoning incident. Instead of telling me that I'll have another chance next year, they tell me how proud they are that I returned to play and made the UK proud. I point out that Princess Brianna was the key to our success because of her skillful doubles play. They nod, patting me on the back.

We're both glowing and animated as we relive various portions of matches with each new group that stops us. For the first time, I'm happy to be here. It's not only because we won, but also because Bri is by my side.

Whether it's our hands touching, my hand on her back, or my

arm around her shoulder, I can't help touching her. The few moments when we're apart, I feel lost.

Eventually, Bri taps me on the shoulder, whispering, "Would you mind if we find our table? I'd like to check on my parents."

"Good idea. My parents and our coaches should be there too."

We wander toward the stage, chatting with more players, coaches, and VIPs along the way. Finally reaching our table, our parents are smiling and talking while Josh and Martina chat with coaches at a nearby table.

We greet our parents and take our seats beside each other for the dinner and program. I keep stealing glances at Bri, enamored with her poise and beauty.

When they call our names, we go forward to receive our honorary memberships to the All England Club. Bri is beaming. I've been so focused on surprising Bri that I forgot about the cherished memberships. Bri will never again have to feel bad about using the members' locker room. She'll be entitled to use it whenever she plays here.

After all the winners are recognized, the men's singles champion dances with the women's singles champion. It's tradition.

My palms start to sweat in anticipation of what comes next.

I quickly dry them on my napkin as the emcee announces, "Please welcome the mixed doubles champions to the dance floor."

Bri turns her head and smiles as our eyes meet.

The audience applauds loudly as I stand, reaching for Bri's hand. The anticipation of holding her in my arms is killing me. I want to jog to the dance floor but know better. Instead, I wrap an arm around her waist, giving her a light squeeze as we walk.

As we step on the dance floor, the music slows, and I turn to embrace Bri.

"What's going on? What happened to the fast music?" she asks in a whisper.

"I requested a slow song for our dance. I wanted a chance to talk," I say, gazing into her eyes with hope. This is it. I have to convince her that she's everything to me. Failure isn't an option.

"Why here? Why now?" She searches my face for answers.

Brushing a lock of hair from her cheek, I'm mesmerized by her. "Because this is where it all started for us two years ago. I've thought of you so many times since. Then we reconnected here, and I fantasized about the future with you. When things went sideways, I was devastated. Then I was mad at myself and lashed out. I should have listened when you tried to explain. I've been miserable since the day we fought. I'm so sorry for everything."

She looks away, sadness clouding her eyes. With a slight tremble in her voice, she says "It's okay. I understand how you could have misconstrued the situation."

Gently turning her face back to mine, I shake my head. "That's not an excuse for my behavior. You've taught me so much about myself. Some things I didn't like very much and will work to change. As for the other things, I'm still sorting them out. There is one thing that I know for certain though. I need you in my life. I play better when you're around. You make me happy and calm. Our chemistry is in the stratosphere. I don't want to live without you. I love you. I can only hope you feel the same."

"You love me?" she asks, uncertain.

"I do."

"Do you still believe that I slept with you as part of the mission?"

Clearly, my accusation crushed her. How could I have been such a tosser? I need to explain.

"No. I know your job was to investigate me. And I looked guilty. Two of my own team members *were* guilty. I was just hurt that you suspected me. But then I jumped to conclusions about you. It's ironic that I was mad at you for doubting me when I didn't give you the benefit of the doubt either."

"When I first heard you were a suspect, I couldn't believe it. Then the evidence started adding up, and I questioned my judgment. I'm sorry I doubted you."

"In your position, I would have doubted me too, but somehow you still fought for me."

"I did. And I've regretted that I didn't have the chance to tell you how I felt. You're the only person who has ever sent chills down my spine, making me want to be with you every chance I could. I also thought of you for the last two years. You're the only man I've ever truly wanted. I love you too. It's destroying me to think I ruined our chances."

"I don't want to lose you, Bri."

"What does that mean for us?"

"I have a proposal."

She gasps, covering her mouth with both hands. She manages to softly say, "Please Blake, don't propose. I love you, but it's too soon."

"Oh! I'm messing this up. I didn't mean that type of proposal."

"What did you mean?"

"Please hear me out before you answer."

I signal to the emcee, and he hands me the microphone.

Speaking to the crowd, I say, "First, this is not a marriage proposal. But I do have an important question to ask Princess Briana. I want you all to be my witnesses. I don't want her to have any reason to question my sincerity. So everyone, can you do that for me?"

The crowd erupts in a collective cheer of "Yes!"

I turn back to Bri, taking her hand and staring into her eyes.

"This evening has a special meaning for us. We met at this event two years ago. Neither of us were here because we were champions but rather because we were expected to attend. You uplifted my spirits that evening and again after I collapsed in the singles match this year. You're the sunshine in my day even when it's raining. You make me a better person. You're the reason I was able to return to play after being poisoned. You even make me want to play mixed doubles. Everyone knows that's quite unusual for me."

The crowd laughs as Bri nods.

"I want to spend more time with you so we can date and learn

more about each other. I don't want us to have a long-distance relationship. I propose that for the rest of this year, I skip my singles
tournaments. Instead, if you agree, we'll play mixed doubles at every
tournament that your schedule allows. The rest of the time we can
spend wherever you would like. The decision is entirely yours, and
I'll understand if you need time to decide. But I wanted to do this in
front of everyone here to show you that I'm completely serious about
making us work. What do you say?"

Someone in the audience yells, "Talk about a grand gesture! Say
yes, Princess Brianna."

Bri pulls the microphone toward her and says, "My answer is a
definite, unequivocal, yes."

The emcee reclaims the mic as the crowd erupts, and the music
changes to an upbeat song to celebrate. Couples flood the dance
floor, but we stand in the middle, embracing each other.

I say, "It was supposed to be a royal-worthy gesture. Prince
Adrian suggested that a grand gesture wouldn't be sufficient."

"Adrian helped you?"

"Technically, Prince Adrian and Prince Stephen both helped."

"I haven't been speaking to them after they let Harrington with-
hold information from me. Maybe helping you was their roundabout
way of apologizing."

"In the spirit of honesty, I should also share that Erin, Fausto,
and our parents helped too."

"Are you joking? What did they do?"

"Fausto made your favorite breakfast to put you in a good mood.
Erin made sure you showed up for it instead of eating in your room.
Your parents invited mine to ride with them, so you would come here
with me."

"I'm impressed. You've been busy."

"I have, and there's one more surprise I hope you will like."

"Don't worry. You know I love surprises."

The other dancers shield us from prying eyes as I press my lips to
hers in a deep, claiming kiss. She's mine now, and I'm not letting go.

# EPILOGUE – BRIANNA

The Champions Dinner was perfect but exhausting. After we finally left the dance floor and rejoined our parents and coaches, we talked forever. Then we mingled with the other players, taking selfies and accepting congratulations on our win and our new relationship. We couldn't stop smiling.

We fell asleep during the car ride back to the house. Stumbling upstairs, we went to my room for fear someone might still be monitoring the cameras in his. It wouldn't have mattered because we immediately fell asleep in each other's arms.

Blake woke early, kissed me, and apologized that he needed to meet his parents this morning before they headed home. Through a yawn, I offered to go with him, but he insisted that I needed my rest for his other surprise. I rolled over and slept soundly for another hour before waking up to shower and dress.

I'm putting the finishing touches on my makeup when a knock sounds at my door.

Blake calls out, "Bri, I'm back."

I hurry from the bathroom and wrap my arms around his neck, giving him a proper welcome-back kiss.

He chuckles, "I could get used to that greeting."

"Then don't keep me waiting any longer. Now, what's my surprise?"

He grins. "Okay, but it's optional. If you don't like the idea, we'll do something else. Your parents offered us the royal superyacht if you would like to cruise to Catalinius rather than fly back. They thought it would give us a break from the press and everyone. Then you can show me around your country. How does that sound?"

My parents know how much I love time on the ocean to clear my head. It's a rare treat for me with such a packed schedule. Their offer also means they must approve of Blake and want us to have time together. That alone makes me burst with happiness.

"That sounds perfect. The yacht is beautiful, and it would be so relaxing not to have to deal with crowds and the press for a few days. Do you like the idea?"

"Absolutely. As long as we're together, I'll be ecstatic." He beams.

Mentally, I start calculating how long it will take to pack, arrange transportation, and notify everyone of my change in plans. Then I slap my forehead.

"Wait a minute. We'll need to wait for the yacht to arrive here from Catalinius. That will take at least eight days."

A sparkle of delight dances in his eyes, "Relax, love. We can start our adventure today, if you want. Your parents arrived on the yacht. Apparently, they were cruising nearby when they found out we were in the finals, so they docked it in London."

Mmm-hmm. More likely my parents found an excuse to be nearby in case something went wrong with my mission. They are a tad—actually much more than a tad—overprotective of their only daughter. Regardless, Blake and I can reap the benefits and enjoy the cruise home.

"That's lucky. It'll also give you a chance to get to know them."

I'm also thinking it's another way for them to keep an eye on Blake until they're sure they trust him.

"Apparently not. They're staying in London for some event. They said we shouldn't wait for them. They plan to fly home."

"Interesting. I guess that means we'll have plenty of alone time," I muse, snuggling in for a hug.

"That's what I was thinking. How soon can we leave?"

"If we pack quickly and Erin can make arrangements, we should be there in no more than three hours, maybe a little sooner."

"Let's make it sooner, I can't wait much longer to show you exactly how much I love you."

"Just how do you plan to do that?" I tease with a playful smile.

"I'm going to worship every inch of your perfect body until you beg me to stop."

# EPILOGUE – BLAKE

We arrive at St. Katharine Docks, the marina in central London where the Catalinius royal yacht is docked. Bri's parents weren't exaggerating when they called it a superyacht. If anything, that was an understatement.

It's a small cruise ship! And a beautiful one at that. The hull is midnight blue and glistens against the water. The deck is pristine white with gleaming stainless steel and glass railings.

Bri is all smiles as we walk toward the boarding area, where the crew awaits our arrival. "Isn't she magnificent?" she asks, gesturing toward the vessel.

"Definitely."

The captain greets us, "Welcome aboard, Your Royal Highness and Mr. Knight. We're pleased to have you sailing on our return voyage to Catalinius."

"Thank you, captain. We're looking forward to it as well."

"Would you like us to give Mr. Knight a tour of the ship before we leave port?"

Bri turns to me with a gleam of mischief. "I'd like to rest before the tour. Blake, you're welcome to take the tour though."

Message received. And if I've interpreted it correctly, we won't be resting if my answer is the right one.

"Captain, I'd love a tour a little later. I'm also exhausted after the two-week tournament."

The captain nods. "Your luggage is being delivered to your suite now. Let the crew know if there is anything you need."

I'm wealthy and enjoy a high-end lifestyle when I'm not playing tennis, but it's nothing like this. Other than the crew and Erin, Bri and I are the only passengers. This is wild. And it's giving me some incredibly vivid ideas for how we can spend our time onboard.

"Blake, follow me. Each member of my family has their own dedicated living quarters on the ship. I'll show you where our suite is."

I happily follow her, counting down the minutes until I can get her alone and naked.

A few minutes later, we step into the enormous suite. A wall of windows overlooks a balcony that faces the dock. An ice bucket with a bottle of champagne, along with a silver tray of chocolate-covered strawberries awaits us on the dining table.

"Would you like me to pop the cork?" I ask, tugging Bri into my arms for a kiss.

"Yes. Let's take the champagne and strawberries onto the balcony for the departure," she murmurs against my lips.

I open the bottle and pour two glasses. Bri returns from changing and picks up the tray as we step through the large sliding glass door onto the balcony. On a regular cruise ship, this balcony would be divided into balconies for at least five, if not more, rooms.

We sip champagne and feed each other strawberries as the horns bellow, signaling our departure. The yacht slowly pulls away from the dock, beginning the next phase of our journey.

When the people on the dock shrink to distant specks, I can't wait any longer. I set my glass on the outdoor table and do the same with Bri's.

Pulling her against me, I say, "Bri, I love you so much. I can't wait any longer to have you again."

"I love you too, and I don't want to wait either."

I pick her up, wrap her legs around my waist, and carry her inside. Pressing her back against the nearest wall, I kiss her with a level of passion that surprises even me. She's my everything, and I want her to know it.

With my teeth, I break the thin shoulder straps on her dress, exposing her bare, plump breasts. I take a moment to appreciate them. I'm in awe.

"Do you have any clue how gorgeous and sexy you are?"

"Show me how much you need me," she demands in a sultry voice.

"My pleasure."

I lick and tease her nipple, and she moans. Twisting slightly, she nudges her other nipple toward my mouth as her fingers lace through my hair. She holds my head firmly against her chest as she rests her head against the wall, eyes closed.

"Oh, Blake. That's so good."

I turn her away from the wall and gently place her on the edge of the dining table. Her long legs stay loosely wrapped around my waist. Retrieving a condom from my pocket, I lower my zipper and free my cock.

I push her dress up and pause. I'm the luckiest man alive. She's completely bare and begging for me.

"Love, I promise we'll make love slowly later, but not this time."

"I don't need slow now," she moans, tossing her head back.

I plant kisses down her beautiful neck as I thrust deep inside, passionately claiming her.

*She's finally mine.*

"WHAT DO YOU WANT TO DO DURING THE REST OF OUR CRUISE?" BRI ASKS after we've showered and changed.

I waggle my eyebrows. "Hmm. I suspect there are plenty of locations to explore."

"By *explore* do you mean what I think you do?"

"Yes. What do you think?"

"That sounds absolutely perfect. Where would you like to start?"

"What about the lifeboat?" I suggest.

"That could be risky, but I'm game."

"I love you. You're perfect."

*What a match.*

# ACKNOWLEDGMENTS

I am extremely grateful to everyone who helped me bring Brianna and Blake to life in *Risky Match*. Thank you to my husband for his willingness to listen to plot ideas over dinner and proofread drafts. Thanks to Molly for all the help along the way. Thank you to my editors for their insightful comments and suggestions. Thanks to the authors who have encouraged and taught me so much. Thank you to Joan, Cathy, Sara, and Gabby for our amazing Friday evening writing sessions. You bring sunshine to my life. And thank you to my friends and family—you make writing possible for me.

The audiobooks in this series and my prior series would not be possible without the phenomenal work by East House Productions. Please download copies of the audiobooks and hear for yourself how Shane East finds the perfect narrators. The production team bring spectacular performances to my listeners. The talented narrators and engineers are the best. I appreciate all of you so much.

And thank you to everyone who helped launch the publication of *Rival Secrets*.

# THANK YOU READERS!

Thank you for reading *Risky Match*! If you enjoyed Brianna & Blake's story, please consider posting a review on your retailer's site, on Goodreads, and/or other sites where lovers of books look for their next read. Posting reviews on various sites helps other readers find new authors and titles, which is appreciated.

**Want more romance and suspense with a guaranteed HEA?**

Don't miss other books by J.D. Carothers

**Love Over Murder Series:**

*Rival Secrets* (Book 1, Standalone)

*Royally Deceived* (Book 2, Standalone)

*Reckless Chance* (Book 3, Standalone)

**Royal Spies Series:**

*Risky Match* (Book 1, Standalone)

*Flawed Match* (Book 2, Standalone) coming soon

**Holiday Series:**

*Christmas on Assignment* (Standalone) coming fall 2025

# KEEP IN TOUCH WITH J.D.!

Don't miss the latest info on new releases,

bonus material, and other updates.

**Subscribe to my newsletter today!**

jdcarothers.com/#subscribe

You can also stay in touch by following me on social media and through my website.

Facebook: facebook.com/JDCarothersAuth

Instagram: instagram.com/jdcarothersauth

Website: jdcarothers.com

# ABOUT THE AUTHOR

When not immersed in her law career, J.D. Carothers loves to cook for her family and friends, read or listen to romance novels and murder mysteries, eat chocolate, and sip wine while watching sunsets.

Late at night or early on weekend mornings, she finds a quiet place to write her next billionaire romance with a twist of light suspense. Writing allows her to trade the stress of real life for a fantasy world where love, food, and clues lead to a happily ever after.

Facebook: facebook.com/JDCarothersAuth
Instagram: instagram.com/jdcarothersauth
Amazon: Amazon.com/stores/j.-d.-carothers/author/B0B25W48TS
Goodreads: Goodreads.com/author/show/22440342.j_d_carothers

www.ingramcontent.com/pod-product-compliance
Lightning Source LLC
Chambersburg PA
CBHW061656190726
48289CB00006B/1896